To

Irene & Duncan

good friends

love

Donald

THE EAGLE'S NEST

Donald Eales White

MINERVA PRESS
ATLANTA LONDON SYDNEY

THE EAGLE'S NEST
Copyright © Donald Eales White 1999

ISBN 0 75410 867 8

First Published 1999 by
MINERVA PRESS
315–317 Regent Street
London W1R 7YB

Printed in Great Britain for Minerva Press

THE EAGLE'S NEST

Eternity is just the real world for which we were made
and which we enter through the door of love.

Chapter One

The Snake in the Heather

When the Minister tripped and fell, they had run and stumbled along the top of the high cliff for several hundred yards, Michael shouting in order to call Musty off. Michael was only just able to pull himself up in time not to fall across him. He caught Musty by the collar, at the same time grasping the older man by the hand and helping him to his feet. As their eyes met, Michael burst out laughing. The Minister laughed too: Michael's laughter was infectious. The Minister himself was not much given to it. They stood side by side; the Minister breathless from his headlong flight and fall, Michael even more so from laughing and trying to stop Musty from barking and chasing after him. He pointed in the direction from which they had come, unable to speak. The Minister nodded.

The glorious light that settles upon the island when the sun is low in the sky and the dusk gathers, cast strange monstrous shadows before them as they made their way back to the spot they had left so hastily. While the Minister climbed down to recover the stick he had dropped, Michael kicked at the vivid green snake coiled in the heather, that had given the older man such a shock: he had almost put his hand on it, as he leant forward to help himself up in his haste to get away from Musty at his heels. The snake was one of those toys designed to be placed in a bed or any-where where its unexpected presence is likely to have dramatic effect. It had had that effect!

The Minister was put out; he was well aware that there were no snakes on the Great Isle and regretted the sudden impulse that had made him decide to take the walk. He lived alone with his mother – separated from his fellow human beings by his calling. He was really familiar only with his own, very small, congregation in church and to a very limited extent, on his infrequent pastoral visits outside it. He had felt quite certain when he had decided to take the walk, that he would meet no one at that time of day and in that deserted part of the island: everyone would be preparing or having their evening meal. He had never taken such a walk before and he certainly never would again.

'Well, well,' he said, as he reappeared at the top of the cliff having recovered his stick. 'So, that is what it was!'

He watched its fascinating sinuous movement, frowning distastefully as Michael playfully held it out towards him.

'That will belong to no one in Foghar. Some child visiting the island from the mainland will have left it there. Strangers and visitors are rare in this part of the world. Let it lie where it was.'

The minister spoke abruptly and somewhat dictatorially but was not altogether unfriendly, despite his continuing uneasiness at Musty's presence and his anxiety to escape from a somewhat ridiculous and undignified situation. However, at that hour of the day and in that part of the island, the only alternative to accompanying Michael back to Foghar, where both lived as close neighbours (Michael in the old, the minister in the new manse), was too go off in the opposite direction, almost as absurd as jumping over the cliff. Michael had bought the old manse about nine months before from the Church of Scotland.

As Musty, a Cairn crossed West Highland terrier, had a tendency to give anyone he met uneasy concern for their ankles and to object loudly to every other dog, on an island where there was a dog in every household, Michael had taken care to avoid human and canine contact as much as possible. This wasn't difficult as this was the most northern part of the long, large island. Wide stretches of moorland surrounded and separated sparsely inhabited village communities, and every house was detached and stood in its own croft. (Even the Minister had a glebe and so did Michael.) Also, there was very little movement between crofts as the crofters spent most of the daylight hours during the week fully occupied on their own small holdings with crofting, weaving and looking after their sheep or cutting peat. Life was even quieter on the Sabbath – almost extinct.

Michael lived by himself – one of several reasons he had had for coming to this part of the island. In the evening or late afternoon after a hard day's work, he took Musty for walks along the deserted shore, climbing from the cliffs to the almost inaccessible bays and beaches. Fortunately, Musty never chased sheep – being more frightened of them than they were of him; he was even occasionally chased by them! Musty could get away with chasing ministers but chasing sheep was fatal – a capital offence on the island.

They had met no one before on these walks. Michael had been lost in thought and had not seen the Minister till his head rose above the cliff top as he came up from the shore. He had scrambled across Michael's path, with Musty growling and barking at his heels. Musty was always protesting at something and Michael had long since ceased to take any notice of him.

'I've not yet made your acquaintance, Mr Gunn.'

The Minister had not called on Michael and Michael had not attended his kirk. The Church of Scotland was but a remnant on the island and ever stricter and narrow degrees of Presbyterianism had broken free from it and formed exclusive congregations, the Free Church by far the largest of them. Rarely a word passed between the members of these various congregations.

'I am not very sociable – too fond of my own company, Mr McAvoy,' Michael replied apologetically.

Malcolm had greatly interested him in religion – in his own deep and universal religious philosophy but never in any particular denomination. What little he had met of church ministers and priests and church services had put him off conventional religion altogether. He had been baptised into the Church of England.

'You are a reader.'

Mrs McIver who came to clean and dust for Michael weekly had no doubt reported back the presence of a considerable library in his house.

'Do you read The Book?' A note of severity entered the Minister's voice.

An outbreak of barking from Musty at his tone did not this time disturb him.

'Yes, but I must admit to finding large parts of it difficult, Mr McAvoy,' Michael replied honestly.

'Mr Gunn, you are speaking of the Word of God, the Book of Books and are crossing your name from the Book of Life.'

The Minister spoke harshly but Michael warmed to him because of the deep compassion in his voice.

Strict Sabbatarianism reigned unchallenged over the whole island and all the separated congregations, otherwise bitterly divided from each other, were united in this, and in a horror of Catholicism. Indeed, they all held the Word of God and the Bible to be one and the same. To the stranger, however, there was no distinguishable difference between any of them: the services were identical and the gloomy, loveless and uncompromising spirit of Calvin brooded over the whole island. Religion had put up a barrier between him and the inhabitants of the island. To him, the spirit of

Woden and Thor still lingered high above the clouds, the rain, hail, snow, wild winds, mountains, moors and raging seas and the Valkyries hovered yet, waiting to carry off the fallen warriors of their choice on their milk white steeds across the rainbow bridge to Valhalla, while the three Norns: Urd, the Past and Vernandi, the Present, wove all day what Skuld, the Future, tore to fragments all night – the web of his life. For him all was not predetermined in accordance with the doctrines of Calvin.

Michael's uncle, Malcolm, had told him that true religion is inward and invisible – independent of anything external, be it church, dogma, doctrine or book, and it was between himself and God only, guarded and cherished in the soul and kept unsullied and undisturbed by the world about him. To Malcolm, God was love, absolute love and the only true and acceptable worship was self-giving love. 'Nothing but love can make a bad heart good,' he had said.

'No church, bible or ritual, only the grace of God, which is love.'

Michael had loved Malcolm, not God. His chief reason for coming to the island had been the social, intellectual and spiritual freedom it offered. He felt the Minister was reaching out to fetter and imprison him in his own narrow confines and load him with his own heavy chains.

They walked on without speaking for a while. Michael put himself into the other man's place: he and Musty had offended him.

'I owe you an apology, Mr McAvoy. My dog and I are both mavericks. I am very sorry to have interrupted your quiet walk. Musty! Come and say you are sorry and that you will never do it again.'

He called the little dog to them and Musty came, wagging his tail. He licked the Minister's hand as he stooped and held it out to him.

The Minister said nothing until they reached the village.

'You'll come and take your tea with mother and me,' the Minister was surprised to hear himself say. It was the second sudden impulse he had obeyed that strange day.

'I'll be glad to, Mr McAvoy, and to meet your mother,' Michael was equally surprised to hear himself say. 'I'll just take the dog away home first.'

'You'll not. He's welcome, too.'

All three turned into the manse.

'This is our neighbour, mother,' the Minister announced in a loud, clear voice.

He introduced Michael to a grey-haired woman with rather too firm and severe a mouth. Her large, expressive brown eyes were too penetratingly observant to leave anyone with anything unworthy to conceal or be ashamed of at ease in her presence. She was much larger and taller than her son.

'Mr Gunn lives in our old home.'

'I have seen you about, Mr Gunn.'

She was a woman of few words which expressed a great deal. Michael was immediately aware of her strong disapproval of his non-attendance at Kirk but not of him as a person.

'What Kirk do you belong to?'

'I was baptised into the Church of England. My mother and father were baptised into it too but I very rarely attend.'

'Not the Church of that "Honest to God" Bishop!' cried the Minister in horror.

None of them had read the book which had just come out and caused such a stir.

'My uncle taught me that the only way to be honest to God is to strip the self to the soul. God does the rest.'

'Mr Gunn will be sharing our tea, Mother,' said the Minister, changing the subject hastily.

There was an instant change in her manner. 'There, you will sit comfortably by the fire till it is ready.'

Michael had been led straight into what was clearly used as a dining, sitting, general living room. The table was already set and there were two easy chairs by the blazing peat fire, before which Musty was already lying on a rug, his back towards them, toasting his paws and presumably fast asleep. Mrs McAvoy's welcome had no pretence whatsoever in it and Michael was soon as much at ease as Musty but not with such abandon.

The Minister excused himself and left to give his mother a hand in the next room, which Michael presumed to be the kitchen. They did not shut the door or lower their voices. Living together and never having been separated since the Minister was born, they were quite unaccustomed to having guests, except the very formal and special occasions when other ministers came to stay in the manse to assist with the communions, celebrated twice yearly.

'You must give him a good tea, mother.'

'Is not your tea always a good tea, Ian?'

'Of course, but there is reason in my asking.'

'What is that?'

'The man's damned, Mother.'

'Damned, you say?'

'Damned past redemption.'

'And he, only in his late thirties, Ian.'

'There is good in him and in his dog, Mother, despite the devil starting out of both with alarming frequency.'

'Aye. I can see it. You'll bring him often.'

There was that note of compassion in her voice that Michael had also detected in the Minister earlier. They were both less harsh than the God they worshipped.

The tea was an excellent one. Mrs McAvoy bought nothing from the baker's van, though Michael had found all baking on the island to be of the very best. She appreciated Michael's appetite and his obvious satisfaction.

'You like home baking, Mr Gunn?'

'I do indeed, Mrs McAvoy.'

'It is time you were married yourself.'

'I'm a settled bachelor, like the Minister here.'

'You are over young to be so decided,' said the Minister. 'For myself, I've never lacked for an excellent housekeeper and I'm past sixty.'

'I am twenty-eight and have always done so.'

'You look older than your years,' said Mrs McAvoy. There was a return of that note in her voice.

'You look remarkably younger than yours, Mrs McAvoy.'

'I am eighty-two. Is your mother not living?'

'She and my father were killed together when I was a baby. They had married very young, both not seventeen, because of the threat of war. He and his twin brother joined up together three months later. My mother went to Victoria Station to meet my father on his first home leave after Dunkirk in August 1940, just after the Battle of Britain had begun. They were blown up returning to the house. A neighbour had insisted on minding me while my mother went to meet my father, or I would have been blown up with them. I was put in an orphanage until my father's twin brother came home from the Far East and could establish a home for me.'

'He wasn't married?'

'No. His first ambition had been to be an actor but after their father's early death from tuberculosis and war wounds in the trenches in the 1914 war, they had been brought up by their grandfather. He had articled them at a very young age in the family firm of chartered accountants, in order to get them settled in life, as he was himself very old and knew he had not long to live. The twins were only just sixteen and had done very well at school. Both volunteered and joined up three days before Hitler invaded Poland.

'My uncle gave up all thought of a stage career to look

after me. After release from the army, he returned to the firm, passing all the accountancy and actuarial exams, taking an LLB and also becoming a barrister. He had a brilliant career. After taking me from the orphanage, except for one short period when we had a self-appointed housekeeper, our establishment remained strictly bachelor: we ate out or had gas ring meals. Malcolm hated being dependent on others and having, in the early days, to make arrangements for me with friends and neighbours when he was at work and during school holidays. He sent me to a good Prep School when I was eight and then to a public school. He was no cook but we foraged and did well enough for ourselves. Nothing like this.'

Michael stopped, surprised at his unusual talkativeness.

'That is twice your father falsified his age,' said Mrs McAvoy, disapprovingly.

'Where is your uncle now?' asked the Minister.

'He disappeared when I was nineteen.'

'Disappeared!' said Mrs McAvoy in a voice that suggested that he had no right to do such a thing.

'He went off to work as usual one morning and never arrived.'

'Didn't he give any indication of such an intention?'

'No. When he left, he obviously had no such intention. It is an unsolved mystery. Something happened between his saying goodbye to me, leaving the flat and the time he should have arrived at work, which decided him to leave his job and leave me to look after myself.'

'Didn't the police trace him?' asked Mrs McAvoy.

'It was never a matter for the police, though they *were* called in at first. The office and I received brief notes from him the next day, stating no more than that, for entirely selfish reasons and with all the good will in the world, he had decided to leave both his work and his home.'

'Had you quarrelled?' asked the Minister.

'Never. I had too much respect for him and for his good opinion. I hero-worshipped him. We always got on very well together. We had recently disagreed for the first time but very amicably. I had won, which I never would have done without his help, a scholarship to Oxford. Then, having for years encouraged and groomed me for it, I was surprised and quite unable to understand why he did not want me to take it up, or even to go to Oxford. He had a dislike for grooves and that one was so deep that once I got into it, I would never get out. "All institutions, universities, schools, class systems," he said, "brand you for life. Total submission," he said, "to any external influence is paid for by a loss of the integrity of the self. Personality and feeling of security are strengthened but real individual spiritual growth is stunted. I must," he said, "develop every potential and native talent, not just one or two in one direction, nor for the reward, ambition, wealth or honour or success they offered but solely for spiritual development and fulfilment. I must grow like a plant and flower, not shrivel and die. Life," he said, "is a means to an end, not an end in itself: it has a very great purpose. Shrivelling begins the moment it becomes an end in itself".'

'How strange!' exclaimed the Minister.

'What happened to you? Did you go to Oxford?' asked Mrs McAvoy.

'No. His partners from the chartered accountancy firm took me over. They paid me a salary during my articles and the rent of the flat my uncle and I had shared together all those years.' .

'You are still with them, then,' said Mrs McAvoy, wondering what he could be doing here on their island.

'Yes. I still have the flat in London but I prefer living here. My work is highly specialised and aimed at individual clients. Given the essential particulars, I can bring most of it away here. A telephone and a tape recorder is often all I need to keep my secretary, or rather my personal assistant, in London busy. Of course, I have to meet clients and pay frequent visits there.'

Michael had not fully understood his uncle but had seen at the time, that to become a chartered accountant as he had done, would be to develop in an entirely new direction. He had been a brilliant scholar at his public school and an all-rounder, passing with top grades in Physics, Chemistry and Mathematics and had then turned to, and won, his scholarship to Oxford in the Humanities. He had not been at all attracted to office work, which he thought must be tremendously boring and uninteresting but he had on the contrary, found it fascinating and developed an extraordinary memory for figures. He seemed to have the same gift, amounting to genius, that his uncle had had, or so he was told by his uncle's partners. He could grasp their significance at a glance.

Michael was regretting his confidences and self-betrayal, almost as the words left his lips. He had never spoken so frankly to anyone in his life, not even his uncle; he could not understand himself. He had broken the resolution and habit of a lifetime. The minister and his mother had set him off and something in him had taken over, despite himself. It felt almost as if he had been committing suicide. He had placed his whole way of life on the island, his social isolation and independence, all the reasons for his coming in the first place, in jeopardy. This was confirmed when after tea, the conversation between mother and son was resumed in the kitchen.

'All those who should have cared and brought him to the Lord were gone before he started his schooling.'

'They were none of them spared. I think he is more unfortunate than he's damned, Ian.'

'I would think so,' said the Minister.

'He has lived too much by himself,' said Mrs McAvoy.

In the silence that followed till they joined him again, Michael could almost hear them working away heart and mind, not with his past but with his future.

★

Michael sighed the next morning. He felt lonely and went to the bedroom door. 'Musty, you little rascal,' he called down the stairs. 'Come up here.'

As light as a feather, the little body came flying up the stairs. Musty's bright black eyes sparkled in their white almond setting. As he leapt onto the bed and made for the pillows, he made a funny little noise, as if so much happiness couldn't all be pent up in such a tiny body – some of it had to escape.

There was clear evidence before the end of the week that Michael had not been wrong about that pregnant silence. He became aware of a distinctly noticeable change of attitude, not only towards himself but towards Musty. The first tangible piece of evidence appeared the second morning after his visit to the new manse. He nearly toppled over a sack, bulging and overflowing with turnips placed at his back door. The next morning he found a sheep's head about a third the size of Musty, clearly intended for him. Their attitude had also changed. Musty did not stop barking but his tail was wagging as he did so, giving the whole game away. As Michael dragged the sack into the large larder of the old manse, a feeling of human warmth more than offset its chilled air. Nevertheless, Michael felt a sense of loss that he too had given the whole show away.

He had not however been a complete stranger to the island: his great grandfather had come from it. Michael had not paid much attention to the details but Malcolm had spoken of it and of him. He had probably been a younger son or brother, seeking adventure or a better livelihood.

After Malcolm left, Michael had been strangely drawn to it, though he had as yet made no effort to find out where the croft was or what part of the island his great grandfather had come from. No doubt they had cousins living there with whom, Michael assumed, all contact had long since been lost. He had made no attempt to establish any family connection but he had taken to the bleak moors, wide skies and the long, lonely shores and the powerful Atlantic as if he were a native. The people, until that moment, had been strangers who, despite being bilingual, were happiest in a language quite foreign to him and which he had no inclination to learn.

Michael felt that he had made a mistake in speaking about himself to the Minister and his mother but was relieved that he had not betrayed his origin and the fact that, with centuries of intermarriage on their remote island, he must be related to many of its small population. Life would be one continuous ceilidh had he done that. As it was, despite a Scottish name and one common on the island, he was considered a Sassenach and expected to be odd and not to conform.

Michael dreaded losing his independence and mastery of his time; he enjoyed living alone, isolated, with almost no human contact. With the exception of Mrs McIver who came and cleaned the house and did his washing, he had until now limited all human contact to a wave of the arm and a passing remark on the weather.

★

Was this life already at an end, gone beyond recall? he asked himself as the two-seater plane took off, with Musty safely secured in the seat behind him. He would return very soon, after a short period of concentrated work in London but not to solitude – never again to a life of isolation. His despondency would have been greater still had he known that his less but still very independent life in London was about to suffer a similar fate.

Chapter Two

Love Story

The two-seater aircraft his uncle had given him, and trained him to pilot, rose above the clouds into ethereal beauty and solitude, that the noise of the engine and the presence of Musty, comfortably and happily secured behind him in no way disturbed. Michael was reminded of Malcolm's love of flying, of the wonderful flights of thought that they had taken together and caught again a glimpse of Malcolm's greatest thought, the Flight of the Soul. Malcolm had inspired him as a child with the love of flying – the freedom that flying gave to birds, butterflies, bees, fairies, angels and men but also to the soul. He had not only taught him to love space but had inspired him with wonderful thoughts of truth, beauty and goodness and of the supersensual and spiritual. Together, they had soared above time and space, travelling at the speed of love on the wings of love, up into the absolute freedom of love. Young and fresh in mind, Malcolm had always seemed more like an elder brother than an uncle or father figure. We either free our immortal souls, our real selves, he had said, by dying to selfishness, sin and evil, and escape into eternity or we imprison ourselves in time, are lost, bury ourselves in the material and the physical.

Then, Malcolm had gone. Michael had fallen back down to earth, no longer walked on waves or rose on wings of love into the kingdom of love but, like those about him, never thought or believed he had a soul. The years in the orphanage and the sensual, material world about him had resumed their overpowering influence over him. He no longer rose into what Malcolm once, laughingly, told him had been described philosophically in the twentieth century as, 'the ontological sphere of immaterial being,' but was lost in a world that only believed in progress and in a purely physical origin and destination of man.

Above the clouds, with the wild elemental beauty of the island below and the vast universe of stars surrounding him, Malcolm seemed closer to him – to repossess him. Michael looked down upon the wild, desolate, uninhabited stretches of mountainous country and recalled Malcolm telling him what he as a child had been told by his grand-father. Malcolm had been told of the life his grandfather's grand or great grandmother had lived and most unwillingly been compelled to leave. She had lived in a community which had been quite isolated with little or no contact with the rest of the island. The sadness and love for that lost life lingered yet in the telling. It was a love story, not between two lovers but of a whole community for each other, in which the most wonderful and exciting thing that ever happened was the birth of a child; the saddest, the death of any one of them.

She had no idea how old she was: time there had been calculated, if at all, by daylight and the seasons. She had never known another life. The community was hidden away in a valley behind mountains that swept down to the Atlantic. It was quite isolated and cut off and there was no road to it, no trodden path or track. There may have been others like it but she did not know of them. There could be none more sequestered. It was separated from the only town on the island by miles of uninhabited country, the only route to which was by sea.

The community had access to a tiny, natural harbour

with a sandy beach, almost completely concealed and sheltered from the sea by cliffs and rocks – a natural protection from human invasion and the violence of the stormy sea. They had escaped invasion for centuries and probably far back in the mists of time, they themselves had been the first and last to invade. The men came down to a huge cave in which they kept the boats, used for fishing, and went beachcombing to gather drift wood, seaweed and other valuable and curious things cast up upon the white glittering sand along the coast. Never a life of plenty, at best of bare subsistence, they had known hunger and its satisfaction but had escaped envy, desire and greed: there was nothing to desire and no one to envy. Their most precious possession and their sole resource was their confidence in, and their love for each other. The survival of each individual member depended upon the love of the community which, the more it was shared, the greater it grew.

They required every hour of daylight for work in order to survive and every hour of darkness for rest. They were entirely self-sufficient, with a water mill and a smithy, spinning wheels and looms and simple sanitation. They had peat for fuel, oat straw to roof and driftwood for furniture and implements. Peat, weaving, sheep, cattle, oats, vegetables and rhubarb were all in common shared amongst one big family.

Occasionally, one of them, invariably a man, disappeared inland and was either never heard of again or sooner or later returned, either alone to die among his own or returning with some material benefit, spade, peat iron, idea or skill that satisfied a need or eased work. Sometimes some would return with cattle, sheep, a pony or a horse. One such man had done well and had made a fortune, which he exhausted bringing into being a circuitous, rarely used cart track which wound round the mountains and the lochs and over the stone bridges he built across rivers and streams for a hundred miles to the town. He had thought to bring a lifeline to the community but it had eventually destroyed it. Most who returned, she had said, behaved like survivors who had been through hell and were so glad to be back that they could never bring themselves to describe what they had seen, experienced and suffered. No one disappeared for years after their return. None could read. There was no minister, no bible, no Sabbath. Every day was a Sabbath. Their religion was love.

Was he looking down on the true source and origin of his being or was it beyond and above in the heights to which he rose, Michael wondered, as he and Musty sped on their way towards London. Malcolm had said that it was neither, that, like a seed, it was within him.

It was a tall man who climbed out of the plane and made his way with a small dog at his heels across the private airfield and, after checking in at the office walked over to a bus stop and waited for a Green Line bus. A keen observer would have been struck by a similarity between dog and master. There was an intelligent brightness and just a little of the scamp in the corners of their eyes that seemed to smile, one with his tongue out, neither betraying what they were thinking.

Arrived in London he went straight to his office, except for a brief pause by a green patch for which Musty was grateful. His secretary, Margaret Smith, was working hard as he entered but interrupted her work immediately and stretched out her arm for a file that she had at hand, ready for his return.

'Good morning, Mr Gunn. Your correspondence.' She handed it to him. 'I have kept this one unopened and separate as it is marked "private".'

He took the file and the letter from her and opened the letter first. It read:

Dear Gunn,

I have decided to remove from your care the heavy burden of my tax affairs. This in no way implies any criticism of the splendid work you have done for me. Quite the contrary. Reading your returns and reports and studying your methods and your remarkable and formidable knowledge in this field, has been an intellectual delight.

I won't bore you with the reasons for my decision. I know that you will all too quickly fill the vacancy. I am the loser.

It has often been a cause of regret to me that we have not met, or even spoken on the telephone. This is not politeness. I should very much like to know you and would be delighted if you and your wife would come and spend a weekend with my daughter and myself very soon. May I look forward to hearing from you?

Yours sincerely
Fairfield Broughton

Fairfield Broughton had one of those 'Count of Monte-cristo fortunes' – inexhaustible and hydra-headed. Even without Michael's protective scrutiny and the very high rate of taxation, Her Majesty's Inspector of Taxes could help himself as plentifully as he pleased and Fairfield Broughton would still remain a very, very rich man, far beyond any consideration of income. His letter of dismissal was both surprising and disappointing yet it was also challenging and interesting. Surprising because Fairfield Broughton had brought great pressure to bear to persuade Michael to accept him. There was an immense demand for Michael's services: his reputation as an expert, approaching genius, on taxation and for his knowledge of the subtle distinctions between avoidance and evasion had proved irresistible to Fairfield Broughton.

Michael had never acted on impulse, never accepted social engagements and lived alone, lost to his work. He was a very quick worker; far from finding them boring, he had developed a sixth sense with figures, read whether they were true or false almost intuitively and grasped their significance at a glance. He understood the financial position of the client, whether individual, company, corporation or government department, ever more speedily in succeeding years. He spent his leisure time looking at the world with interested amusement from a position of distance and objectivity. He was not at all shy of people, despite rare close contact. Since leaving the orphanage, he had lived with two people only: his uncle until his disappearance, and the woman they had taken in for only four months. He thought he knew both but in fact he knew neither. Since the disappearance of his uncle he had lived in the flat as he did in the old manse, alone, until Musty arrived. The Minister had now broken the long spell by inviting him into the manse at Foghar.

Impulse now led him to accept another social engagement. This was not out of curiosity to discover why Fairfield Broughton had withdrawn after making such efforts to become one of his select clientele. It was rather the man himself that attracted him, or rather what he had heard and read about him. He reached for the telephone.

The secretary who answered had a pleasant, friendly but very efficient voice. 'Mr Broughton is out, but will return shortly, Mr Gunn. May I give him a message?'

'I have a letter of invitation for a weekend and wondered if he could lunch with me today to discuss it.'

Her answered surprised him.

'He will be delighted to lunch with you. At what time and where?'

He appointed a time and place where he occasionally lunched with clients.

'He will be there on time without fail,' she said with firm assurance.

Michael could visualise her straightening his tie, brushing his jacket and seeing that he was at the restaurant on time. He was.

His own secretary was fairly new but neither she nor her predecessor, who had been with him for years and had left to get married, would ever have presumed to make such a decision for him without first consulting him. Michael disliked having his own life run for him and, put off by this, was inclined not accept the weekend invitation. He dismissed all thought of refusal, however, at the appearance of his guest at the entrance to the lounge bar ante-room. Their recognition of each other was immediate, though they had never met before and neither had any doubt or made any enquiry after the other's identity.

In point of attraction, Fairfield Broughton exceeded all expectation. In his middle fifties, he gave Michael the impression of a man who had not only lost nothing with years but was gaining in stature all the time. He was splendid – strikingly impressive with thick greying hair and eyes that missed nothing, penetrating, keenly observant yet full of humour. He was a magnetically attractive figure.

They were in great contrast to each other. Michael's thin, strong face gave him a rather 'Sherlock Holmes' appearance without the pipe but the intellectual tautness of his features was made completely human by the expression in the corners of his eyes. Fairfield Broughton's amused expression revealed a sense of the incongruous, the ridiculous and an ability to discern all self-deception, hypocrisy and inconsistency, any nonsense at all but good-naturedly and entirely without malice. Both were instinctively and intuitively attracted to each other.

'You would have been surprised to receive my letter?'

'You were so pressing for us to take on the job.'

'For *you* to take it on.'

'I don't understand. It still has to be done.'

'I thought you the last person to support an idea which, to be honest, is not mine and which I don't yet fully understand but which revolutionises my policy towards the Inland Revenue.'

'I'm not quite with you,' said Michael, his interest awakened, beginning to see what was coming.

'I no longer wish to evade or avoid taxation but to pay what the law demands.'

'That is precisely what all my clients do.'

'You are remarkable at finding weaknesses in fiscal law to enable them to avoid taxation.'

'Only to protect them from minds as keenly interested in exploiting weaknesses to their disadvantage, before the slower moving legislative machine can rectify them.'

'In future, I want to pay all that the law demands in the spirit, not the letter. My aim is to increase wealth, reduce unemployment, raise living standards and improve living conditions, more by redistribution than by accumulation. Would you be prepared to carry on in this spirit?'

'You remind me of my uncle – what he would want to do in your position. The answer is yes, but it would require frequent consultation to clarify any difficulties.'

'Good. That is settled. Now when can you and your wife join us for the weekend?'

'Next weekend? If the invitation is not conditional on my being married!'

'Then there will just be the three of us.'

On his return to his office, Musty was in the same place he had left him, lying with his head between his two front paws, his ears pricked, staring straight at the door. He did not stir when Michael entered. He never did, not until Michael bent down where he stood at the door, about five yards from him, and fixed upon him an identical stare.

Then for a second or two they would stare each other out until Musty yawned, got to his feet and walked slowly over to receive the attention he regarded as his by right, knew he was going to get and took completely for granted, reminding Michael that he too had taken something for granted.

'Michael Gunn, here. Can I speak to Mr Broughton?'

'I'm sorry, Mr Gunn. Mr Broughton is out and won't be in this afternoon. Can I give him a message?'

'I'm spending the coming weekend with him. He said that the invitation was not conditional upon my having a wife but I forgot that my acceptance *is* conditional upon my bringing a dog.'

There was a distinctly perceptible pause of surprise at the other end of the line and then came that pleasant but very efficient and assured secretarial voice.

'Of course, you must bring your dog, Mr Gunn. Has he or she any particular tastes?'

'He has developed a strong partiality for sheep's head recently.'

Michael rang off, even more surprised especially now he had met Fairfield Broughton, that any secretary, however efficient and long in his service, should presume to make such a decision without consulting him.

★

His telephone was ringing as he entered his office on Friday morning. He recognised the efficient voice at once.

'Mr Gunn? Mr Broughton is very sorry, a technical fault has grounded his plane and will delay him in Yorkshire. He wonders if you could leave earlier, preferably after lunch, to avoid the weekend traffic. The car will collect you as arranged, but take you all the way to Broughton. He will go straight there from Yorkshire. He will see that you are back in your office on time on Monday. Could you be ready at two o'clock this afternoon?'

Michael was ready but not for what met his eyes when, with Musty at his heels, he opened the door of his flat that afternoon at two o'clock precisely. Standing there was the most beautiful woman he had ever seen.

'Mr Gunn?'

He knew instantly who it was but gone was that efficient secretarial voice and all his thoughts of secretarial presumption. He was surprised Fairfield Broughton had any mind of his own at all with such a creature as his secretary. He stood looking at her and only the normal reaction of smiling and shaking hands gave him his usual appearance of self possession.

'I'm Elizabeth Broughton. I've left the car in an awkward place. If we run, we may beat the traffic warden and reach it first.'

She turned and ran, Musty and Michael after her. The noise of the flat door slamming behind him reassured Michael that he had remembered to shut it. She was already seated in the driver's seat of a perfect Rolls Royce when they caught up with her.

As he got in and sat down in front with Musty on his lap, silence seemed natural. It was an uplifting experience, moving off into the traffic in that beautiful car with such a beautiful companion. Fairfield Broughton had had the car specially designed to retain the spaciousness of the splendid vehicles he had known all his life, without losing its graceful modern lines. Michael had not had to twist and dump himself like a sack into his seat, his legs raised before him as if in a dentist's chair but sat, in full control of his limbs, in a position from which he could extricate himself with ease at the end of the journey and could meanwhile appraise the driver at leisure and in comfort, without embarrassing her.

Elizabeth Broughton had that rare natural beauty and

composure that expressed her whole being perfectly. One couldn't imagine her ever disturbing or being disturbed. In feature, form, body and soul, she expressed intelligence, goodness, charm and strength of character.

'How long have you been your father's secretary?'

'About ten days.' She turned for a second and glanced at him with a smile. 'Why do you ask? I persuaded my father to let me take Angela Quail's job while she went on holiday. She comes back on Monday. I had just finished a course in child psychology, not with any intention of becoming a child psychologist, just to be with children and learn more about them.'

'They all want shooting. Not children! Child psychologists!'

'Not all, surely.'

'All, without exception.'

'Why?'

'What children need is love and understanding, not psychology.'

'Of course children need love and understanding. Why the blood lust for child psychologists?'

'I've known one all my life.'

'What's her name?'

'Dorothy Kennedy.'

'Ah!'

'You know her?'

'Yes. She lectured in the Wonderland Home where we did all our practical training. She has just retired at least ten years after the normal age for retirement. Where did you meet her?'

'I was in the Wonderland Home as a child.'

'An orphan?'

Michael told his story.

'And your uncle never married?'

'He is waiting for the right woman to come along.'

'What sort of father did he make?'

'I have no criterion. He was more like an elder brother. He had no criterion either. He was brought up by the now extinct species, a maiden aunt. He and my father were twins. My father married very young, before he was seventeen. I suppose the right woman came along early in his life! My grandfather was the headmaster of a Prep School. He disagreed with my grandmother over the appointment of a school chaplain. She claimed that Christianity should not be taught by a specialist but by the cooperative effort and responsibility of the whole staff. He said a chaplain looked better on the school prospectus.'

'Who won?'

'Ultimately neither. Or perhaps I should say my grandmother. A chaplain was appointed who not only baptised but was godfather to both my uncle and my father but the next year my grandmother ran away with him and neither has been heard of since.'

'It must be in the genes.'

'What must be in the genes?'

'Disappearing – in your family. What happened to your grandfather?'

'He died very shortly afterwards, it was said, of a broken heart. The Doctor diagnosed influenza. I think it was mortification.'

'Over the prospectus.'

'Yes.'

'Perhaps your uncle went on the stage after all.'

'No. He only wanted to go on the stage to get experience of the world and of people, and the war gave him that. When he became a soldier, he realised that what you do or become doesn't matter. Life itself is enough and so is wanting to know what it is all about. He still thinks that all the world's a stage and all the people in it merely players, playing many parts, only they have forgotten their origin and have to learn who they really are and what they are here to do or become. He used to take me to lots of shows, theatres, cinemas, operas and ballets – gave me all his free time and a very happy life. He was very intelligent, exciting too. I didn't always understand him—' Michael paused.

'You have missed him?'

'He was the only real person in my life. I haven't met anyone like him since. Until now,' he added naturally.

'And my father.'

At this point, he became aware of a pair of very bright eyes fixed upon his, Musty's paws planted on his chest and his little cold nose and red tongue on his cheek.

'When did you start mentally shooting child psychologists?'

'When I was about three!' he laughed.

'Dorothy Kennedy?'

'She is my only experience of one, till this afternoon. I am quite certain I would not have felt the same had it been you.'

'I'm glad of that! But don't you think it very unfair to generalise from only one, and that one Dorothy Kennedy?'

'Dorothy Kennedy was and is a whole heap of evidence.'

'Aren't you worried about your poor old uncle! How do you know he hasn't been washed up on some beach, buried in concrete or burnt to death in some fire?'

'He is not the type. He isn't very old. Remember, my father was his twin and married when he was not yet seventeen. He'd only be in his very early forties. I've never worked it out. He was always young to me and had a great sense of humour. Always exuding wisdom, of course.'

They were nearing the end of their journey. They had been travelling north at considerable speed and had turned off the main road into an expanse of unspoilt country of great estates, which the wealth of their owners had so far protected from development: they were not yet cleaved apart by motorways and had absorbed the railway and beautiful little stations completely.

They had fallen into a pleasant, companionable silence when they turned off the road into an entrance with stone pillars on either side, surmounted by griffins. Wrought iron gates stood open and they were suddenly plunged into a shady mass of foliage from trees overarching the driveway. Hundreds of rooks rose up, giving that atmosphere of 'peace disturbed' to the countryside, that gulls do to the sea. They went through deep forest and were sheltered by trees until, after two or three miles, they entered open parkland and were exposed to a view of a rambling warren of a house, so beautiful that it could only be greeted by silence.

Michael knew at once that this was not an acquired home, brought by wealth into the possession of Fairfield Broughton and his daughter, but their ancestral home. Though they were both different in character and temperament, he knew intuitively that this was the source of the unique quality they had in common.

The house was so old that the latest structural additions to the original medieval manor house were Tudor. The whole place had grown slowly through the centuries and had spread in all directions, without any plan, and stopped sometime in the reign of Henry VIII. Tudor chimneys stood out here and there, at different levels and Tudor bricks and windows had been added to stone and half timber. Time had beautified the whole.

Inside, similar changes and additions had gone on into more modern times – cumulative, with nothing being discarded. Staircases, galleries, wainscotting, tapestries, furniture and furnishing – everything had found a place and function, so fitting that any change, alteration or removal would have had the effect of sacrilegious disturbance or violation.

Elizabeth Broughton seemed an intrinsic a part of her

home as everything in and about it. She led Michael, with Musty at his heels, through the main entrance into a low roofed hall with a perfectly proportioned staircase, ascending with broad, low steps to a gallery only nine feet from the ground and only seven feet from its floor to the carved oak ceiling. The whole interior was panelled. Two great, carved heraldic birds stared straight across the hall from newel posts, guarding the way up two flights of stairs, at right angles to reach the gallery. Passageways under identical Tudor arches led off from both gallery and ground floor. One, central and immediately opposite the entrance, led directly into the heart of the house. They crossed and went through this and into a long, wide corridor, past several doors on both sides and into a large, rectangular room with windows from floor to ceiling. It looked out on to a lawn, which ran for about one hundred and fifty yards until the eye was stayed by an old stone wall, over which spread the branches of great elm trees. Above these trees, the rooks still wheeled, squawked and complained of their disturbance by the recent arrival of the car.

'When does his lordship require his sheep's head?' Elizabeth addressed Musty.

He responded by looking straight back at her with an expression so strikingly similar to Michael's, that she could not help glancing at the latter with a little laugh. The little white stub of his tail moved once and then once more, slowly and indecisively, as Musty's eyes searched hers, questioning whether there was something imminent and exciting going to happen so that he could wag it vigorously.

'I'll leave you both here a minute while I get things going, and then show you your room and how to find your way back here for tea. I really won't be a minute.'

She left Michael looking out on to the lawn. The noise of the rooks outside intensified the tranquillity inside the house, taking possession of them all.

There was some domestic help but it remained invisible. Michael never saw any servants and the only indication of any help was at dinner, when dishes were handed to Elizabeth through a deep hatch in the dining room. He gathered, during the course of the weekend, that one of the gardener's wives cooked when needed and Elizabeth was helped with all the cleaning and polishing by the wives and daughters of a gardener and of two gamekeepers who all lived in houses within a mile of the Hall. Elizabeth was chief cook, cleaner and housekeeper. A first class engineer and a mechanic, both married, lived near the small airfield and were responsible for the maintenance of the aeroplane, three cars and the electricity plant at the house. No one but Elizabeth and her father lived in the house.

Both men drank moderately and left the dinner table with Elizabeth for the drawing room – the room into which she had led Michael on their arrival. Despite its size, there was a pleasant intimacy about the room, enhanced by the light of the fire, although it was early summer.

'What is the name of this house?' said Michael, upon whom it was making a deep impression.

'Just Broughton,' said his host. 'It has been called that for a long time now. In Norman times it was a castle and was then called Broughton Castle. Part of the moat is still there and the lower part of the original keep is incorporated into the house and covered by subsequent roofing. It is easily identifiable by the original stone spiral steps which lead to long since disused servants' quarters. Then, later it became a manor house and the great hall was built, which you must see. It was called Broughton Hall until, in time, it just became Broughton.'

'It must have been very difficult to keep the estate intact and pay death duties.'

'My grandfather only just managed. It was a lifelong struggle.'

'A wonderful way to spend a life.'

'Elizabeth says we can't choose our parents, the place, or the circumstances into which we are born but we are free to choose how we react to them and to the succeeding events and situations in which we find ourselves all our lives. Well or badly.'

'Fall or do not fall into temptation,' laughed Elizabeth.

'That is almost word for word Malcolm's teaching. He said, "We are free within limits. We can choose between loving or hating, good or ill will, right or wrong. That applies to how we spend our time: we can do good, evil or nothing at all with it, waste it."'

'Did he learn that from the War? Elizabeth was telling me about him. Would he have considered my grandfather spent his time well? Or should he have sold Broughton and given the proceeds to the poor?'

'Only if he was too attached.'

'Like those stockbrokers to their fortunes, who threw themselves from their skyscraper office windows during the Wall Street Crash,' said Elizabeth.

'I think I'd take to the windowsill if I lost a place like Broughton,' laughed Michael but he was really thinking of Elizabeth. 'What do you do about security?'

'Take every precaution against fire and burglary. All is covered by insurance but everything here is irreplaceable and it is impossible to calculate its real value. We don't keep a safe full of jewels and negotiable bonds and so far the house has never been burgled or broken into. The dozens of easier, more accessible houses to burgle all around us may account for that. The park is surrounded by forest and there is only one way in.'

'No security staff?'

'Only guardian angels,' said Elizabeth.

'Don't they only do night duty?' asked Michael.

'Ours work twenty-four hours a day.'

'That's on good authority. Elizabeth took a first in Theology.'

'Then the course in child psychology?'

'That came after a doctorate in philosophy.' Fairfield Broughton laughed. 'Elizabeth is first and foremost the philosopher.'

'You wouldn't learn much psychology from Dorothy Kennedy's lectures. I found her terribly boring as a child.'

'She had no understanding whatsoever of the mind of a child!'

'Difficult to imagine her ever being one.'

'It is remarkable you even remembering her, after all these years,' said Fairfield Broughton.

'She kept in touch with us.'

'Had become attached to you in the home?'

'She never noticed me or took the least interest in me, or in any of us individually and only gave us very boring talks, which never meant a thing. The only thing I remember of them is her telling us that there are two dialects spoken in Albania – Geg in the north and Tosk in the South.'

'Did she and your uncle become friends when he came to visit you?'

'I don't think Dorothy Kennedy has ever made friends with anyone. Her turning up was as complete a surprise to him as it was to me – a shock in fact. She just turned up at the flat six months after he took me away from the home and asked to stay with us until she could find another house or flat. We often discussed it. We came to the conclusion that I must have been the only orphan anyone ever came to take away from the home and that she had got our address from the office. She insisted on keeping house for us. Her cooking was quite terrible. All her meals were appalling. We had to eat hundreds of little hard rock buns. She stayed four months and my uncle nearly stopped laughing. I think Malcolm was thinking of leaving himself. Perhaps that first put the idea into his head! She could have solved her housing problem and had our flat had she stayed another month.'

'Was she lonely?'

'No. She very soon made it clear she preferred her own company. She was glad when we went out and left her alone and she never came with us. Needless to say, we went out as often as we could! Malcolm took me out even more than usual those four months.'

'Did you see much of her after that?'

'That was quite unpredictable. Sooner or later she gets on the wrong side of everybody about her – thinks they are hostile, dislike her or are out to cheat her and is desperate to get away and change house. For some inexplicable reason she latched on to us.'

'She must have been struck by your uncle and seen him as a sort of lifeline,' said Elizabeth.

'She never showed the least curiosity or personal interest in either of us. We never even exchanged Christmas cards. We only heard from her when she wanted to move. We would both go round together, and she would give us a rock bun and a cup of lukewarm tea while she complained about the people upstairs, the landlord, the neighbours, even the postman, the milkman and the paperboy. We never knew where we were with her, one minute agreeing, the next changing her mind. She left everything to us but the final decisions. She was a nightmare! Often she wouldn't even leave the car but took an instant dislike to a property and wouldn't even view it. Worse still, she would decide to take it without viewing it! And then opt out at the last moment when all but legally bound.'

'Why on earth did he put up with her? I say, you didn't take her on after your uncle disappeared, did you?' asked Fairfield Broughton, anxiously.

'My uncle said she was good for the soul. It is only too

easy to love the loveable and turn your back on the unlovable.'

'Only to disappear,' said Elizabeth sadly. 'We find this uncle of yours intensely interesting but you haven't answered our question. Did you carry on the maddening work after he left?'

'Yes,' admitted Michael. 'I plead guilty.'

'But insane,' said Elizabeth. 'What an influence he must have over you still. You must have missed him terribly.'

'His disappearance was like the light failing suddenly everywhere. A complete blackout. A feeling of total loss.'

'It was cruel to leave you suddenly like that.'

Michael looked at her in surprise.

'Oh, no! Malcolm is quite incapable of hurting anyone. He heals wounds, never inflicts them. He was always helping lame ducks over stiles. One of his partners told me after his disappearance that when I was away at school, he used to spend his nights visiting all the places in London where the homeless were living rough on pavements and in bus shelters, and giving the alcoholics and drug addicts the only food they had that day. Coming back from a night club once, a friend told me he had seen Malcolm trying to persuade some young people to return home and face up to whatever it was that had driven them away. He left because he thought it best for me.'

'How could that be?'

'To make me stand on my own feet, become independent of him, learn to stand back from life, not be caught in its machinery, catch at the overhanging branch and not be swept downstream and out to sea.'

'Perhaps that's why he disappeared. He caught hold of the overhanging branch to stop himself being swept out to sea,' said Elizabeth.

Michael looked at her thoughtfully, both interested and struck by this idea.

'He always gave the impression of being very firmly in charge from the tow path but I think you may have something there. You would know about that, wouldn't you? He may have gone to climb a mountain and left the river altogether.'

'Have you ever thought of looking for him?'

'No. He'll turn up at the right time, if there is a right time.'

'You have the highest opinion of him,' said Fairfield Broughton.

'Increasingly so since he left. I never tried consciously to form one before.'

'Took him for granted, perhaps.'

'No, appreciated him too much, I should say,' said Elizabeth. 'It must have been terrible for him to lose his twin brother and your mother because being a twin he must have loved her too. He must have loved you too and found it difficult to part from you.'

'I've never thought of that. Malcolm would have done that. He was so much bigger and stronger than I. I depended on him too much. I hadn't a real being of my own.'

'Do you still feel cast adrift?'

'No. He had taught me self-reliance. He had made sure I would find myself, stand on my own feet and could face life alone; could swim before he shoved me in the deep end. I didn't like it at first – not because I couldn't swim but because I missed and wanted him. I had to replace him with myself and to come into existence in my own right, start off on my own and be content to know that I was only at the starting point and had a long way to catch up if I was to find myself where he is. Now I'm glad. I wouldn't like it any other way. I have even coped with Dorothy Kennedy on my own!'

'Have you found friends?' asked Fairfield Broughton.

'None like him. Business friends really. I haven't had

any social life. My first experience of it since he left was afternoon tea this past week with the local minister and his mother on the Great Isle where I live. This is my first weekend stay with anyone!'

'And I hope it won't be your last,' said Elizabeth. 'You've got Musty! Where did you get him?'

'A pet shop in the shopping centre I go to, which I've passed hundreds of times without looking in, until one day I found a shoe lace undone and stopped close by the window to tie it. There I found his face, then a tiny puppy one, a few inches from mine, fixing me with that same look he has now, his head between his paws, all bright-eyed, and giving nothing away. I went straight in and bought him and went round the self-service shop, him sitting in the metal shopping basket!'

'You must bring him here often. You and he will always be welcome. Any weekend you are not in Scotland. Remember, you and Elizabeth will be dealing with my tax matters now. That was her chief reason for taking over from Angela Quail while she was on holiday. You will be aware now who is responsible for my change of attitude towards the Inland Revenue. To be frank, I don't fully understand why but I am a trustful soul and place myself entirely in her hands. I haven't had time to take a doctorate in philosophy.'

'Perhaps a course in child psychology is all that is required. In the Wonderland Home!'

'Imbibing the original thoughts of Dorothy Kennedy!'

'No thoughts ever originated in Dorothy Kennedy! Only resentment. She has a genius for taking offence, nursing a grudge and generally being negative.'

'Couldn't Malcolm change her?' asked Elizabeth.

'Could anything?' asked Fairfield Broughton.

'Malcolm thought it was too late. She has petrified before she has learnt that she must change herself and not her circumstances. She has taken life as an end, not as a means to an end for too long. She has worn a groove too deep to get out of. Things go wrong for her because she does not know herself or see herself in others. We can only change ourselves by knowing ourselves. Dorothy Kennedy is a complete stranger to herself. She needs to know herself and no one can do that for her. Hers is a lonely, loveless life.'

'No use inviting her down here for a weekend?' asked Fairfield Broughton.

'I can hear her complaining of those noisy birds and wondering why you don't have them all shot,' said Michael, pointing through the great windows to where the rooks were settling in for the night, as the long summer evening drew to a close.

Chapter Three

The Minister's Niece

The girl, who was about five feet four and dressed in a white shirt and jeans, with slightly longer than shoulder length dark brown hair, had climbed to the top of the cliff about twenty-five yards behind him. She had an unusually interesting face, sparkling with liveliness, laughter and intelligence and was watching him with an unusually interesting expression. Musty had given him no warning: he was lying on his back wagging his tail ecstatically, trying with all four pads to ward off the long fingers gently tickling, caressing and doing altogether delightful things behind his ears and underneath his collar. Michael had stopped at the place where the Minister had thrown down his stick and turned, almost a full circle around in her direction, to pick up the vivid green snake and was playing with it. He was holding it out horizontally by the tail and making it writhe. His face too had an unusual expression for he was at that moment recalling the Minister and his mother with affection. His was a very attractive face, at the first sight of which a girl could fall in love, especially when it lit up with good-natured laughter. Indeed the expression on the face steadily regarding his, was that of a young girl falling in love and quite unselfconsciously revealing what was going on within her.

As he glanced back for Musty, their eyes met, lingered and locked in one single glance, along which a swift current passed between them but cut instantly by Michael at the thought of Elizabeth. The girl rose to her feet and came towards him. Her dark eyes had caught his attention but he had not observed her closely.

Michael had considerable understanding but little direct experience of women. Malcolm had taught him to appreciate their attractions and their manifold and subtle differences of character. He had also from a very early age introduced Michael to all the great characters in both fiction and drama, taken him to countless plays, cinemas, to all the great national events and to social engagements with the wives and daughters of his business partners and some of their friends, but Michael had had no family life – no mother, sister or aunt and he had had partners at dances and parties but no girlfriends. Then, at that most impressionable age when he was emerging from childhood, Malcolm had dazzled and inspired him with a vision of perfect love.

'The right woman will enter your life at the right time when she is right for you and you are right for her,' he had said. 'Meeting the right partner is one, if not *the* most wonderful thing that can happen to you in life. It is impossible to overestimate the joy of uniting with the woman you hold in the highest esteem and respect.

'Eternity is the real world into which we enter through the door of love. Love is in eternity, perfecting love in time. The purpose of life is to rise out of time into eternity. Man and woman are divided in time but perfectly united in eternity. Division is in time.

'True marriage is removing all that stands between us and perfect love; it is not perfecting our partner but ourselves. Freeing ourselves from the imprisonment of the false personality that we have acquired by imitation, ambition, greed, envy, conceit and vanity – all that stands between us and perfect loving, all that we accept unconsciously and uncritically, take as our real self, all that is assumed, that is not real. We become one by loving one another and by becoming perfect in love, drawing nearer and nearer to each other until we become one in eternity. That takes all our time together. We take selfless love into our hearts and our hearts into the world so that they may shine and become perfect in love. All other love that does not belong to this eternal process is illusory and false, and sinks from the heights of exquisite beauty to the depths of avaricious lust, squalor and oblivion. The flight of the soul on its way to God is grounded.'

Malcolm's philosophical ideal still had a powerful influence on Michael. That one woman had not so far entered his, nor as far as he knew, Malcolm's life, unless Malcolm had met her on his way to the office that morning and they had run away together. He himself had been enormously impressed by Elizabeth. She seemed to him to be the incarnation of the woman he had visualised when Malcolm had described his own vision to him. But that was Malcolm's vision, not his. He had never visualised for himself the woman he should seek. Elizabeth Broughton was quite wonderful. Was she that woman?

Since his return to Foghar from Broughton, Michael had continued to see as little of his neighbours, as before, but he had not tried to avoid them and his attitude to them and theirs to him was quite altered. The exchange of greetings was friendlier and more cheerful and he realised that the barrier between them had been almost entirely in himself. Those premonitions he had had, that life on the island as he had known it was at an end, were confirmed. He was glad and was no longer concerned.

'Good afternoon,' she said. 'My uncle said I might find you here. My grandmother has sent me to ask if you would care to come back to tea. I am the Minister's niece.'

'Right now? This afternoon?'

'Yes.'

She rose to her feet and came up to him. Musty followed her.

'I should love to.'

'Let's go then. Are you having fun?' she laughed, looking at the snake.

'Enormous fun. But I ought to find the owner. Have you any idea who it might belong to?'

'No. I've been away for five years. Only came back yesterday.'

'Do you live at the manse?'

'No.'

He did not ask her name or where she had been those five years. She felt his lack of interest in her. 'Leave it where you found it,' she said. 'The owner might come and look for it.'

She sounded just like the Minister, he thought.

He put it down again in the heather, coiled as before. They did not speak any more and parted at the manse. Mrs McAvoy opened the door and glanced swiftly to either side of him. 'Is Mary Ella not with you?'

Michael became uncomfortably aware that she had been sent to invite him on the spur of the moment in order that they should meet. Their simplicity touched him but only distanced him from the girl even more. He was glad to bring a new interest into their simple, quiet life but he disliked any invasion of his private life, especially what had become more and more a sacred part of it. Yet it also warmed him: they were guileless and had from the start treated him naturally and sympathetically as a friend.

'She was coming for her tea. No matter. The Minister will be glad that she found you and that you have come.'

Musty made his way to the same rug in front of the peat fire. There was always a fire burning in every home on the island, winter or summer.

'Mary Ella can't prefer their company to ours,' said the Minister to his mother.

'Not her. She will have gone to lift the peat. She will be back because of her father's accident. She may make their tea but she'll not be staying in the house.'

Michael neither felt, nor expressed any curiosity in Mary Ella but the mention of peat did interest him. 'What do you mean by lifting?'

'When first cut, the peats lie wet on the ground where they have been thrown. They dry on top and all round but not underneath. When dry enough, the pieces are lifted and placed against each other so that the whole piece dries. You should cut your own banks.'

'Takes a lot of time, I should think.'

'Yes, but it is very good firing.'

'The womenfolk do most of the work – throwing, lifting, loading, stacking, and barrowing it every day from the stack to the house for the fires and every day they have to get rid of the ash. Mary Ella did all that and much too much more when far too young,' said the Minister.

'I'll cut my own banks next year. It will be too late this year,' said Michael.

'There's still the lifting, bringing in and stacking. You might give a hand where it's welcome. Learn to get the way of it. Do all but the turfing, cutting and throwing.'

'Turfing?'

'Removing the top layer – the heather – from the top of the bank before cutting.'

'Mary Ella must have gone to prepare their tea, not to lift the peat,' said the Minister to his mother.

They had gone out to the kitchen and left him as before.

'I hope it is not to that terrible life and appalling treatment that she has returned,' said his mother. 'I fear she was not taken with the lad.'

'So, it was taking to one another that you were after, was

it, Mother?'

'They'd suit one another fine; she the sweetest looking lass the island has bred this hundred years and with the voice of an angel.'

*

Instead of going straight back to the old manse, Michael went out on to the moors where the long dark walls, sometimes shining wet, and where the peat, recently cut, indicated the peat banks surrounding Foghar. The peat was lying drying where it had been thrown for anything up to six weeks before, according to the weather. Lifting had scarcely begun but some had made a start. He stopped by a bank where someone had started and began to lift himself, following the pattern of that already lifted. As he worked he continued to think of Elizabeth Broughton.

Before Malcolm had disappeared from his life, he had only been a disciple – sewing new cloth onto old. Now, he felt himself emerging, no longer merely an aggregate of acquired characteristics, attitudes and principles that life and Malcolm had taught him – no longer a copy but an original. He had replaced Malcolm in his life by himself and he no longer needed him. He needed someone else. He needed too to get away from himself, lose himself, forget himself, discover himself, his real self, in someone else. That was the true purpose of life – not wealth, ambition or any mundane purpose. He could no longer be satisfied with wholeheartedly involving himself in people's financial or external affairs, whether Fairfield Broughton's or Dorothy Kennedy's. He wanted someone, not something, to care about, someone other than himself.

He had always worked hard at school, university and at the office and had tried to develop and to make something of himself but had until now lived only to and for himself.

There had been too few people in his life – only Malcolm and Dorothy Kennedy. Malcolm had taught him that there is something good to be found in everyone. Michael had found another and more vast world in Elizabeth and Fairfield Broughton. He had found a great deal in Malcolm but very, very little in Dorothy Kennedy. That was perhaps his fault, not hers. Now, he was beginning to find something in the people of Foghar. Hitherto everything had been external: he had developed considerable power and ability to deal with people externally, manage them and their affairs but he had never yet developed any inner power to understand either them or himself.

He had first become conscious of changing at Broughton but it was not until after his return to the Great Isle that Michael knew his life was becoming radically different. He was really changing. His attitude and reaction to everything and everybody was changing. He was no longer at the mercy of external circumstances but was conscious of a growing inner strength deep within him, that came from far above him and that had entirely replaced Malcolm in his life.

After half an hour, he decided to finish the lifting the next day instead of going for his usual walk. Musty cocked a leg at Michael's last effort and followed him home.

The next afternoon, Michael almost completed the bank before returning to the old manse for tea. He stopped and stood looking across the moor to the low, unbroken skyline. It swept on beyond to the sea, ten or twelve miles the other side of the island, and then on across another thirty to the mountains of the mainland. His thoughts stilled and a great silence closed in round him. Musty was lying on his coat. It was warm working in the sun. The sky over the treeless moor was vast and blue. Michael's back ached and yet he did not want to stop, nor was he drawn with his usual zest to the very different work that waited unfinished in the old manse. Musty was not on his coat when he turned to pick it up, for the very good reason that he was once more on his back kicking, no less ecstatically than on the previous day, at the long, quickly moving fingers of Mary Ella, who was regarding his master as calmly as before but this time with a smile of pleased surprise.

Their eyes met again. The only one of the three to remain at all at ease was Musty. Mary Ella saw at once that he had not come to do the work that he had just done to please her.

'I'm trying to learn this peat business,' he said, feeling a complete fool for the first time in his life. 'I must get back to the manse.'

'Thank you,' she said flatly to his departing back, with so little volume that it is doubtful he heard her. She did not finish the work herself but returned to the croft on the far side of the manse.

He did not, however, escape thanks. Mrs MacLennan, another sister of the Minister who lived in the croft house nearest to the old manse, was standing in her gateway. She was a woman whom he had seen before with prematurely white hair and periwinkle blue eyes. She gave him the impression, that most of the other women on the island gave him, of always being busy, always working, always doing something for somebody else. She was nodding her head at him with beaming approval.

'Bless you, Mr Gunn. That girl needs all the help she can get with that useless father of hers and her three brothers helpless most of the time with drink.'

All Michael could summon up in reply was a weak smile and quickened pace. He returned very late that evening and completed the work. He had lifted five banks in all. He resolved to master all branches of crofting but without neglecting or getting behind with his own work. He wondered if there was any possibility of getting secretarial help on the island. As Carnach was thirty miles away, it seemed very unlikely. When he was posting his letters and buying stamps the next morning, it occurred to him to ask the subpostmaster, Angus MacDonald, if he knew of anyone in the district with any secretarial experience. He did not but said he would ask around. A man he had often waved to accompanied him out of the Post Office and Michael told him of his wish to learn crofting.

Late that afternoon, when Michael was deeply engrossed in intricate work trying to make up for lost time, he was interrupted by a loud whistle and an outbreak of barking from Musty. It was the postman's whistle but not the postman. Instead it was the subpostmaster himself in the post van.

'There is a Miss Murray, Mr Gunn. She lives here in Foghar. Shall I ask her to call and see you?'

'Please do, Mr MacDonald. I should be grateful if you would ask her to come tomorrow morning. I am learning to hoe potatoes this afternoon down the way at Mr Morrison's croft.'

'You are welcome to do the like any time you care to, on my croft, Mr Gunn,' he laughed. 'Have you had any lessons in neep hoeing yet?'

'I have you in mind for the haymaking this year, Mr MacDonald.'

'I'll be keeping you to that, Mr Gunn.'

Musty did not give any warning of the arrival of Miss Murray for her interview the next morning because he was lying on his back, with those long fingers skilfully delighting and refreshing his spinal column. When Michael answered her knock, both were waiting expectantly at the back door.

'Good morning, Miss Murray. So you were a secretary the five years you have been away. Typing and shorthand?'

'Yes, working in my uncle's office in Glasgow. He is a lawyer.'

'You did not by any chance, have anything to do with accounts?'

'I kept all the books.'

'Office management?'

'I was head clerk the past eighteen months.'

'What is your uncle doing without you?'

'Tearing his hair out!' she laughed.

Right out of nowhere he had on his doorstep an Angela Quail. 'What did your uncle pay you?'

'Forty pounds a week and board and lodging.'

'Board and lodging! Will you accept fifty without board and lodging?'

'No board and lodging?' she laughed.

Looking down on her lively laughing face, something leapt in Michael at the thought of her lodging with him there. 'No board and lodging,' he said firmly.

'Office hours?'

'Usual but I suggest elasticity to fit in with other commitments. You have a father and brothers to look after and peat and crofting, and I often go away to London. When there, I shall need to get in touch with you and will telephone you here regularly but at convenient times. When can you start?'

'Right away.'

Michael turned and led her into the house. Like all the croft houses, the old manse faced the road and had two gateways – one for pedestrians leading to the front and back doors, and the other through a gate leading into the croft itself, for tractors, trailers and farm machinery. There was only one road through Foghar, with crofts running in narrow fenced strips on either side, towards the moor or the sea on one side the machair and the common grazing extending along the coastline on the other. Sometimes the house was divided from the croft and faced it, with the barn across the road. Crofts ranged in size from four to ten acres and there were three small farms there of forty to sixty acres. Michael had bought the glebe of twenty acres with the old manse but had so far left it in the hands of the Church. He was now thinking of crofting it himself. He would only be evicting a few sheep that the Minister had allowed one of the crofters to graze on it. It was in fact, good arable land and a previous Minister had kept twelve cows and provided Foghar with milk.

The old manse stood very close to the road. All the croft houses were double fronted, with a room each side of the front door and two attic bedrooms upstairs, lit by skylights. The old manse was much larger with four rooms downstairs – two at the front and two at the back and four bedrooms upstairs with ceilings and windows.

As Michael led Mary Ella into his office at the back, he saw a look of doubt cross her face and immediately understood. 'The house is practically empty. Choose either of the two front rooms for the office instead of this and arrange it as you like.'

She turned and led the way. In the front room there was only a very worn chaise longue, with tufts of horse hair sticking out in several places and a very shabby armchair, both abandoned by a former Minister. The other was quite bare, with a very wide bay window, looking immediately on to a tiny patch of grass between it and the road. Another window at one side stared straight down the road. Neither window had curtains and anyone walking towards or past either room could see into the interior. Both reception rooms were so exposed to anyone passing by either way and the manse was so lacking in privacy, that no Minister had ever persuaded any woman to live in it. No wife, mother, or sister had ever lived in the old manse (to which Michael had yet to give a name) until the present Minister had persuaded his widowed mother to come there while a new manse was being built and she had brought her own furniture. All had been bachelors.

Mary Ella chose the bare, exposed room without hesitation. They moved a large table from the back room and she placed a typewriter on one side and a large piece of blotting paper on the other. At work together, she would have her back to the window at the side of the house and they would be seen seated opposite each other with the table between them in the bay window, in full view of anyone passing up and down the road.

'That certainly won't stop tongues wagging but it may save you getting punched on the nose by one or all three of my brothers.'

'They are very aggressive, are they?'

'Only when very drunk.'

'I hope they don't drink often!'

'They never stop!'

'How can they afford to?'

'Social security.'

They spent the next day together; he introducing her to the work and being introduced by her to a temporary but quick and efficient filing system. Michael decided at once to ask her to go to London as he wanted her to see how the London end worked and to get all the office equipment she needed.

'I suppose you can't drive?' he said after a moment's thought.

'More havering and blethering!' She was laughing at him. 'The right thing is to suppose I can do anything and be very surprised, in fact, astonished, to find I can't.'

'I shall never haver or blether again.'

'That's better.'

'Did you learn to drive when you were away in Glasgow?'

'My father and brothers have all had cars.'

'And they were kind enough to let you drive them?'

'They clouted me if I didn't. When I was too young I had to drive without a licence. When I was old enough to return clout for clout, they begged me on their knees.'

Michael looked incredulous.

'How come?'

'They had no option. Alec had his licence taken away for the third time for drunk driving for fifteen years. He also served four months in prison. Ian served only six weeks for much the same offences, which Alec thought very unfair. His licence was taken away for only five years. Murdo was convicted for the fourth time for driving an unlicensed vehicle, belonging to the local policeman without his permission straight into the river when under the influence of alcohol. To be honest, I don't know what happened to him. He was awaiting sentence when I left.'

'So they were all disqualified from driving and you had to drive them to work?'

'What work?'

'What do they need cars for then?'

'To get their drink. They need a constant supply. I used to drive them to the bothan.'

'Bothan?'

'An unlicensed drinking hovel. It's on the edge of the moor, isolated like a medieval leper's hut, where the heavy drinkers meet and get drunk together.

'All on social security?'

'Father has a pension. Hey, aren't we getting remote from the point? Why do you want me to drive?'

'I want you to go to my office in London, learn all you can about our work, buy any office equipment you need here and then buy a Land Rover and trailer and drive it all back here. You go by air and return on the ferry.'

'What about furnishing the whole house properly?'

'Could you undertake that too?'
'Given a free hand.'
'You have it.'
'Can I go round it now? I'll fetch my measure.'

★

Three days later, she was gone and Michael had resumed working on his own. The next day he had just finished work for the day, when there was a knock on the door and an outburst of barking from Musty. On opening it, he found the Minister standing on the doorstep of his former home for the first time since leaving it.

'Come right in,' said Michael warmly. 'I am about to make a cup of coffee. I hope you don't mind the kitchen. I am going to get the house furnished properly.'

'Mother has sent me to ask you to tea this evening.'

The Minister took a hard Windsor chair, one of two by a kitchen table. These and almost all the little furniture in the house had belonged to former ministers and probably some of it to him and had been abandoned when he and his mother had moved to the new manse.

'There are several good furniture shops in Carnach. I should get some good advice. Mrs McRitchie who teaches domestic science at the Junior Secondary School in Clachan would be helpful. She lives in Foghar on her father's croft near the Post Office.'

'I'm going to leave the whole thing in Mary Ella's hands.'

'Mary Ella!'

'She's my new secretary and is away to London to fetch new office furniture and equipment. She is going to furnish the rest of the house on her return.'

'You have a way with you! In regard to myself from the moment we met, you set your dog on me, tripped me up, and then made me laugh. Now you astonish me out of my wits. How in the name of all that's wonderful did you manage the Captain?'

'I didn't. Should I have done?'

'You will regret the day you did not.'

'He is your brother, isn't he?'

'Indeed he is not. To my great shame he is my brother-in-law. He and her three brothers have given Mary Ella a terrible life until my brother in Glasgow rescued her five years ago. They did her mother and my sister before she died. He was a Captain in the Merchant Navy until he quarrelled with the owners and had an accident. He was retired early with a pension some years ago. He took to drink and beating his wife, and Mary Ella too, full time instead of only on shore leave, and to making her three brothers even worse characters than himself. Mary Ella was treated worse than a slave and it is only the great goodness in her that has brought her back, since he has taken to his bed with a terrible liver complaint that is only getting worse. The man cannot stop tippling.'

'Why object to her working here?'

'They are fellows for rights! Like all worthless layabouts they are fânatically zealous about their rights – human rights in the community and society, and family rights in the home. Having abused and ignored all her rights, and their duty and every natural obligation to love and care for her, they demand every right and claim they can make upon her as a daughter and sister. As for common rights, they treat them the same as they do or have done Mary Ella. If any dog but theirs strays onto the moor or the machair during lambing, they won't rest until the owner has shot it. With their blustering and bullying they have appointed themselves "overseers". They have taken the monopoly of beachcombing and there's trouble for anyone who picks so much as a match stick to a plank or anything at all from the shoreline.

'They don't care a pin for Mary Ella herself but regard her as a piece of their property. Before she went away to Glasgow, they gave young William MacDonald a terrible beating on his way home in the dark for taking her out to a dance, though it was never proved against them. Alec and Ian are big powerful men, but Murdo is the worst of the three, though no bigger than Mary Ella herself. He is a sneak and a thieving little wretch, and is waiting for sentence this minute. The court has asked for a report on him but he will get away with it. His kind always do.'

Michael looked at the Minister with astonishment.

'There was nothing browbeaten or cast down about the girl I have just interviewed. She struck me as remarkably independent and cheerful. She never mentioned any difficulties about her going to London and she said she had organised the district nurse, who is an aunt, to look in on her father while she is away in London and Mrs MacLennan, another aunt, also to keep an eye on him.'

'The lass never lacked spirit. There never was anything browbeaten about her. But that is very good news. The lass has grown more than strong enough to deal with, perhaps even strong enough to quell them. You have nothing to fear from the lass herself, not a thing. None of their nastiness has brushed off on her. The girl has goodness of nature and moral strength. Five years away, being treated with the love and respect that is her due will have been the making of her. May we expect you this evening?'

'Please thank Mrs McAvoy. I accept with pleasure.'

★

'I think we should warn you to expect a visit from my three grandsons before long,' said Mrs McAvoy at tea that evening.

'I am very surprised that you have not had one already,' said the Minister.

Michael had. He had been visited in his absence and his visitors had not gone away. When he arrived back at the old manse, he found three men waiting for him on his door-step. Mary Ella's three brothers had called to escort him to the Captain about half an hour before. They did not greet him but just stared as he came straight up to them. They were deliberately trying to disconcert him and might have succeeded, had he not been forewarned of their existence, the likelihood of their visiting him and of the kind of men they were. Musty, like a very small motor engine, gave audible expression to feelings very similar to those his master was forming.

Two were large men, one nearly as tall as himself and both were much more heavily built. The third was a very small man. The eldest, Alec Murray, had an overbearing, dark expression and he would have been a fine looking man if he had had strength of character, instead of bad temper. The second brother, Ian, was quite different and altogether weaker in every way. What little impression he made was little more than that of a henchman: his only purpose in life was to echo whatever his brother said and to do what he was told. The third, Murdo Murray, was a very self-assertive little fellow who had very little or nothing to assert. What there was, was slippery and sly and expressed by an utterly false, badly timed smile, switched on and off rather too quickly. Michael, usually of an entirely peaceful and non-violent disposition, found himself suddenly obsessed with thought of the toe cap of his right foot making forceful contact with the seat of Murdo's blue jeans.

The three, taking their cue from Alec, the eldest, did not move as he came up and made no reply to his look of enquiry but regarded him instead with expressions of rude indifference, standing and lounging in his way. He had to pass too close to Alec to do it but he firmly placed his hand on the handle of his front door.

'Captain Murray has sent us to fetch you. He wants to see you,' Alec declared, leaning with his back against the front door. His expression of surly indifference did not change.

'Miss Murray's father?' Michael instinctively referred to Mary Ella with the greatest respect. 'I want to meet him myself. You are Miss Murray's brothers?'

The eldest brother acknowledged their relationship by tilting his head back a fraction against the door, the second just stared and Murdo switched on and off.

'You'll come now,' he ordered.

'No. I will not come now. Tell him I will call on him in the morning.' Michael spoke firmly with quiet assurance.

There was a pause, a certain tightening between them and a very brief struggle between moral superiority and bullying ill will. Without a word, they moved off and Michael entered the old manse. Why, he asked himself, had Mary Ella left her uncle in Glasgow and returned to live with such ruffians? How could such a girl, whom he had found increasingly attractive, so much so that he had at times almost forgotten his prepossession for Elizabeth Broughton, have grown from the same stock as Alec, Murdo and Ian Murray? What sort of man would her father, Captain Murray, prove to be? He decided to postpone going to London the next day.

It was Mary Ella's aunt, Mrs MacLennan, the woman he had met on his return from lifting Mary Ella's peat, who opened the door of Captain Murray's house when he called there at 10.30 a.m. the next day. She looked very surprised to see him.

'You are very early, Mr Gunn. The men are all asleep. There will be no movement from any but the Captain until

four this afternoon. But I heard him a while back clattering
his crutches on the floor above. If he's awake still, I'll tell
him you are here. He will be some time dressing himself:
he is very crippled. He fell all the way downstairs again
three weeks ago.'

She ushered him into a room in which everything
looked not so much new, as unused. It was a room in
which all formality was quarantined and where the coffin
lay in state before the funeral and from which, after the
service in the house, it was borne forth to the head of the
long, all-male queue of waiting mourners to escort it to the
grave.

There was a cabinet with glass doors full of quite useless
objects lacking interest, taste or even the attraction of
novelty. A varnished table with four varnished chairs, two
facing and one either side of a window, which itself looked
as if it had rarely, if ever, been opened and was there only to
admit light and certainly not there to look through, in or
out. It was hung with heavy green curtains and covered by
thick lace courtesy curtains. There was a shiny leather
three-piece suite in front of a tiled fireplace with a bronze
fender, bronze coal scuttle, bronze fire irons and a brightly
patterned spotless rug in front. All indicated that no fire had
ever been lit in the hearth. On the mantelpiece two enormous green china dogs sat on either side of a light oak
clock. The hands stood at four o'clock and the thought
occurred to Michael that they had done ever since it had
been placed where it was. Immediately over the clock hung
an oval mirror, with so much opaque ornamentation round
it that Michael felt quite sure that no one had ever tried to
look at themselves in it. Three pictures, one on each of the
other walls, otherwise bare, immediately caught his attention.

A cargo ship, of considerable tonnage, sailed across a sea
of orange wallpaper in a long rectangular frame on one

wall, and must originally have been intended for a much larger room, perhaps a shipping office or a hall. It dominated the room. If this was Captain Murray's last command before his retirement, he had clearly held a post of considerable responsibility. The other two pictures were very large, full length portrait photographs which faced each other across the room. One was of a middle-aged man in the uniform of an officer in the Merchant Navy. The other was of a handsome woman, slightly younger but with the deeply unhappy face of someone who had found life disappointing and had a disgust for it.

Michael had scarcely taken all this in and was still standing looking at her when a violent blow struck open the door which Mrs MacLennan had left ajar and banged it against the wall, revealing the pyjama clad figure of Captain Murray lowering a crutch. A powerful smell of whisky preceded him into the room, emanating from large patches he had recently spilt on his striped pyjamas which were all awry, leaving him indecently exposed. He had not bothered to dress and stood glaring at his visitor in a violent temper.

'So you've come at last, have you?' he shouted. 'I sent for you last night. You come at once when you're sent for!'

Michael said nothing at all but stared at the man in amazement, too astonished at the startling contrast between the smart figure in the portrait and the flabby, bloated mass he watched clumsily propel a huge, unwieldy body into the room and collapse onto the couch. The Captain put one crutch along its length on the floor and clapped the other on top of it.

'What's this about you and my daughter? How dare you come where you're not wanted! Sit down, Sir!'

Michael had turned and started towards the door, overcome by repugnance and disgust.

'Sit down, Sir!'

'Good morning, Captain Murray.'

The situation was embarrassing and ridiculous. As he left, he looked about for Mrs MacLennan and, glancing up the stairs, caught a glimpse of Murdo Murray on his hands and knees peering slyly down into the sitting room through the bannisters. Taken by surprise and startled by Michael's sudden exit, he furtively dodged back out of sight, still on all fours.

Michael let himself out by the front door. He met Mrs MacLennan hurrying up the path from the back door to the front gate.

'Come home with me, Mr Gunn. Come and have a cup of tea. You will be needing it.'

Nothing was said while she buttered two large, round and very thick biscuits, cut two large slices from a cake and put them on two plates and brewed the tea. Then she poured out two cups, brought and placed one at his side with one of the plates of buttered biscuit and a piece of cake, and took another beside her and sat down at the table. There was a long silent pause and Michael had just inserted one of his huge biscuits into his mouth but fortunately not bitten into it, when he noticed that her eyes were shut. Mrs MacLennan began to give a blessing. Whipping the biscuit quickly back onto his plate, he was just in time to shut his own eyes when she finished. She started talking easily and freely at once.

'The Captain is not the easiest of men and was a wicked father. Many a time has Mary Ella run to me here with her face taut with pain from the beatings she has had from him. Never a tear, just taut with pain and then smiling again. She is a brave lassie and incapable of self-pity. I could never take the place of the mother she'd lost, poor darling. No one will ever do that.'

'When did she die?'

'Mary Ella will be twenty-two next month and her mother died when she was eight but she will never forget her. There was great love between them. I tried to help her through those terrible years but her father came home for good from the sea at about that time. That was soon after the accident that crippled him. He smashed himself up in his car under the influence of drink. He and Alec ran the house, with Mary Ella doing almost all the work. Fortunately, she was brilliant with her school work and, with all four of them drunk most of the time, able to work hard at her lessons and to get away to the manse to my brother, the Minister, and to the schoolmaster's too. She was the brightest and most successful pupil the school has ever had and she was to have gone to the university, but the Minister advised her to take the first opportunity to become fully independent and to get away to my brother in Glasgow, who is a lawyer. They have been such good years for her in Glasgow and she has done so well. My brother will be lost without her.'

'Why leave him? Why has she returned?'

'It is her faith that has brought her back. The commandment to honour father and mother. My father was a Minister and his before him. Mary Ella has her mother's faith. It was only her faith that made life bearable for my sister and Mary Ella too.'

Michael did not doubt that but her faith must be different from that of her mother. Her mother's was the support of an unhappy woman. He could not imagine Mary Ella ever being unhappy – not even when having a rough time with her father and brothers and she certainly wasn't unhappy now.

'Even though he has never been more than a beast to her? What about her brothers? Why are they so much older? Surely she doesn't have to honour them?'

'Alec, Ian and Murdo were born in the first years of the marriage before the Captain went away and left my sister to bring up the three of them on her own. It was said that he had other wives in other ports around the world. Mary Ella came many years later. The brute of a man suddenly turned up at the house, forced his way in when drunk and without love, and went away the same day. He did not return till years after and first learnt Mary Ella had been born. He came back for good when he came out of hospital after his accident and took to living the way he has ever since and no doubt much the same, as he had all the years he was away. My sister did not live long. The Captain beat Mary Ella too and worked her so hard that she is now wonderfully strong from doing man's work. The four men were mostly incapable of any work, with drink.'

'But what has made her decide to return now to that terrible life?'

'Dr MacBeath does not think he has long to live. He won't heed his warning to stop drinking. She thinks it is her duty to look after him. She doesn't stay in that house. She lives here with me.'

He thought Mary Ella was too clever and sensible to credit the hair-splitting, doctrinal disputes that had led to division after division on the island. She had too great a sense of humour and too much common sense. Like the vast majority of churchgoers on the island, she would be on the side of good and against evil, and that was why the island was such a haven. But there is no knowing what garments hereditary religion can put on a child. Michael had not himself been attracted to the religion of the islanders: it seemed to him too forbidding and based more on fear than love, and more on what neighbours thought than God. Malcolm was right: true religion is essentially love and founded in the lives of the multitude of women whose selfless love has saved and continues to save the world. Men turn religion into boring argument, bitter dispute, violence and war. Mary Ella couldn't ever be narrow-minded or fanatical or a bore.

'Every minute of our lives is full of purpose and meaning. Every minute is discovery. Every time you're bored or angry, criticising or sneering, you lose an opportunity, slam to a door but if you recognise the fact immediately you retrieve and strengthen yourself. Don't miss the bus, Michael,' Malcolm had said. 'Reach for the stars! That's what you have been born into this world to do. So has every single individual in it, so get down to it and start by boiling that egg for three minutes the way I like it.'

'Do the Captain and her brothers attend church?' Michael asked MacLennan.

'The Captain not at all. Her brothers stopped going when their mother died and they started drinking with their father instead. They attend all funerals, though often unsteady on their feet carrying the bier.'

Michael himself had not attended Church at all since coming to the island and had respected the Sabbath by keeping out of sight on Sundays. What now was the right thing to do? Malcolm had given him the answer to that too. 'When in Rome do as the Romans, unless it is evil. A worse evil often comes of refusing to conform.'

Michael found himself looking forward to his next visit to Broughton the forthcoming Sabbath. There had been no question of attending church there on his recent visit, but that might be the reticence of English hospitality – not wishing to embarrass a guest with whom they were not yet on sufficiently familiar terms. Would he welcome attending church with them there, more than he would with Mary Ella on this island?

★

All thoughts of Mary Ella were soon dismissed by the arrival the next morning of a letter from Dorothy Kennedy.

★

At tea that evening, he asked Mrs McAvoy if there were ever any houses for sale on the island, knowing that he himself had bought the first house ever sold in Foghar. The other houses were crofts and were hereditary in the family or under the crofting commission or part of an estate. The old manse was in a separate category altogether, having belonged to the Church.

'Well, you are the only—' She stopped herself but not before the word she was going to use to describe Michael had gone forth in the spirit as powerfully as if it had been spoken. '...the first that was not born in the district that has come to live in it. You'll not be the last. There is a law just passed that permits all the crofters to buy the feus of all their houses and for new houses to be built. The grants for new houses will leave the old house empty and up for selling, if there is need to sell. Andrew MacDonald and Malcolm Murray – no relation of Mary Ella – have applied to buy the feu for their old house, not to sell but for their own son and his family. They will themselves move into the new one. There will be many more houses on the island for sale now that there is nothing to prevent the old house from being separated from the parent croft. However, the old houses are damp and in a poor state, with the old, tarred felt roofs and bad sanitation and drainage. Are you looking for a house for someone?'

'I may have to find a house for an elderly woman but it would have to be in very good order, not in need of any renovation.'

At that moment a vicious gust of wind hurled heavy rain, mingled with hailstones, violently against the window panes. A wicked thought entered Michael's mind: he had only to mention the possibility of water pouring through her roof onto her furniture and carpets and drenching her house to be quite sure of Dorothy Kennedy never entertaining a thought of coming to the island. She had dropped vague hints of her considering coming to live near him in the past and the thought of having to endure her fastidiousness and fussy ways, and run all her errands, replenish her supplies of cigarettes and fetch her fortnightly half bottle of whisky, in the totally dry district on the island disturbed him. Perhaps Mary Ella's three brothers might help in that direction! These thoughts were interrupted by the Minister addressing his mother.

'What about Foghar Farm, Mother? Mr McPhail got two grants and has just completed the work to convert it into two flats – one upstairs and one down. He will never get a tenant for either. They will have been inspected and passed by the Council and should be right up to the high standard demanded.'

'Well, now that is the truth. They will be fine and dry and well drained, with all the modern conveniences we have here in the manse.'

'How accessible is it?' asked Michael hopefully.

'The farm is up a rough track and quite a way from the Post Office but all the vans call there, and Mr and Mrs McPhail live in the modern bungalow they built nearby when they took over the farm. They go themselves to Carnach at least once, and more often than not twice, in the week. Any elderly person living there would by no means be cut off,' said the Minister, in that helpful way Minister's have when referring to other people's affairs.

Dorothy Kennedy would contrive sooner rather than later to live quite cut off in the centre of New York, London or Paris. Why not in Foghar?

Chapter Four

Dorothy Kennedy

Dear Mr Gunn…

Michael wondered if Dorothy Kennedy knew or cared which of them it was, Malcolm or himself. She had never remarked on Malcolm's absence when he had turned up without him, although he, Michael, had always been a silent spectator before and was only nineteen. She had merely continued this form of address and treated him as if he were Malcolm.

> *I can't stand this place a minute longer. Lorries roar through day and night, shaking the house to its foundations. I must move before the roof falls in on me.*

Damn, said Michael to himself. Then he remembered Malcolm's tolerance of her and laughed. Thanks to Mary Ella's temporary filing system, he found the house agent's telephone number quickly and dialled it.

'There is no hope whatever of selling that house with the good lady in it, Mr Gunn.'

The Manager himself answered the phone. He put an entirely different meaning into the word 'good' to that in general use. He and Michael were old acquaintances and were in full sympathy, both having shared previous experience of Mrs Kennedy.

'She insists on showing prospective buyers round herself; tells them she can't get rid of the place quick enough and why! Is there any possibility of her moving out and leaving it vacant and withdrawing it from the market meanwhile?'

'I don't know that there is,' said Michael untruthfully, the thought of Foghar Farm looming large in his mind, 'but, I'll see what I can do. I shall be in London very soon. I'll phone you again when I get there. I should meanwhile quietly suspend operations.'

★

Dorothy Kennedy was living in a village that had been almost completely swallowed up by expanding London and stood between the City and an ever increasing load of traffic. It was also only five hundred yards from a tube train terminal. Michael had moved her there – her third move since Malcolm had left. Some years before, an enterprising developer had bought the old village shop, house and barn from the octogenarian granddaughter of the last of the family, who had kept the shop for generations. It had survived into the modern world, unchanged, unmodernised and nearly derelict. The developer had transformed the whole property into three period houses; all the seventeenth and eighteenth century timbering, beams, doors, staircases and panelling had been treated for woodworm, restored, repaired or replaced. He had installed modern kitchens, bathrooms and central heating and sold the two largest at an enormous profit but not the third, originally the corner shop. It had no garden whatsoever and was surrounded by pavement, the corner of which divided the very busy highway into one way streets. Single line traffic went one way down the street at the front and the other up the street at the back where the pavement was very narrow.

Heavy vehicles did indeed lumber past the rear windows very close by the house.

Michael and Dorothy Kennedy had agreed at once that this was too great a disadvantage and also the price was beyond what she could expect from the sale of her existing home, so they had gone off, viewed and bought a bungalow on a new estate nearby. Michael had instructed the estate agent and her solicitor on her behalf, arranged for her furniture to be removed and left her until the day fixed to move her. But shortly afterwards, the developer decided to realise the capital locked up in the remaining house, enquired at the agents for Mrs Kennedy's address, called her and easily persuaded her to buy it at a price temptingly below what he had originally asked. The developer had gone himself to see her solicitor and cancelled her purchase of the bungalow. Michael was presented with a *fait accompli* and had subsequently moved her there, instead of into the bungalow.

Michael knocked at the imposing eighteenth-century door on the evening of his arrival back in London and stood waiting patiently. A normal reaction would be to have gone away after a reasonable delay, assuming that she was out but anyone at all familiar with her habits, knew that Dorothy Kennedy was never out. Anything she needed that could not be delivered or ordered through the post, she did without. This was however, only until the 'intrusive' neighbour, unsuspecting salesman, casual visitor, paper boy, milkman, man who came to read the meter and of course Michael himself (and Malcolm before him) could be persuaded to run the errand for her. When she could find no one reliable or trustworthy to draw her weekly pension, she left it to accumulate until someone turned up. Finally, she had decided to follow Michael's repeated advice to have it paid direct into her bank account. Once, just before leaving, she had been reduced to asking the vicar on his fourth and last visit, without her once having attended his church or encouraged his treasurer, to get her the half bottle of whisky she allowed herself every two weeks from the pub on the corner.

Dorothy Kennedy had three faces: sociable, professional and discontented. When sociable, she expressed amused tolerance, disdainful indifference and deliberately misunderstanding mockery. She assumed her professional face when exercising her ability not to appear to be talking nonsense by juxtaposing abstract polysyllabic words, mostly of Greek and Latin origin (which had lost all their original meaning and now had no meaning at all) lecturing and practising child psychology at the Wonderland Home. This face had ceased to exist abruptly on the day of her retirement or fell into disuse. It was her discontented face, full of gloom and resentment, that she now presented to Michael after a very, very long wait. She held a headscarf, wrapped round under her chin with one hand, and the door, as uninvitingly open as was humanly possible, with the other. This was the face currently in most frequent use, with which she exhausted all the patience and charity in any neighbourhood in which she happened to be living and eventually made her situation quite untenable. Her face expressed without words but with startling clarity, that she was now regarding him as wholly responsible and to blame for her ever having come to live there and was at its most tense and reproachful.

'That woman was here again this morning,' she said, suddenly turning its whole force in another direction and as if continuing a conversation she had been having with him in the house. She jerked her head, as if in the direction in which the woman referred to lived.

'Asking if I wanted any shopping done!' she snorted. 'As if I'd ever bother her. You should try living here yourself in this dreary, noisy place! Can't stand it any longer. That vicar never calls now.'

Another jerk brought to his attention a gentleman in a dog collar hurrying past on the other side of the road. 'Only after your money, that lot.'

'Coming in?' she asked, as if he had just stopped on his way past and had not made a very long journey especially to see her, and in reply to her letter. 'Taking the dog for a walk?'

She managed to convey in this remark a dislike of dogs and a contempt for their owners who employed their time in such a useless way. At this point, Michael became aware that transition was taking place to her socio-sceptical face.

'Time for a cup of tea?'

'I have come to see you and the agent before returning to Scotland.'

'You do rush things, don't you? Always in a hurry.' She spoke as if she knew him intimately.

Michael realised that neither had any real knowledge of the other one at all. He had merely sat and watched her at the Wonderland Home, listened but not understood a word she had said. She hadn't noticed him at all – not at the home, nor the flat, nor when he had gone with Malcolm to organise her moves. He had always just sat and watched her, even on the subsequent moves he had organised.

'Always in a hurry,' she said again.' You must learn to take things calmly and quietly. Been on another holiday? Always Scotland. You must like the place. They don't give you much work to do, do they?'

She had no idea who 'they' were or what work he did. She set out cups and saucers and, opening a tin, took out six rock buns and put them on a plate and then transferred one to another plate which she placed before him and left the room to make the tea.

'I live in Scotland now,' he called out. 'Only visit London on business.' As he spoke, he surreptitiously passed the rock bun to Musty who took it away under the table and gnawed it appreciatively.

'You know,' she said in an entirely different tone of voice when she came back with the tea. 'That's where I want to live. I want to finish my days in Scotland.'

Michael looked directly at her, clearly and objectively for the first time. Had she a soul? Did she ever fly? She seemed so destitute of wings, grounded, almost pedestrian. She trampled on everything with heavy boots. Had he himself a soul? Malcolm said we all had souls and are free all our lives, either to nourish or starve them. They could be seen in the eyes of a child, before the good and evil that it sees, hears and experiences is assimilated and become part of it. The body is given only to house the soul, but can become its prison. Bad nourishment, such as moral evil and preoccupation with the body, and vice brought spiritual sterility and imprisonment for life. The stronger and better the nurture of the soul, the greater the freedom of spirit. Had Dorothy become impervious to truth, beauty and goodness for life? Had she never absorbed but instantly and instinctively rejected them? Had her body become a prison, a condemned cell from which only love could release her? He remembered: she was a complete materialist, a dedicated follower of Darwin and had taught the Wonderland Home children that man is wholly descended from apes and is an animal.

Malcolm had taught Michael the reverse. Apes are descended from men. Monkeys descend from men, not men from monkeys. Men descend to their level. Malcolm's ideas suddenly flooded back into his mind. Men descend lower – much lower – than animals, lower than the level of the most utterly selfish and cold-blooded of living species. The spiritually dead are those who have lost all ability to love even themselves. The process is going on all the time. Outwardly, men and women have the appearance of men and women and make pretence of being men and women but inwardly, they have descended to what they have become in the course of their lives; as Circe discovered to Ulysses on the island when she turned his men into the swine they inwardly were. Ulysses himself would have turned into a fox, had he not been given a charm against her spells, probably self-knowledge. Malcolm had said this was an everlasting process in time. Like the angels on Jacob's Ladder, men and women are ascending and descending, not evolving. From childhood onwards they are descending or ascending to Man and above, or descending from Man and below and repeating the process everlastingly in time. Ascending is rising out of time into eternity, realising the eternal purpose of time, the realisation by free will in time of God's eternal purpose. 'Eternity,' Malcolm had said, quoting some old spiritual reformer of the sixteenth or seventeenth century, 'is the real world for which we are made which we enter through the door of love.'

At this point, his thoughts were interrupted by Dorothy Kennedy offering him another rock bun.

Malcolm had said that there was always something in everybody. He had never before asked himself what there was in Dorothy Kennedy – about her soul. What about her flight, her other half and the purpose of her life? There had been an absence of love in his and Malcolm's approach. Though they had never shown or felt dislike, neither had they shown any personal liking for her. There had never been any exchange of love between them. Was that the reason for her bleak and negative acceptance of their help from time to time? They had never given her what she really wanted. They were perhaps her only resort. Without knowing it, she might be seeking love and fulfilment like everyone born into this world. All else was false and substitute, and led to spiritual death.

He not only took the rock bun but ate it and looked

straight at her and gave her a smile as he did so. He did not notice the look Musty was giving him.

Why not a flat at Foghar Farm? He had, until now, thought that the idea of her coming to live on the island would be as horrifying and unwelcome to her as to him and was about to dismiss the thought as quickly as he dismissed her from his thoughts, immediately after leaving her presence, or having satisfied any demands she made upon him. Now, it struck him that it was as good a solution to her housing problem as any; better in that the possibility lay immediately before them. Why not the flat at Foghar Farm? It had too, the advantage that she could move soon or at once and so solve the estate agent's problem. It was as good alternative as any. He would put it to her and would fully inform her of all the advantages, disadvantages and stress all the difficulties of living on the island in its very different social and physical climate. He would be fair to himself and to her, by exaggerating all the island's disagreeable features and put her off to the best of his ability. If she insisted on moving there, as the signs showed that she would, he would organise her move there at once.

Chapter Five

The Night Watchdog

The rooks were once again disturbed by the arrival of Michael Gunn at Broughton but this time he drew up to the house in a modest estate car, not in the beautiful limousine in which he had been brought before. Fairfield Broughton had flown him in his plane from London, as had been arranged, and it was Fairfield Broughton who drove the car and not Elizabeth Broughton.

They found her in the garden, or rather Musty did as he ran through the drawing room and out through the French windows on to the lawns. She came in with him at her heels and greeted them. There was now no trace of the efficient secretary who had spoken to him on the telephone; here was a queen who had formed her own realm and was in full possession of it. There was a thrilling power in her presence. Without being the least ill at ease, Michael felt an inclination to worship and adore her and he realised that she had never been far from his thoughts since he had last left her here at Broughton. There was no doubting her pleasure at seeing him.

There were just the three of them this time, with no domestic help. Elizabeth herself cooked the dinner and her disappearances were clearly responsible for the appearance and disappearance of the dishes through the hatch. Both Fairfield Broughton and Elizabeth showed a genuine interest in, and prised every detail of Michael's life out of him. He found himself, to his surprise, opening up and responding yet they were learning, not so much about himself as about Malcolm. After dinner, he found the conversation turning the other way and it was he who was learning about them, and then the conversation concentrated on a particular topic.

'Wain House and Scanton have both been broken into and robbed this past week. The police were here today warning us to keep a look out and take every precaution. They suspect a particular man and say he is very dangerous, armed and doesn't hesitate to use immediate violence. He apparently carries the usual sawn-off shotgun. These last two robberies have definitely connected him with similar robberies all over the country. The police pointed out that if he was planning a third raid in this area, our isolation would attract, rather than deter him.' Elizabeth did not sound at all alarmed but serious, as she passed on the police warning.

'I've been round the whole house checking security.'

'We'll go over the whole place again before we go to bed,' said Fairfield Broughton. 'Ought to do that before it gets dark. Mind giving us a hand, Michael?'

'I'll lend a hand and a dog too. I suggest we make up a bed for Musty in some strategic place where he is free to run about. He'll give us instant warning of any intruder. He usually sleeps downstairs but I let him up occasionally. I've resisted the temptation to let him sleep on the end of the bed so far.'

'Give into the temptation. I can't wait to get a little darling just like him and have him at the end of my bed. When I'm settled and decided what to do with my life, which is going to be soon, very soon, *I'm* going to. I wonder what significance this armed robber has in our lives?' Elizabeth added, thoughtfully.

Michael was surprised at the question. Fairfield

Broughton was not at all. 'No hunches?' he asked her.

'None whatsoever!'

'Not even a theological, philosophical or psychological one?' asked Michael. 'What about intuition?'

'Father has a low opinion of women's intuition.'

'Except Elizabeth's. You know that, Elizabeth,' he said reproachfully. 'I have the greatest respect for Elizabeth's intuition,' he said to Michael. 'Though I have no idea what intuition is,' he added with a laugh.

'Immediate insight without reasoning? Something true as opposed to something contrived? Much more than a sixth sense, I should say,' said Michael.

'Berdyaev thought that no true philosopher should be without it, that every true philosopher had an original intuition of his own and that no religious or scientific truths were adequate substitutes for it,' said Elizabeth.

'Is it intellect working at the speed of instinct?' suggested Fairfield Broughton.

'I don't even think that is doing justice to it. It is instant, effortless, complete understanding. It is not memory. It's not just intellect or mind and is certainly not emotion. Intuition is whole and works instantaneously, effortlessly and inerrantly, from the depths of our inner being and carries absolute conviction. Intellect is slow, laborious and inaccurate in comparison. Also the degree of consciousness is altogether different. Intuition instantly puts us into a higher state of consciousness.'

'To get back to this robber. Malcolm said everything is designed for a purpose, to an end. Too much that is utterly pointless seems to me to be going on all the time for me to believe that. This worries me because everything Malcolm ever said is important to me. I always feel he must be right and that I must be wrong.'

'The vast majority of things just happen because they must and they are insignificant or significant only on the level of material existence on which most of us are content to live our lives,' said Elizabeth. 'But there is another level, a higher level – the level of values, of quality rather than quantity on which nothing happens without a purpose. On this level, everything is altogether different and intuition replaces intellect and instinct.'

Michael glanced at Fairfield Broughton as Elizabeth said this. He realised that Elizabeth lived wholly and consistently in this world of values she was describing. He wondered if this was as true of his host.

'I am beginning to understand your change of attitude towards the Inland Revenue,' he said to him, smiling.

'You are ahead of me then! I am far from understanding. I don't think I have ever lived exclusively on either level. I only decided recently to try to live more on Elizabeth's – the level of values. I let her lead me like a blind man up a slope. I can't yet see, even in imagination, what is over the top on the other side but somehow it seems right and exciting.'

'Can you remember more of what your uncle said about things happening for a purpose?' asked Elizabeth.

'More from what I sensed from his whole way of life than what he said directly, and from what he hoped, and was always expecting of me. Time was not to be wasted: every event and meeting has significance. I followed him from afar, like you Elizabeth,' he said to Fairfield Broughton. 'Sometimes still do.'

'Now? When he's not with you?'

'I believed in everything he did and said when he was with me. I didn't have a mind of my own. Mine just reflected his – was a carbon copy of his.'

'But you won an open scholarship to Oxford. You can't do that without a mind of your own,' said Fairfield Broughton.

'You can without understanding, without independence

of mind,' said Elizabeth.

'You can go to a university and get by without any mind at all. Take for instance Dorothy Kennedy,' said Michael.

'You have both independence of mind and understanding. All that you have told us about Malcolm and yourself proves that,' said Fairfield Broughton. 'But all this time it is getting darker and darker and the man with the sawn-off shotgun is getting nearer and nearer,' he laughed. 'He may have already taken up a position in the woods nearby and be waiting until it is quite dark and all our lights have gone out.'

'It might be a good idea not to put our lights out at all tonight and put a few more on. Wouldn't the rooks have given us some warning if he was waiting in the woods?' asked Michael.

'It is too early in the evening for our early warning system to work and they won't stir after dark.'

'That just leaves Musty,' said Elizabeth, 'but on the end of your bed. Not all by his brave little self downstairs. Let's all go round together checking. That will give you an opportunity of seeing all over the house.'

All three took the job seriously, and Michael found himself examining every door and window throughout the house critically from a security point of view. The easiest room to break into was undoubtedly the drawing room from which they started, but no room presented any real difficulty to an experienced and determined intruder – not even on the first floor and above. Even the attics were of easy access, owing to the rambling and uneven nature of the roof line with its many gable ends. They had an immense number of rooms to check and Michael got a wonderful impression of the whole house.

On their return, Musty ran out onto the lawn of the walled garden and they all followed him into the late twilight of the summer evening. The trees on the other side of the wall were full of dark shadows; the rooks' nests were beginning to disappear into the blackness of the coming night.

'This twilight is what I miss most when abroad in the tropics and subtropics,' said Fairfield Broughton, 'and missed especially during the war when repatriation seemed only a remote possibility, years and years ahead, and the Japs seemed unbeatable.'

He spoke with undisguised love of the stillness, peace and warmth that seemed to shelter and surround them in the present, even though the remote possibility of an armed robber lurking brought the future closer and made the gathering darkness silently threatening. Michael got the impression that nothing ever disturbed his host and that he had never taken anything for granted but had observed, absorbed and appreciated everything.

Elizabeth left them and went on alone and disappeared into the shadows by the wall at the far end of the lawn, followed by Musty.

'Where were you during the war?' asked Michael.

'Mostly in India and Burma.' A sad, nostalgic note crept into his voice.

'Arakan?' Michael spoke as if remembering something.

'Arakan? Yes. Most of that campaign. Why do you mention Arakan?' Fairfield Broughton was surprised, alert, questioning.

'The name stuck. My uncle was there. He would be very young.'

'He was in the Burma campaign? In the Arakan? What did he tell you of the Arakan?'

'He never told me anything at all about the war. Never spoke of it. The only time I ever heard him speak of it was to someone he met soon after had taken me from the Wonderland Home to live with him at the flat. Everything seemed fresh, intensely alive and wildly interesting after the orphanage at that impressionable age. He often took me out.

'One day we went to the zoo and were looking at the backside of a rhinoceros, standing with its back to us – very disappointing as it just wouldn't turn round. Suddenly, someone gurgled out a terrific Tarzan cry behind us and the rhinoceros turned right around and so did my uncle. The cry was aimed not at the rhinoceros but at him. A man had recognised him. They had served together in Burma. I remember every detail of their meeting. I was as fascinated by the man and the Tarzan cry as I was with the rhinoceros which had turned full around. I particularly remember them mentioning Arakan; the word came into their conversation not once but many times. They had both been very young and the cry had been a frequent joke between them at finding themselves really in the jungle. It seems that it had been an awful experience. Conditions were frightful: the British were bewildered and lost in the jungle, while the Japanese were quite at home and very well trained to fight in it, especially at holding out in intricate positions they called "foxholes". They spoke a lot about the toughness of the fighting and of the Japanese, and how frustrating it was, especially at the end when Akyab fell so easily. The other chap had his family waiting nearby for him in the Monkey House and left us. My uncle started telling me about rhinoceroses and fascinated me. That was the last I ever heard from him of the war and Burma but I never forgot it. He so seldom spoke of himself and the past, however curious I might be. Something in him inhibited me from asking him questions about himself. I instinctively knew that he didn't want to talk of himself ever, and certainly not of the war. If ever I did venture to do so, he would divert me and laughingly lead me off in some other direction.'

'Elizabeth!' Fairfield Broughton sounded moved and

there was a trace of excitement in his voice.

'What is it, Daddy?'

It was the only time Michael had heard her called him that.

'Let's go in.'

Michael felt he was about to say something to her but had deferred saying it. When they were all back again, seated in the drawing room with a drink beside them, he turned towards her and engaged her full attention.

'Michael has just told me that that interesting uncle of his was in Burma and in the Arakan – in all the fighting and particularly those last months of the fighting before the fall of Akyab.'

'Ah,' said Elizabeth and Michael knew that there was a lot that they did not tell him going on in both their minds.

Hitherto, Fairfield Broughton had remained the contented, good-humoured host. On neither of his visits had he given much evidence of that dynamic and forceful personality that was so often in the news. Michael remembered that he had first made a name for himself as a leader in the war – the start of that colourful career that had so often caught the attention of the press but he could not recall any details. Now Fairfield Broughton suddenly seemed to glow.

'I suppose you have no idea what unit he served with in the war?'

'None at all. If he had any choice I'm sure it would have been a Scottish regiment.'

'He would have been called up and would not have much choice, I'm afraid.'

'No. He wasn't called up. I do know that. He volunteered right at the beginning of the war with my father.'

'You aren't Scottish, are you?' asked Elizabeth.

'My uncle's grandfather and my great grandfather came from the Great Isle. The Gunns originated there. I haven't yet found or visited the ancestral croft, farm or whatever gave them their livelihood. It can't be all that far from the old manse in which I live, although it is a long island, and I am right up in the most northern part of it.'

'Is this old manse your holiday home?' asked Fairfield Broughton.

'No. I am making my home on the island and will be doing most of my work there. I have just appointed someone local as a secretary. I was going to suggest you meet her. I sent her to London earlier last week to work in the office in London with Margaret Smith for a couple of weeks, and to bring back all the office equipment she needs in a Land Rover I am buying for local use up there.'

He told them of their meeting, of her father and brothers and all he knew of Mary Ella and her exceptional ability.

'Bring her next weekend. She's not going back before?'

Michael noticed with a thrill of pleasure that both accepted him and automatically assumed that he would spend any or every weekend he could at Broughton with them as a matter of course.

'She is a very strict Sabbatarian. Like all on the island she never misses church on Sunday.'

'Nor do we. Father is one of the churchwardens and is sidesman on duty tomorrow. You will have to put up with me while he is away tomorrow.'

'If you have no objection, I'd like to come with you. I was baptised but have never been confirmed in the Church of England. I should hate to keep you from going.'

'That would be nice. It is a lovely church and you will like our Vicar.'

'And you will like Mary Ella.'

'If I telephone your office on Monday morning will I get her?'

'She'll certainly be there all the morning—'

'To get back to your uncle,' interrupted Fairfield

Broughton. 'His name is Gunn like yours? May I know his full name?'

'Just Malcolm Gunn.'

'And he'd only be about eighteen in Burma?

'A bit older than that. He and my uncle both joined up together, under age, in September 1939. Both survived Dunkirk.'

'...And he qualified as a chartered accountant and as a barrister after the war, Elizabeth told me. He never married. I wonder why? Helping to bring you up would attract many women. He may be now of course, wherever he is.'

'I doubt it,' said Elizabeth. 'I think you would mean everything to him, not only yourself but because he would have been very close, exceptionally close, to your father and mother. It would take him years to get over the loss of his brother and your mother.'

'Intuition speaks again!' laughed Fairfield Broughton.

'I was a full time job and took up all his spare time. We met many women socially but none became more than friendly acquaintances, who we were glad to see next time, except Dorothy Kennedy, whom I regret to say neither of us were glad to see next time! Malcolm will marry when the right woman turns up. That's what he always said would happen; she would just turn up. It was a jest with him. "Come on Michael," he would say. "Get those laces tied. Three times round the park and a cold bath for both of us. Can't have a paunch, double chin and a bald patch when she does turn up. She might not recognise her other half and take me for some other chap!"'

'And did he have a paunch, double chin and a bald patch when you last saw him?' asked Elizabeth.

'Not he!'

'I should think he'd be much the same as you to look at, only older?'

'Not much older. Not a generation older. He always

looked much younger than he was and the other day I was told I look much older than I am. He is wiser, stronger and taller by an inch and a half. I have never got over not catching up that inch and a half, particularly the half! He will only marry when the right woman comes his way.'

'My guess is that he is married, not will marry,' said Fairfield Broughton. 'Especially now he has no ties.'

'I am quite certain he isn't and that when he does he will be right back in my life. I can hear him saying, "We'll make a god-fearing citizen of you yet, Michael, marry you to someone who will take you to Church every Sunday and make you say your prayers regularly."'

'Joking?' asked Elizabeth.

'Not about real prayer; that is when we breathe the breath of life, spiritual life, nourish the soul and expel all that stands between us and God. God is love, every kind of love that has the least element of selflessness. Real prayer is prayer for love, for God himself. The other form is, consciously and unconsciously, all we ask of life for ourselves. It can adulterate real prayer, almost always does but can be elevated by it, and often is. Our lives reflect both forms – what we ask of life for ourselves and what we ask of God. Real prayer is an attempt to get away from ourselves, to suspend the self that stands between us and God and get it out of the way altogether. It is not communion with ourselves, it is communion with God. Going to church may be no more than what we ask everyday of life for ourselves, even thinking ourselves better than others like the Pharisees. Then it's not loving nor praying for love, not even praying for love in a loveless situation, but living without it and dying. In Church, many do both – living two lives.'

'You are talking as if that's what you yourself believe,' said Elizabeth.

'I wish I did. Sometimes I do. I always did when I was with him.'

'And when you recall vividly the thoughts he expressed to you.'

'It's time we all went to bed and said our prayers,' said Fairfield Broughton. 'We must get some sleep and sufficient rest to tackle that man with the sawn-off shotgun when he comes.'

All three had taken the warning seriously but had not really believed he would come and had dismissed the threat from their minds. Musty slept on his own blanket, which Michael always carried about with him so that he knew instantly, wherever they were, where he was to sleep and felt at home. He slept at the foot of Michael's bed. Not one of the three gave the burglar another thought and all three were fast asleep when he did come.

Michael was awakened by Musty growling by the door. He got up, hurriedly put on his dressing gown and slippers; and decided to follow Musty wherever he led him. There was no sign of Fairfield Broughton or Elizabeth: they were sleeping in adjoining rooms in the same wing of the house. Musty ran straight down the stairs to the inner hall and then along the passageway to the green baize door that led to the kitchen quarters. It was locked and bolted top and bottom. Musty began to sniff and scratch at it, and then started to bark so fiercely that he seemed to lift himself off all four feet as he did so. Michael examined both bolts and also tested the key in the massive lock and, finding all three strong and secure, decided to leave well alone. This was the only way into the kitchen quarters and by which anyone could enter the great house from that part of it.

Almost immediately Musty stopped growling, barking and sniffing and lost all interest in the green baize door. It became obvious from his behaviour that the intruder had left the kitchen area. Musty ran back the way they had come and Michael followed him up the staircase, straight past their room to Fairfield Broughton's bedroom door where he started to bark as fiercely as he had at the green baize door. Michael, without a moment's hesitation, flung the door open and switched on the light.

Two men, about equally matched, confronted each other. Neither hesitated or lost his head but the intruder was at a disadvantage for he had not yet got into the room and was precariously situated on the sill of the window and not – as had been reported on previous robberies – inside holding a gun and in command of the situation. He was quite unprepared for an attack and quite unable to attack or defend himself as Michael ran straight at him, but like Michael, he did not hesitate. He reacted instantly and smashed the window in, with the gun he had intended to point at the sleeping body of Fairfield Broughton.

Michael realised later that he must have planned the robbery carefully, previously reconnoitered the house thoroughly and learnt a great deal of the habits of Fairfield Broughton and his daughter, and the exact location of their rooms. Musty and Michael rushing at him completely surprised him. He fired wildly without aiming, as Michael grasped his gun with both hands, twisted it round and then gave him a violent push with it. He fell backwards, let go the gun, leaving it in Michael's grip, lost his balance and tumbled onto the low, sloping roof up which he had easily and quickly climbed from the kitchen quarters. Michael could hear him slithering back down. He had disappeared. The whole incident had ended in seconds. Michael turned to the bed to find Fairfield Broughton staring at him with a look of amazement.

'You again,' he said, talking as if still in a dream from which the blast of the shot had woken him. 'My God,' he said, shaken fully awake. 'The blighter really has come, sawn-off shotgun and the lot, but he's hit you, and Musty too!'

Elizabeth had entered the room and picked up Musty.

Blood was streaming from one of his front paws.

'I'll telephone the police right away and get a vet and a doctor.' Fairfield Broughton had his dressing gown on and was already through the door as he spoke. 'Do what you can, Elizabeth.'

Michael and Elizabeth examined Musty's wound.

'It's a pellet lodged in his paw,' said Elizabeth. 'I don't think it's serious. What about you?'

'Much the same as Musty. Shot in the leg. It's all numb. I think he got me in the thigh.'

'He's got you badly in the thigh! Look at all that blood.'

'He has cut the telephone wire somewhere,' said Fairfield Broughton, returning. 'The line is dead. I'll dress and go by car. Where's that gun?'

He examined it and saw that it was still loaded with one cartridge. 'Keep that handy – but he'll be well away by now. The way he came. Anyway it's loaded so you can give him a warm reception if he isn't.'

The police were there almost immediately. Their car had actually been approaching the house up the drive on patrol. They summoned an ambulance which took Michael to the district hospital ten miles away. Fairfield Broughton drove Musty to the vet himself and brought him back very soon after.

'We'll hear no more of him,' said Elizabeth to her father, when they were alone together with Musty, later that morning at Broughton. 'He has played his part. Everything is ordained, not determined. Everything happens for a purpose. Not a sparrow falls. Not a Musty is shot. Michael would have lost that leg before the war. I'm afraid he will always have a limp. No amount of physiotherapy will get those thigh muscles right. He deserves a medal. I wonder if he will be allowed to keep that gun!'

'I hope the man gets caught and it's used as evidence against him,' said Fairfield Broughton. 'But I have a hunch that you are more than right this time, darling, and we are on the right track at last.'

'I shall be back tomorrow night before Michael gets back and only be away while you and Mary Ella are here to look after him. I shall have time enough to start things moving and fast.'

Michael was kept in the hospital for two days and returned to Broughton in the care of the district nurse. All shot had been removed and his wounds were healing but needed dressing. Elizabeth had been right: the muscular mechanism of his right thigh had been devastated. Michael did not therefore go to church until the following Sunday when, still very sore and in considerable pain, he limped very slowly from the lychgate with Fairfield Broughton and Mary Ella. Elizabeth had taken care of him on his return from hospital at Broughton till they arrived, when she had then returned to London on some pressing business.

'Do you think your uncle really believed that there is only one woman for you and for him?' She had asked him this the evening before when they were alone together.

'Yes, but I think he had already lost her,' said Michael.

'So do I. And I know who she was.'

'You know who she was!'

'She was your mother.'

Chapter Six

Elizabeth and Mary Ella

Fairfield Broughton was a discerning man. He had listened with growing interest to Michael's description of his life on the island, and in particular, his recent meeting with the Minister and his niece, Mary Ella. He was intrigued by Michael's references to Mary Ella. A young woman emerged strikingly fresh from Michael's description, with a distinctly lively and independent personality. She had risen high above the most adverse circumstances and, however difficult and unkind those surrounding her had been, she had remained untouched. But what he discerned was that Michael had allowed his feelings towards her to be affected by her background. Despite discovering in her an Angela Quail and a very attractive person, Michael had allowed her unfortunate circumstances, unhappy childhood, his experience of her father and brothers, and their appalling treatment of her to diminish her appeal, instead of increasing it. He had not seen a jewel gleaming all the more brightly in the darkness and did not fully appreciate her qualities – influenced probably by admiration for Elizabeth and her entirely different background and qualities. Mary Ella more than interested Fairfield Broughton. He was determined to get to know her and asked Elizabeth to invite her to Broughton the weekend following the attempted robbery.

Her reaction to Elizabeth's invitation pleased him: she

refused the invitation because she could not be ready to
start back to the island on the following Monday morning
by the weekend. He telephoned her himself that he would
be in London on the Thursday and that Angela Quail
would give her every assistance to enable her to complete
the work, and that he would wait for her and collect her
himself, however late she finished on the Friday evening.
He would take her to Broughton by car and would personally see that she was right on time at her starting point on
Monday. It would be a splendid opportunity to get to know
her at leisure and in comfort. They met at Michael's office
at six o'clock that Friday evening and drove off together,
heading for Broughton.

He was entranced with her straightforward and innocent
directness and they got on very well together right away.
She appreciated his genuine interest, respect and understanding, immediately recognising in him someone she
could trust and confide in, as she had never been able to do
with anyone before. They had established a strong liking
for each other long before they reached the hotel where
Fairfield Broughton had ordered a very good dinner, during
which they broke down all remaining barriers to their
becoming really good friends. She reminded him of a
flower that had sprung up, despite the most adverse
conditions and bloomed fresh and exquisite and untouched
by its surroundings – like a soldanella melting the snow in
which it grew to perfection.

They arrived at Broughton late. The rooks remained
silent and undisturbed. Mary Ella did not see Michael on
Saturday at all. He was still recovering and needing dress-
ings. He was up but could only walk painfully and
uncomfortably with the help of a stick and remained in his
room until just before they all set off for Church on Sunday
morning. Fairfield Broughton had taken her round and
showed her the estate on the Saturday.

★

Canon Drew had not led his flock on to the shifting sands of change. The only alteration he had made since he had taken the living thirty years before, was to shorten the sermon so that services never exceeded the hour and Holy Communion half an hour. He was neither High Church nor Low, nor indifferent but deeply spiritual. In his short sermons he tried to illume the form and letter of a religious service with the light of the Spirit. The small market town with its ancient church on the green, separated from the vicarage by the graveyard, an old, mature orchard and a broad, sloping lawn, still heard the cadences of Cranmer, the exquisite prose and poetry of the Authorised Version and the most beautiful of hymns, both ancient and modern. Canon Drew had continued the practice, long established by canon law, of holding the three main services of Holy Communion at eight o'clock every Sunday, followed by Morning and Evening Prayer and Holy Communion after Morning Prayer on one Sunday in the month. His evening services were quietly beautiful.

As he had faithfully evoked the spiritual beauty of the Bible and the Book of Common Prayer and taught his congregation to love God and not himself, his ministry had always been appreciated and successful, and he had never known the sadness of preaching to empty pews. Mary Ella was impressed. She appreciated the atmosphere and beauty of the ancient building, which had been allowed to grow old with dignity and not been subjected to the ravages of renovation and restoration and Church party politics. She knew the Bible so well that the almost wholly biblical nature of Morning Prayer quite overcame her unfamiliarity with the seventeenth century formality – minimal ritual and black and white cassock and surplice – of the Anglican service as it had been for centuries. The only colour was the striking red of Canon Drew's hood. Mary Ella was also grateful to Fairfield Broughton and Elizabeth for introducing her into their peaceful and lovely home. It was a contented and cheerful party that returned to Broughton.

At lunch the conversation turned upon life in the Western Isles.

'You still produce most of your food on the island?' asked Elizabeth.

'And fuel. Most of our basic needs – fish, meat, eggs, milk, oats, potatoes and hay for cattle and sheep.'

'Isolation and tradition must conserve old values and ways of life,' said Fairfield Broughton.

'And living in constant touch with the land and the sea,' said Michael.

'Language too,' said Mary Ella. 'Gaelic is still the first language and the *only* language of many. Life hasn't changed much but I found in Glasgow everything is changing all the time. Everything is man-made and manhandled, and so different in the cities. Even the air is polluted. However, technical advance is so rapid it will soon destroy isolation on the island. And intolerance, too,' she added, laughing.

'Lack of change produces narrow-mindedness and religious intolerance, sadly.'

'Malcolm said that love is the main product of the Western Isles: love of the old and the young and of neighbours and of love itself.'

'Who is Malcolm?' asked Mary Ella. 'He is right. We've never needed the welfare state and social service there. It has been, and is being, thrust upon us. The family care for the old and the young.'

Michael recalled that she had, without any hesitation, given up a happy life in Glasgow to look after that worthless father. 'Talking of care of the old and at the same time breaking the Sabbath,' he said to her, laughing. 'I have taken the ground floor flat at Foghar Farm for Dorothy Kennedy.

I haven't yet told you about her. She was to have flown to Carnach at the end of this coming week and I was to have met the plane there the day after her furniture arrived and seen it into the flat. Now I am grounded here for another few days, under doctors orders, and must recover lost ground in the London office. Her move will have to be postponed— '

She did not let him finish. 'I will take care of her move and meet her. Mr and Mrs McPhail and all the family will give her the kindest of welcomes. There will be no trouble or difficulty at all. Fires will be lit and they will have some peat stacked ready for her.'

Michael and Elizabeth's eyes met.

'I think I ought to warn you that Mrs Kennedy was, as the sparks fly upward, born to trouble. Can't leave the bellows alone.'

Mary Ella smiled with that superbly provoking air of self-confidence and efficiency that Michael had failed to appreciate to the full on the island, and which now delighted Fairfield Broughton.

'Now is your finest hour,' he laughed, while Michael and Elizabeth's eyes met and they slowly shook their heads ominously in unison and grinned at each other.

'The chance to prove your worth to the young chief has come. To remove one Dorothy Kennedy, bag and baggage, from Putney, or wherever she lives, to the Outer Hebrides in one piece and there before her cottage door present her, overflowing with gratitude, to her young benefactor.'

'Overflowing certainly but not with gratitude,' said Michael.

'That's my second, not my first commission. I have yet to deliver the office equipment to the old manse in the Land Rover and trailer and furnish the whole house.'

A sudden look of doubt appeared on Michael's face. 'That room your aunt showed me into, when I went to see your father—'

'Will bear no resemblance whatever to any furnishing of the old manse,' said Mary Ella, giving him a very reproachful look that left no doubt in any of their minds that she was very hurt. Elizabeth quickly put a hand on hers.

'I'm going to hold the fort here and take over everything till you come back for Mrs Kennedy and you must come and stay here again, as soon as these jobs are completed.'

'And I'll fetch you here wherever you are and at whatever time,' said Fairfield Broughton.

Michael murmured, 'I'm sorry,' to her as they left the room.

She looked up at him with a smile. 'My uncle and aunt will have done all the groundwork and have furniture shops and departments ready with things for me to choose from and approve, and have arranged for their collection and removal to the island. I shall have plenty of time to return to oversee the loading of Mrs Kennedy's furniture and to drive her to the island. Mr and Mrs McPhail will have everything ready for her to stay in the flat above hers at Foghar Farm, if her furniture hasn't arrived in time to unload the day we arrive. They can easily make up a bed and anything necessary for one night. I shall be stopping on Monday night with my uncle and aunt in Glasgow.'

She left that evening, with Fairfield Broughton, to return to London so that she could make a very early start on the Monday. Michael remained in Elizabeth's care but insisted on her taking him with her to London the following Thursday morning and on staying there till the weekend when they would return to Broughton together. She reluctantly agreed, although he could see she was anxious to join her father on some pressing business which, Michael gathered, was of especially keen interest to them both.

The only sign Musty showed of his wound on arrival at

the office in London, was a pathetic and endearing little limp. Michael had to walk very slowly with a malacca stick, chosen from the great number of walking and shooting sticks that had accumulated in an old closet in the hall at Broughton.

He arranged to return to the old manse at the end of the following week and meanwhile worked hard to recover lost ground. On arriving at the office on the Friday morning, Margaret Smith handed him a letter.

Dear Mr Gunn,

All the furniture has arrived and has been unloaded, both at Foghar Farm and at the old manse, and Mr and Mrs McPhail have been wonderfully kind and helpful. Mrs Kennedy has not had to do anything. They have even come and helped me with the curtains at the old manse, so all will be in good order when you return. However, I am very sorry to have to write and tell you that I found that all the windows in the old manse had been broken when I got back, and even more sorry to have to write that, though it is impossible to prove, they were certainly broken by my brother Murdo. As you can imagine, nothing can happen in Foghar without it being seen and known to everybody.

I don't know what happened between you, my father and brothers, but am very sorry to learn from my aunt that they were troublesome and ill-mannered. I have had all the windows reglazed and I can assure you that it will never happen again but I cannot say the same of the bearing of my father and brothers towards you.

You must decide on your return whether, under these circumstances, I should continue as your secretary.

Mary Ella Murray

Michael's feelings towards Murdo Murray, last glimpsed on the landing upstairs as he was leaving his father's house, were entirely out of sympathy with those inculcated by Malcolm towards a fellow creature, and more recently by Canon Drew in his short address. He wondered how Mary Ella could be so certain that it would not happen again.

He did not telephone but wired at once that he needed her and wanted her as his secretary under any circumstances, and then forgot her completely. He was looking forward to returning to the island and the old manse but even more to the coming weekend which would be his last at Broughton with Elizabeth before his return to Scotland. His thoughts were full of Elizabeth. Their relationship had always been easy and comfortable when together but strangely he did sometimes feel in considerable awe of her, when away from her, and thinking constantly of her. She did not fit into any category: she was unique – a fusion of unusual beauty, great intelligence and strength of character, yet there was also an exquisite gentleness in her. Roughness and coarseness seemed to shrink away out of her presence. She had rare grace which gave a fresh enjoyment of life to all about her, however familiar, even to her father.

Michael had sensed, when they had all three been together at Broughton, that Fairfield Broughton was under her influence, not the reverse. The thought struck him that, though enormously attracted, he himself was not under her influence – not yet anyway – and that gave him a strange feeling of freedom, of relief. Quite unconsciously and without wishing to, Elizabeth would hold the reins. He suddenly felt the tremendous force of her beauty and knew that he would never dare to ask her to give herself to him for life. She was beyond his reach, far beyond, above even the ideal Malcolm had once so strikingly described. He knew that there was something in or about him that she found attractive, liked and welcomed, something more than the effect her gentle interest in them had upon anyone about her. There was no suggestion of any deep feeling for him, although they were close friends and all barriers were down.

'Why haven't you married before now?' she startled him by asking, interrupting these very thoughts on the evening of his arrival.

They were sitting out in the open before the drawing room window on deck chairs and Fairfield Broughton was not with them at the time.

'Mind you, I am in no position to ask the question, being thirty-two and still single.'

He was twenty-eight and surprised they were not, as he had supposed, the same age. 'I have had to discover for myself, chew over and accept consciously, things I had taken from Malcolm and swallowed without question. I've found many to be as much a part of me as they are or him. One in particular. There is only one woman for me, as there is for Malcolm. The only difference between us is that she is an unknown to me. Malcolm already knows her and loves her and is absolutely confident that she will come to him, whatever he is doing and wherever he is.'

'How strange. That is just how I feel. There is only one man for me whom I already know and love. You are very like Malcolm, aren't you? You said your father and he were twins. His father was the headmaster who died of mortification. What about your grandmother's parents? That side of the family.'

'Another blank there. Malcolm never knew anything much about her family. He thought she was a refugee from France. Malcolm himself is the only relative I know.'

'Are you and he alike to look at?'

'He was very often taken for my elder brother. It usually caused great surprise when I said he was my uncle.'

'How is he different from you?'

'He was always so completely commanding, had a very strong personality, even stronger than your father but in an entirely different direction – if you can talk of personalities having direction. In the same direction as yours. He never asserted himself. It asserted itself. He was always just himself: gentle, yet tremendously strong, like you are.'

In describing the effect Malcolm had on him, Michael realised that it was the same as the one Elizabeth had on him, but her beauty had, until that moment, screened that realisation from him.

'You still haven't answered my question.'

'There is an unusually strong likeness between us but I should think I dim somewhat in his presence.'

'I think you are now entirely your own man. What he did for you is all anyone of us can do for another. He gave you as much sunlight and good soil to grow in as he could, then let you grow your own roots.'

'Malcolm believed that we are born as we really are but remain so only for a very short time. What we are, however, never dies in us; it becomes obscured and the world takes over. We lose our integrity and, more and more, we see ourselves through what is acquired, not what is intrinsic. We are shadows shaded by imitation, attraction, fantasy, by our circumstances and the times we live in. We are shaped by events, novels, drama, and a million other external influences that stand between us and an internal reality. We cease to be real. Only what we are within, what we are in the eyes of God, matters to Malcolm – what cannot be taken away. The child unconsciously and innocently sees reality and then grows up in the ways of the world. It absorbs influences, good and bad, and becomes quite unconscious of reality. Millions, good and bad, live and die in that state. They do not achieve the purpose of life.'

'Malcolm is clearly not one of those. He is seeking to achieve it. How?'

'If I knew that, I would be following his example. I think that's why he left. We have to find the way ourselves. It is always directly between ourselves and God.'

'He never tried to convert you, or steer you into any denomination?'

'No. He said that was the worst thing we could do. We must awaken ourselves and find the way ourselves. Unless we awaken to the real purpose of life, to become a member of a denomination, though flooded and brilliant with artificial light, is to enter the darkest tunnel of all, to become blind, deaf and dumb like the Pharisees. The vast majority of churchgoers have utterly shelved their responsibility – passed it on and never discovered the real purpose of life for that very reason. They are building, if building at all, on sand, though if they are fortunate in their minister or are utterly sincere, they may awaken to the real purpose of life. We did go to church but not often, or always to the same one. Malcolm taught me to read the Bible, the Christian Calendar, the Prayer Book and the history of the Church and many other things but he never preached to me. Instead he always stressed that all that was knowledge only, and must not be mistaken for religion. That, he said, we must find for ourselves.

'He taught me about the other great religions – even Norse and Greek mythology – to respect them, recognise higher values, spiritual values and the absolutes: beauty, truth and goodness, wherever I found them. But most strongly of all, he stressed that we must never think we have arrived and stop seeking. True religion is recognising and resisting everything artificial, the self, that we imagine we are or have become, that stands between us and reality – the truth. The real purpose of our lives is to free ourselves from that accumulated self and discover our real situation. We can only do this by seeing what we are, what it is that stands between us and God – real understanding.'

'Did he tell you how?'

'Yes, but I didn't understand him. If I had, I'd be doing it but I don't think he expected me to. We can't use the very self that hinders, blinds and misleads us! Prayer? Praying to know the real purpose of life? But mustn't we first become aware of the purpose, then try to know ourselves, what we have become? Find our real selves by getting to know what is real in us, what is false, what we have become in the course of our lives as we have developed and followed other purposes only to sacrifice it all? On what altar? I can understand why so many just eat, drink and try, most failing dismally, to be merry! And even that is the most difficult thing to do in the world! Pride and vanity stand in the way.'

'Nevertheless, true religion is the way, as he said. And from the moment of realisation to the end of life. He puts everything else second. Do you realise this now?'

'After he left I turned to facts and figures, the intricacies of accounting and fiscal legislation and to closer study of our materialistic, scientific western civilisation.'

'I don't believe you are such a materialist,' she laughed.

'Whatsoever things are solid, whatsoever things are empirical, whatsoever things are scientific, whatsoever things are rational and demonstrable, if there be any certainty, any proof, I think only on these things.'

'And still do?'

'Not since I met you.'

Chapter Seven

Foghar Farm

Michael achieved something remarkable on his return. Despite having Musty with him (now without even the suggestion of a limp) who usually declared their presence in no uncertain way, Michael arrived and settled into the old manse without anyone in Foghar aware of the fact. The reason for this was that he had acted on a sudden impulse. He was not expected.

Mary Ella was to have met him at the airport at Carnach with the new Land Rover on the Thursday but on his return to London from Broughton on the Monday, he suddenly decided to fly home at once, quite against all medical advice.

With Margaret Smith's help, he packed up all unfinished work, got a taxi to the airfield where he kept his plane, took off and, after landing hours later at Carnach, got another taxi and arrived late in the evening at Foghar. No one observed the taxi stop, Michael get out and ferried two suitcases, walking, or rather limping, on the malacca cane stick Fairfield Broughton had given him on his return from the hospital. While he was paying the taxi driver, Musty paid disrespectful attention to the two gate posts.

Inside the house, he found that there was an electricity cut but there was still sufficient daylight. He went over the house with increasing delight. Everything was neat and in order, and the house completely furnished throughout in perfect taste. He returned to each room again and again, especially to the office, which was a masterpiece of order and comfort. Gone altogether were the horsehair relics and all the shabby emptiness. Only the table in the bay window, across which he and Mary Ella had glanced at each other as they worked, remained.

He sat down in his own place. By this time it was very dark inside but still light enough for him to recognise a small figure furtively open the front gate and hurry straight to the window through which he was looking. With a spring, which caused him great pain, Michael leapt from his chair, sprang across the room, out of the door and across the hall into the front room opposite, which Mary Ella had furnished as the lounge. He made for the matching bay window from which he could watch the intruder without his being aware of his presence. It was Murdo Murray, the smallest of Mary Ella's brothers.

The small man raised the centre sash of the window of the office wide enough to insert his head and shoulders. He put something he had been carrying onto the table, twisted himself round and pushed up the window as far as he could from beneath. He was trying to get onto the window ledge and worm his way in. His feet were off the ground and only his lower half from his waist downwards, consisting of jeans and boots, remained outside, when suddenly there was a fierce outbreak of barking, preceded by a ferocious growl. The rest of Murdo Murray suddenly and swiftly re-emerged. He touched ground and ran for the gate, closely pursued by a very indignant little Cairn crossed West Highland terrier who had all this time been visiting familiar smells and scents and thoroughly enjoying life. Kicking him off one trouser leg to which he had become fiercely attached, Murdo managed to shut the gate on him before he could return and attach himself even more fiercely to the other leg. Leaving him on the inside barking frantically and trying to get at him through the bars, he disappeared in the direction of the Captain's house at great speed.

A ceilidh nearby was disturbed. These friendly social evenings start at ten o'clock and seldom finish till the early hours and it was only twelve o'clock of a midsummer night. Within minutes there was no one in Foghar who did not know that Michael and Musty had returned and that Murdo Murray had been at it again. The report was that he had been surprised and worsted by Musty and thwarted in an attempt to wreck all Mary Ella's fine furniture in the old manse, a report verified by Michael's finding a sharpened butcher's knife and a heavy iron-headed builder's mallet; tied together, which Murdo had put on the table before trying to hoist himself in.

Any feelings of dismay Mary Ella may have had at her brother's behaviour, were dismissed by the genuine enthusiasm with which Michael greeted her and showed his appreciation of what she had done for him. He expressed unequivocal pleasure and unstinted admiration at the total transformation of the interior of the old manse. She had created a home for him and an efficiently equipped office in which they were at once very happily and busily working together. That afternoon he left her working and made his way in the Land Rover up the track to Foghar Farm.

The house had been an old shooting lodge, one of many in the island originally only occupied in the season for grouse shooting. It had since become a farm house, with about fifty acres of arable and grazing land surrounding it. The McPhails had built a modern bungalow nearby and had just taken advantage of a new government housing development policy of renovating old properties by providing grants and loans to modernise and convert the old house into the two flats. Government stores were established in remote areas, such as the Highlands and Islands, to sell building materials at very reasonable or cost price to crofting communities.

Almost every croft house and the dry stone walls surrounding the crofts, had originally been built by the crofters themselves with stones cleared from the land and brought up from the beaches. They themselves now supplied much of, and sometimes all of, the labour and many of the skills required. There was very little local employment to supplement crofting and weaving on the island, and the young had to seek it either fishing, on the mainland, or in the services. In the event only the annual cutting of peat and the seasonal work on the crofts; the crops, the dipping, clipping and lambing and the care of the cow, interrupted an almost universal rebuilding, reroofing, roughcasting and rehousing in all the townships.

On the Great Isle, widows still went into deep mourning and wore black for the rest of a hard-working life. Silhouetted against the background of the profoundly religious community in which they lived, their special status was recognised, and as assured and respected as it had been in the days of the early church, as described in the Acts of the Apostles. They continued as head of the household, looked up to by all their children, and *their* husbands and wives. This was at a time when as a class, in the rest of Britain, together with maiden aunts, they had long since faded into the background and become indistinguishable from all other women – married or unmarried.

The last occupant of Foghar Farmhouse many years before, had become one such widow. She had survived all kith and kin and had lived, almost without modern amenities, with old, worm-eaten furniture mouldering about her, and wallpapers of long ago peeling off all the walls. They had continued to moulder and peel off for about ten years after she had died. Mr and Mrs McPhail, living in the new bungalow they had built nearby, had been very good to her.

Now they had given the house she had lived in an entirely new life. Only the shell of the old house remained and that had been roughcast to keep out the damp. A new roof, guttering and drainage system, white pebble-dashing, a large sun porch with an enormous window and flat roof, and a new front door, with frosted glass panels, had transformed the outside. New floors, ceilings and walls of plasterboard, cheerful wallpapering, tiled bathrooms and stainless steel kitchenettes had transformed the inside.

The widow Kennedy did not wear black widow's weeds, nor had she faded into any background or become indistinguishable from other women, married or unmarried. But she did wear a very black look. After keeping him waiting a long time outside the porch, she at last slowly opened the door a few inches. Her third face, wrapped in a pale green scarf, unwelcoming, unsmiling and full of resentment, made her look as if she was suffering from toothache.

'How is everything?' asked Michael.

He ignored the fact that it was face number three and pretended to talk to face number two, which could smile resignedly with lofty and amused tolerance. Given time and patience this trick invariably worked.

The door remained open an intractable nine inches. One half of Mrs Kennedy full length was visible, as if she had been cleft down the middle, and the expression on her face looked as if that was just what had happened to her and she was in agony.

'Mice!'

Her cry of agony was so great that Michael saw them in her expression as big as elephants and herds of them.

'They are under the sink and in the cooker. They are everywhere. All over the bedroom. I can't wash up. I can't cook. I can't sleep. They are in the cupboards. I shall have to throw all the food away. I shall starve to death in this terrible place.'

'Mice! We'll soon get rid of them,' said Michael reassuringly. 'They are only field mice – beautiful, clean little things, just exploring and making for shelter when it gets wet and cold. Their fur is fresh and shiny. They are little pets.'

'Pests, you mean. Filthy vermin! I can't stand the horrid little beasts.'

While he had been waiting patiently outside, one of those sudden weather changes, so frequent on the island in all seasons, had taken place. Rain had begun to fall heavily; a violent wind, gathering to gale force, had sprung up and the temperature had sunk with the bite of the wind. Michael and Musty were still standing outside getting very wet and cold. He continued patiently to address face number two, despite the unmistakable evidence and persistence of face number three. It was a struggle of wills. He won at the expense of getting soaked.

'You coming in?' she asked at last, and then acknowledged the presence of Musty. 'Taking the dog for a walk?' She ignored the Land Rover standing not five feet from the door.

'I'm just back from London. Came to see how you are settling in.'

After a guided tour and a thorough inspection of the flat for mice, and finding two or three dirts under the kitchen sink, Michael was sitting at the dining room table with a glass of sanatogen wine, listening to endless complaints. Musty was underneath it with his rock bun.

He learnt that so far she hadn't been able to get any whisky and had brought a large supply of groceries with her as a precaution against being cut off from the mainland and running out of food. She ignored his telling her about the Gulf Stream, and that it is not intensely cold in the Outer Hebrides at all times of the year. The result was that from being cold and wet on her doorstep, Michael now found himself in a subtropical atmosphere in her dining room. She had put all the storage heaters on in the flat and a very large and powerful electric fire, which she had brought with her in the room in which they were sitting. He very soon had to take off both his raincoat and jacket.

'That girl!'

'Girl?' said Michael surprised. 'Do you mean Miss Murray?'

'Does she always wear those awful tight trousers?'

'I expect, like most girls now, she prefers jeans to skirts.'

'Can't tell whether she is a man or a woman wearing those things.'

Michael, who had found no such difficulty, did not reply. He was surprised to discover how very much he liked her in them. She had never worn anything else on the island, except on Sundays. He then recalled with growing pleasure what she had worn at the office in London. She had looked very attractive indeed in a three-quarter length black skirt, black shoes and stockings. He found himself in no hurry at all to dismiss her from his mind. She had looked very smart and attractive in them. He found himself also recalling with pleasure what she had worn at Broughton. He returned from these engaging thoughts to the present with an effort.

'Nothing went wrong with the move, surely?'

'Except my ever moving here at all! The fire in the lounge smokes. All the windows are open to let smoke out!'

'Depends on which quarter the wind is in. Smoke won't always come down the chimney. It won't always smoke. The wind will change. You haven't been here very long.'

'Too long.'

'You're the first tenant. The place will have teething problems. I am sure Mr McPhail will put a cowl on it, if it is troublesome.'

'That man!'

'Mr McPhail?'

'Always at the door. Any excuse to get in. Am I all right? Do I want anything from the store or from Carnach? One day he'll just push past me and take a good look round.' She paused, '…How do I post a letter in this place?'

'The postman will take any letters when he delivers. And you can always give them to Mr McPhail; he and Mrs McPhail are kindness itself. They will do anything for you.'

'I don't want them poking their noses into all my business.'

'I'll post them for you,' said Michael. He knew well that they would only be a few business letters in which he would probably have advised her what to say. He had made out her tax return for some years.

'This must be one of the last places in the world where you'll find honesty and kindness everywhere; very different from the mainland. There has not been a single robbery or murder or any need of a policeman in living memory in Foghar. If you dropped a pound note on the road you could pick it up next day if the wind hadn't blown it away.'

A cross between a sneer and open incredulity appeared on face number two.

Michael· found himself getting indignant with her but suddenly recalling what Mary Ella had told him of her brothers and Murdo in particular, he paused and didn't answer.

'They can't even speak English!'

'They speak English better than most English people. Their native language is Gaelic. It is we who can't speak Gaelic.'

'I can't stay in a house riddled with mice!'

'We'll get rid of the mice. I'll use one of those traps they can get in but can't get out of, and I can release them on the moor. Not one of those snap traps which breaks their backs.'

'And they all come back again!'

'I'll show you the next one I catch. You'll see what sweet little things, they are.'

'You'll do no such thing! Quite enough here without you bringing any more.'

'They are clever too. Some manage to get out.'

'I won't have one of those traps in the house.'

'Cats keep them away. Mrs MacIver has two. Hers had kittens last year and she had managed to find a home for all but one. She offered one to me when I first came to the island but I can't keep a cat because of Musty. He chases them and I couldn't take it with me when I go to London as I can him. It'll be fully grown now. I'll ask her to lend it to you. The presence of a cat is often enough.'

'I'd have to feed it!'

'You must not feed it! Not on any account. It would stop hunting the mice.'

'Not feed it! I'd have the RSPCA on me. Not feed it indeed!'

'Only for a couple of days. Give it lots of milk in the morning when you let it out but don't let it out at night and don't forget to put it out in the morning for obvious reasons. It won't catch the mice if you feed it, just roll on its back and play with them. You can keep it as long as you like. She'd be glad if you kept it for good.'

She wasn't listening, he realised. She was one of that great multitude of people who automatically edit, what they want to hear and are oblivious to the rest. But Michael went straight off to Mrs McIver in the Land Rover and fetched the cat. On his way back, he called in to see and thank Mr and Mrs McPhail.

'The poor old thing. She'll be frightened of them. I'll set traps in the flat above and put a cowl on the chimney this week. I expect smoke blows down when the wind is in the north, although we never have smoke in the bungalow. I'll go to Cartiach tomorrow and get a cowl. I'll call in first. She might like to come with us or we can get anything she needs for her. She ought to have television.'

'When you see her you might remind her to put this cat out every morning. I do hope she doesn't feed it tonight. She has never kept a cat or a dog before. I'll try to come up again the day after tomorrow.'

Mr and Mrs McPhail stood there looking so benevolent that Michael was conscience-stricken. What had he done to these good, kind people who were probably blessing him for finding them a tenant. There was some consolation in there being no sign of one for the flat above.

'I hope she won't be too much trouble to you.'

'Don't you be concerned. We are used to old people. We looked after old Mrs Fraser who lived there till she died, and she became very odd in her ways. Mrs Kennedy is just the tenant we want here. No children and no dogs to worry the sheep.'

He found Mary Ella had gone when he returned but there was a note to remind him of several things requiring immediate attention. The letters she had typed were neatly set out in order, ready for his signature. He was finishing these when he noticed Mary Ella's three brothers hovering about the gate, keeping a wary eye out for Musty. They moved off when they saw that Mary Ella's place in the bay window was empty. He learnt the next morning from Mrs McIver, that the Captain had died late that night and they had come to tell Mary Ella that he had been taken seriously ill.

★

All but housework stopped when there was a death in the community, until after the funeral. Only basic and essential outside activity took place. The children went to school but otherwise all became still, silent and solemn. Death was still an event of tremendous significance in the small community. Like the wind and the rain and the wild seas and wilder moorland it was elemental and stark and a much rarer and more dominating visitor on the island than on the overcrowded mainland.

Chapter Eight

The Burial of the Sea Captain

Death dominated and paralysed Foghar until Mary Ella's father was in his grave. All work ceased and each day became as sombre as the Sabbath. The mood changed the expression on the faces of all the women as they made their way, dressed in black, to the Captain's house carrying packets of tea, biscuits, scones or a newly baked cake. The men in hats, dark suits, overcoats and shoes instead of blue denim trousers, overalls and boots, were transformed into strangers.

It was Michael's first experience of Death. It had had an enormous effect upon his own life but he had been a baby when it had deprived him of his father and mother. He had not thought much about it and it meant little more to him than ceasing to exist, almost like disappearing. Malcolm's going had seemed like Death.

Mary Ella came over early that morning to tell him that she would not be able come to work until after the funeral. She offered to stop and do anything urgent there and then, all she could, before going back to her father's house.

'Of course not,' said Michael. 'It is very good of you to come. You should have sent a message.'

She looked so unhappy that he murmured. 'I'm sorry about your father and upsetting him so recently.'

'You will not be believing in life after death?'

The unexpected question brought the reality of it startlingly close to him. He realised that he had never thought about it himself but had accepted everything Malcolm had said about it without question. 'I don't believe in Hell, if that is what you mean.' He remembered Malcolm saying that.

'But it is in the Bible.'

'Not the Hell we always think of. That comes from Milton's *Paradise Lost* and Dante's *Inferno*.'

'You don't really believe, do you?' she said sadly. 'Like so many nowadays, you do not believe in spiritual life and spiritual death, only in physical death, the end of everything for the individual, the end of a life – long or short, of the senses.'

'I believe God created Heaven and Earth but not Hell. We do that. He doesn't punish us. We punish ourselves. And each other,' he added. He was again quoting Malcolm.

'You mean my father punished himself!'

'Malcolm said we all do that. Hell is on earth. He said there are different degrees or circles, like Dante's Inferno but they are on earth. Hell is the absence of love; meeting situations without love. Heaven is love and is present everywhere, and is nearer to us than breath itself. It is at the heart of every one of us. It is where evil is entirely absent. I remember Malcolm quoting from Dean Inge, "Heaven is not a faraway place to which we hope to go but the presence of God in which we ought to live." God is love and we are in heaven whenever we really love.'

'And are loved?' added Mary Ella. 'But what about all the millions and millions all over the world who don't believe in God – in either Heaven or Hell and are quite indifferent?'

'We are all interested in loving and being loved, even though unaware of the fact. Malcolm said that most people are indifferent or too preoccupied with their daily lives to think about such things. They are in a sort of material limbo and might go in either direction at any time – blown hither and thither by the wind of hate and the wind of love. He also said that many of those who go to churches or mosques and temples are no different. They are spiritually dead and loveless, like the Pharisees. But he also said that we can enter eternity, rise above time by absolute selfless love at any moment. In fact, we can only do so in the present – now, not in the future and, of course, not in the past. Only now. Eternity is above and out of time. So while there is life there is hope. Men and women who give their lives for others in war or peace rise from the dead. They don't join them. They become immortal; part of eternal love. The little girl who runs to save her dog which has fallen under the ice, the passing stranger who doesn't hesitate to go in after her and is drowned too, instantly achieve the purpose of life.'

He felt himself what Malcolm said was the truth – luminous, limpid and still. Above time. It becomes darkened, confused and obscure in time. Time passes and is never still.

He was looking into her troubled eyes and something jumped inside him. Suddenly he found himself powerfully disturbed. He cared that she was troubled. Everything in him wanted to make her happy again, as she had always been with him. He faltered and murmured 'You mustn't be unhappy. It will all be over soon.'

She smiled at him and they parted.

He kept to the house and worked sporadically, unable to settle into his normal routine. The man who had died and the scene he had had with him kept constantly returning. He was acutely conscious of what was going on outside. He could see the entrance to the Captain's house, and the visitors coming and going. He felt like an outsider, a foreigner. He was not part of it. He did not want to be part of it yet he was acutely aware that Mary Ella was part of it, acutely aware of her absence, of wanting her in her place at the desk as part of his world, not of her world. He wanted to be part of her. He had a strange feeling of sadness, mingled with excitement at the thought of her. An extraordinary yearning for her, mingled with the feeling that he was being drawn apart from her and yet they were not apart. He passed the next two days in that state of utter loneliness until the morning of the Captain's burial.

For the first and last time in their lives, Alec, Ian and Murdo became objects of sympathy. Death made them temporarily respectable and they took full advantage of this. Under the cloak of mourning, they indulged in a steady orgy and a comfortable soak. Alec, until the burial of his father the third morning after his death, could freely gratify his two principal weaknesses: forcing his will upon others by making them drink too much and drinking too much himself, without feeling the usual pressure of strong social disapproval, or at least the fear of it being openly expressed.

He exercised his first weakness immediately by interfering with, and taking charge of the funeral proceedings. He falsely declared that his father's last wish on his deathbed had been that his body should be laid out on the bed in which he had died, his coffin on trestles beside him. Not, as was customary, for his body to be placed in his coffin and to rest in the parlour. He was, he said, bound to respect his father's last wishes. Only at midnight on the eve of his funeral was he to be laid to rest in his coffin and the coffin borne downstairs by his three sons to the parlour for the funeral service the next morning.

In order that he might freely gratify his second weakness, he also stated falsely that his father had wished Mary Ella to receive the main stream of mourners who came, as of custom, during the day to pay their respects to the dead and console the bereaved. However, from seven in the evening onwards, the custom that had nearly fallen into disuse should be revived and the men of Foghar come to pay their last respects to the Captain in his house each evening before his burial.

It was true that his father had expressed last wishes on his deathbed. It was not true that these had borne any resemblance to what his eldest son claimed them to be, and certainly not that they had been limited to only two. Captain Murray's last wishes on earth had been repeatedly to ask that his glass should be filled and his last wish of all had been that he should be propped up, the glass held to his lips, as he had become incapable of holding it himself, not because he was dying but because he was dead drunk. And it was not Alec, but Ian and Murdo who had granted him this last wish; Alec had been dead drunk too. After this, the Captain had lain back, dropped off and died in his sleep some hours later.

To remind all visitors of his father's past importance and reflect some of it upon himself, Alec moved the picture of the ship from the parlour and placed it immediately below the brass faced, mahogany cased ship's clock, over the fireplace in the living room, where all visitors were received and refreshed.

Normally, time had little authority in everyday life on the island on arrivals or departures. Buses never arrived or left on time. It had slightly more respect on the Sabbath, when work was taboo, the daily routine was suspended and the whole community went to Church. When death struck and there was no more time for the principal figure in the house, it became all important. Nothing must be done in it that was not connected with the funeral and mourning.

Mary Ella, assisted by her aunt, Mrs MacLennan, made tea and gave the visitors refreshment between sessions of hushed talk, and prayer when a minister or an elder was present. Alec Murray and his brothers, having indulged themselves without stint the night before, spent the day sleeping it off and were not to be seen until seven o'clock in the evening, after both Mary Ella and her aunt had left. They then took over until the early hours of the morning and, with the men of Foghar, paid their respects to the Captain by refreshing themselves, not with tea but with neat whisky.

The whole island was dry except for two or three small hotels in Carnach which had, in the interest of the tourist trade, been granted a licence to serve alcohol with meals. The only places where, men, like the Murray brothers and their father, could meet and drink outside their own homes were the isolated stone-built bothans on the fringe of the townships where, like outcasts from the rest of the community, they could abandon themselves to drink and drunkenness.

An unfamiliar sense of real importance added a ridiculous dignity that did not make the expression on Alec Murray's face any the more pleasant. Nor did his even more overbearing behaviour make his company any more acceptable. He abused his position as host to force his will upon his guests, as he always did upon his brothers. He made the unwilling drink more than they wished and drank far too much himself, especially on the last evening when the company was joined by the undertaker from Carnach and his two assistants. They had had to accept Alec Murray's hospitality by his insistence on obeying his father's last wishes.

Although under the cloak of mourning and, unrestrained by the presence of a woman or the disapproval of the elders, they could and did indulge themselves in a steady orgy and a comfortable soak, there was also the restraint of a house of mourning. All must accept a code of conduct, long established and deeply respected in the community and sanctioned by the presence of Death. Death took the chair, even though the most serious attention was paid to drink. Never more than one speaker at a time held the floor and he must address the whole company. There must be no smiling and no laughter, no dissension whatever and the speaker must be heard with attention, however dazed was his audience and however dull of comprehension, as the evening progressed. The voice of the speaker must be subdued and he must be listened to in absolute silence and without interruption. To a listener in another room, the steady droning sounded like the intoning of prayer in a monastery. Silences were rare and the amount of intelligent attention required being minimal, the evening passed in uninterrupted enjoyment. Dram went down by dram and not by the bottle and, though as many bottles were consumed and their ultimate condition was the same, it was a steadier process. At the end of the evening, almost all mourners finished in their own homes and in their own beds instead of on the floor of the bothan and the company was just capable of breaking up in the early hours with regret but without disorder. The more temperate and all those with wives waiting at home had departed by ten o'clock.

On the last evening, when prayers had been said by the Minister and Mary Ella and all the women had gone, the all male company was joined by the undertaker and his two assistants from Carnach, officially to supervise and ensure that the Captain was placed in his coffin by his sons, according to his last request. Alec Murray became conscious of the brass and mahogany ship's clock as he had never been before.

Torquil Morrison, a local artist who painted pictures in oils of rough seas, ships, cliffs and the sky over the moors and who, though he did not attend Kirk, had painted one of the Captain's ship which hung in the Minister's parlour, never missed such rare evenings. He had been the first speaker and had all evening performed the important office that Alec, as host, had long since become incapable of performing: that of preventing silence from becoming absolute. When it got late, when there was considerable danger of it doing so, he spoke again.

'It is difficult, it is indeed, to accept that the man who lies dead upon his bed up the stairs above us is the same that strode in all the power of young manhood upon the bridge and in command of that great vessel.'

Alec interrupted his spilling of whisky into glasses to turn unsteadily and glare, not at the picture, but at the clock. At midnight precisely he and his brothers would leave the rest of the company and perform their important duty. They and they alone would place their father in his coffin. It was eleven thirty.

'Thank you, Mr McKay, for reminding me,' said a small, elderly man with a very red face, whose name was Gillies, to the very red face of another man at his side, who had not opened his mouth.

Mr Gillies was a natural actor and drew attention to himself by pretending his neighbour had addressed him instead of the company. He stared straight before him with unseeing eyes which, in the condition he was in, presented no difficulty. He paused dramatically and then continued in a voice that, had the company been sufficiently conscious, would have struck them all with fear. The monologue which followed was his party piece and always reserved for the last night, and as near to midnight as possible. They all entered into the spirit of it, though no one believed that he had really been overtaken by the phantom funeral procession and thereby received the fatal summons and forewarning that his own death was imminent.

'It came up behind me when I had but barely crossed the bridge. I felt Death's chilling touch upon my shoulder. The clutch of Death held me in its icy grip. Whether I would or not, I must keep with it along the way by the coast till we reached the ford of the river and beyond that, follow the path to the graveyard upon the hill. I felt my hand upon the bier and the weight of the coffin in the cradle. I dared not look upon my companion on the other side, or did I look upon the man who stood beside him, waiting to take his place when he and I must pass to the rear, till the eight of us had been relieved by the long columns of men on either side. In silence, we changed down the four grips along the cradle, till I took my place by the wayside. I stared out to sea as the coffin in its cradle passed on, borne, turn by turn, by the long column of men until the tail of it caught up with me and I must turn back and fall in with it to bear it again. I felt not the weight of it, nor the coldness, nor the darkness of night; I felt only fear and horror. I saw not men but shadows; I heard no sound but silence. I had no will of my own but was in the irresistible grip of a ghostly power that held me fast. It was as if the chill of ice had clutched and stilled my heart, and Death in all its shadowiness held all its sway over me and all about me. I thanked almighty God for the river. My toecap had scarcely touched water and I was myself again but never again to be the man I was. Never again.'

He took a deep draught from his glass. Not a glass had been raised as he spoke and every man was looking at him with uneasy fear. However, though the tradition was that the victim of a phantom funeral died sixty-one days later, old Mr Gillies had been recounting his supernatural experience for almost as many years!

'When was it this happened to you Mr Gillies?' the red face of Mr McKay next to him asked, speaking for the first time.

Mr Gillies had sunk into absolute silence.

'Was it not your own father's brother that heaved the stone?' another asked.

Another man answered for him. 'He found it upon the

moor, seven miles from his home, and every time he went out that way for the next twenty years, he moved its great mass, just its length, until it reached the wall of the grave-yard that stares the seas out with those sightless eyes. And within the week he died. It is now his own tombstone and stands yet upon his grave.'

The hands of the mahogany clock stood at midnight and Alec rose with his two brothers, neither in any condition to perform their father's last wish.

'You'll bide where you are!' he ordered him sternly. The undertaker had half risen at his words. His two assistants were incapable. 'It is my brothers and myself will do this last service to our father in his own home and not yourself.'

The undertaker sank back between the two assistants, seated either side of him, and indicated that they were not to move by putting an arm round each of their necks and settling back between them. The two were brothers: one drove the hearse and both took charge of the entry and exit of the coffin into the vehicle. The other was also a reserve gravedigger, whose services were only called upon when insufficient help was forthcoming from relatives and friends, by whom this office was usually performed. As they were in the same case as himself and scarcely able to stand, all three complied with Alec's wishes without question.

Murdo rose unsteadily to his feet. 'I wish for a few min-utes alone with my father,' he said and left the room unsteadily.

Alec and Ian granted his request by taking a full bottle of whisky each and turning back to their guests, filled each glass to the brim. They then put what was left to their lips and drank it down – the first lapse into bothan behaviour that evening.

Alec then put his hand on Ian's shoulder and both turned abruptly and aimed themselves at the door. Alec looked surprised to find it and gravely traced his way to the handle, and supported himself by it until he had opened it. Both tried to pass through the door together astonishingly successfully, if there was still anyone in any state to be astonished. It shut very slowly and carefully behind them.

They were away a long time. During their absence, their guests continued to fix the door with a serious and steadfast gaze, quite lacking in interest or curiosity. In still silence, their attention remained unbroken and undisturbed by the heavy noises and thumps which came from the Captain's bedroom immediately above them. A murmur and muttering came from the landing and a bump, bump, bump was heard as the coffin came down the stairs and finally came to rest in the neighbouring parlour.

The two came back as unsteadily as they had left; Alec with a 'mission-successfully-accomplished' expression upon his face, Ian with no expression on his face at all. Murdo never returned and there was no sign of him for the rest of the vigil, which finished in the early hours of the morning.

'You'll screw down the lid tomorrow,' said Alec to William MacDonald, the undertaker.

His good sense in not requiring him to do it there and then, and the fact that Peter and Andrew McRitchie, his two assistants, would have made poor work with the screwdriver (had they been able to find one at all) would have been quite apparent.

*

Despite a strong wish to support Mary Ella, Michael decided not to join the long column of men waiting outside the Captain's house to bear the coffin at one o'clock the next morning. Instead, he watched the procession leave the house. The service within was mostly attended by the women, seated on rows of chairs provided by the undertaker both in the parlour, the sitting room and wherever it was possible to place them without blocking the hall or passageways. The coffin, now screwed down, rested on trestles in the parlour to be carried, after the service to the bier standing by the gate surrounded by men, waiting in groups from all over the district and the island. The bier was a wooden structure of a design unchanged for centuries; it suggested a very small catamaran. The coffin was laid in a cradle flanked by two parallel poles each of which had handholds for the eight bearers (in four pairs) side by side, separated by the structure.

The service was long but at last William MacDonald appeared, leading. He was followed by Peter and Andrew, his assistants, and three other pairs including the three brothers and three other male relatives bearing the coffin on their shoulders to the bier. When the coffin had been placed on the bier, the four ministers present, the brothers and another male relative took the eight places along the poles of the bier and all the waiting men began to move into position to form the two long columns behind. With the two leaders of each column walking beside the leading bearers, the procession set off. After about twenty or thirty paces, the leaders of the two columns took over from the two leading bearers who passed down the poles to the second handholds vacated by the two bearers behind them. The two rear bearers fell out and stood clear of the columns on either side, looking away from the road. They waited until the rear of the column caught up with them, when they rejoined at its tail. This process continued as others fell out and waited, as they had done, until once more they found themselves at the head of the column and again took over from the leading bearers. The whole process repeated itself until the coffin arrived at the motor hearse on the borders of the township and was driven the rest of the way to the graveyard. All embussed at this point or got into cars parked near by.

Michael watched the cortège move off and the roadway empty. All the women came out of the Captain's house and made their way home – Mary Ella with her aunt, Mrs MacLennan. Minutes later, he saw her returning alone from her aunt's house and coming towards the Captain's house, no doubt to clear up and clean it thoroughly of all traces of the past three days of visiting. He hurried out to intercept her and caught up with her as she was entering it. He found himself lamely and apologetically pouring out excuses and explaining why he had not attended her father's funeral.

'Please excuse the rush but I have to get everything as clean as possible before they all return. Of course I understand. After the way they behaved to you, you could not possibly have come.'

'But that wasn't the reason. I didn't want to intrude and rouse their ill will or resentment further by my presence.'

As he followed her in, she turned and looked up at him.

'Do you yourself really believe what you said about Heaven and Hell; that Hell is on earth and Heaven is living in the presence of God or are you merely repeating what your uncle Malcolm thinks?'

'I am finding myself wholly agreeing with Malcolm as I come to experience and think for myself. I don't believe Hell is a place but a state of mind that we all experience in this life. I am sure Heaven is too but, whereas I have come near the one, I can't be sure I have to the other but the thought has that a ring of truth in me that convinces. I am almost certain that it is love and I came nearest to it in my love for Malcolm and nearest too to hell when he went out of my life.'

He was looking at her with love and the experience was heavenly.

'Evil is in time, and in man, and entirely absent in eternity. It is negative and I am sure love is positive and indestructible. Creation is positive and an act of love. Good and love cannot be destroyed. I am grateful to Malcolm because he has made me think positively and know when I am thinking negatively, and for convincing me that the world was created for a purpose and that that purpose is positive and must be love which cannot be destroyed. We are all made for a purpose. Evil too has a purpose: it is a means, not an end. It has a purpose, the same purpose as love. It is a cleansing process, a spiritual cleansing agent, purifying the individual soul. The world is a great distillery.'

'A laundry!' laughed Mary Ella.

'That's it! It is a great washing machine!' They were gloriously close, and smiling at each other.

'And evil is only washing powder?' she laughed again sceptically. 'I think it is a lot worse than that!'

'Only if we make it the end and not the means. When we make it an end instead of a means, evil is the dirt. Time and events in our daily lives are the washing powder with which we cleanse ourselves, or are defiled. By ourselves, Malcolm means our real selves, our souls which life surrounds with thicker and thicker coatings of forgetfulness. Forgetfulness is worldliness and selfishness, personal conceit of ourselves. We grow cleaner and cleaner till our souls shine in eternity, or we grow dirtier and dirtier till we disperse and become biological dust in time – fertilise the earth, become bacteria, microbes and part of the living and dying world of time.'

He had followed her upstairs and was now talking to her back on the landing on which he had spotted Murdo skulking on all fours, furtively spying to see what was happening between her father and himself. It came to him with a shock that the last time he had been in that house he had left her father drunk and repulsive on the couch in the parlour.

'We have forgotten who we really are and have to wash our souls until they are pure and shine again and we can see God.'

His heart filled with love for her as he spoke and one thing more he knew to be true that Malcolm had said and that was that between man and woman, pure love can reach to the height of Heaven on earth. Malcolm had taught him to reach for the summit of human happiness – heaven itself. Love of woman for man and man for woman can be heavenly, a spiritual marriage, if it has not been muddied and defiled.

She had her hand on the door of the Captain's bedroom and looked up into Michael's eyes. Their eyes met. He was very close to her. She had turned the knob and the door swung open. As she let it go, he followed its swing with his eyes, surprised at its opening. She was startled by the sudden change to shock expressed on his face. He was no longer looking down on her but straight across the room. She followed the direction of his eyes. Laid out on the bed was the unburied body of Captain Murray. She gave a gasp of horror.

Very early the next morning before dawn, in the all too short period of darkness in the Outer Hebrides at that time of the year, three men in black, furtively but expeditiously, made good the shortcoming of the previous day. William MacDonald and Andrew and Peter McRitchie carried the body to the waiting hearse and took it to the graveyard where Alec, Ian and Murdo, standing beside the coffin with the lid raised and unscrewed, were waiting to receive it.

Very soon, it was known to everyone that Alec and Ian had not turned on any lights when they had gone upstairs to put the body in the coffin and to carry it downstairs. The body that they had lifted and placed in it had not been that of their father but of their drunken brother Murdo, who, on going into his father's room, had lain down beside him and passed out. On waking some hours later and finding himself in the coffin he had pushed up the lid, climbed unsteadily to the ground and gone off to his own, more comfortable and less unprepossessing, resting place.

Chapter Nine

Of Mice and Women

'There is one woman for you and for me. I will know her instantly but will you? You mustn't overlook her when she comes, pass her by in a daydream or a brown study, pat her dog or talk to her mother, Michael. I am myself incapable of doing such a thing but you my boy, just at present, have it in you to do just that very thing. You must be on the look out – be the watchman on the tower. You are liable to become too abstracted and focused in one direction and put yourself in solitary confinement. She might come and go and you miss her.'

There had been no close attachments in either of their lives. They had led a very bachelor existence but Malcolm had taken every opportunity to teach him to be sociable, to introduce him to girls, to appreciate women, enjoy their company and to try to understand them.

Michael had been almost certain that he had known her at once. But not quite certain. Was Elizabeth that one woman? He had never yet completely recovered his customary equanimity since the moment he had opened the door of his flat and seen what he had thought to be Fairfield Broughton's secretary standing there. Like a searchlight, she had dazzled him, blinded him too much to enable him to observe her objectively and appreciate her fully and rationally. She had put him at ease but she was so overwhelmingly beautiful, so intellectually lucid, positive, strong yet full of gentle humour and kindness – a quality he had found most lovely in women. She was the most attractive woman he had ever met. No other woman could compare with her, but could he ever be worthy of her? Stupid word 'worthy'! Would he ever think about the things she did for himself, search the same horizons, and not, as he had with Malcolm, only when they were together. Would he merely be inspired by her and seek to follow her, as her father did perhaps?

Malcolm had warned him not to philander. Then he would certainly never find her – would lose her, pass her by or worse still, she would pass him by. Had she, would she, come into his life or had Malcolm been talking nonsense and there was no such woman?

Since Malcolm had gone out of his life, Michael had thrown all his energy into making a successful career. He had developed his mental powers, an ability in practical matters and great patience and efficiency in tackling tremendously difficult and intricate problems. He had grown rich, though he had never sought wealth and spent little. He had been undaunted, determined, and reached levels that were very worthwhile. He had refined and brightened his mind and developed qualities that Fairfield Broughton also possessed and had appreciated in him.

Elizabeth and her father had introduced him at Broughton into another world, where everything was quiet beautiful and still. She lived on a higher spiritual level – discontinuous with that on which he lived. Like her father, he could only glimpse along it when he was with her. She was ahead of them both and saw more distant and loftier horizons. When not with her, he could not see where she was going and could not be sure that they were even going in the same direction. It had been the same with Malcolm. He looked at things on earth, they on things above but never from an opposite point of view. The difference between them was that they were seeking the kingdom first, he only in their presence. Was that why Malcolm had gone out of his life and why Elizabeth had come into it?

What he wanted was a sparring partner, a helpmate, a lover. He could never take on Elizabeth. He would be knocked out in the first round in the unlikely event of his even getting into the ring.

Here on the island, he had come to appreciate Mary Ella more and more. They worked together like two first class tennis partners, winning game after game and set after set without faults, with a confidence in each other and satisfaction in successful achievement that drew them closer and closer together. He began to notice things about her: her voice telephoning, her fingers touch-typing, the intelligent efficiency with which she dealt with, and quietly concentrated on, the intricacies of their work. His mind in London and at Broughton had been prepossessed by Elizabeth. It was so still to a considerable extent but the presence of a woman with the strength of character and personal attractions of Mary Ella could not be disregarded – certainly not by Michael, whose powers of observation and discrimination had been schooled by Malcolm.

★

The morning after the Captain really had been buried, the shock they had experienced together had begun to fade but Michael had not quite recovered and was quite unprepared for another.

He usually took Musty for a short walk before coming into the office and was back before she arrived but either she was early or he was later than usual. She was sitting in her usual place opposite his as he came in, working away with the same calm, quiet efficiency. She looked up.

Her presence struck him with overpowering force. It

was as if he saw her for the first time but not as a stranger. It was as if he had suddenly been translated into an entirely different world and yet everything was the same. She was transformed. She had become a different person and yet was the same. He became intensely aware of how gentle she was and her gentleness hurt him. His heart suddenly began to beat fast and his breathing quicken. He stopped working, completely lost his self-possession and found he could not stay sitting there opposite her. He had to get away. He had to make an excuse to get away. He chased through his mind and remembered that he had forgotten to go up to Foghar Farm. The very thought of Dorothy Kennedy brought him to his senses.

'I must go up to Foghar Farm,' he said quietly. 'I've completely forgotten Dorothy Kennedy. Shan't be long.'

As he drove off, widening the gap between them and separating himself from her, he suffered an excruciating mixture of pleasure and pain that was almost unbearable. Yet at the same time, he was wonderfully happy, elated.

The porch door was wide open. He passed three rugs hung over two chairs and a clothes horse and knocked on the door to the inner hall. Not unexpectedly there was no reply, no movement and not a sound, not even from the wireless which he had often heard when she kept him waiting in patient expectation of the usual pantomime. At last he heard her approaching. She was wearing her not-amused, long, shawl-shrouded face when the inner door opened nine inches to reveal it. This time, the silk scarf was pale grey.

'I see you have let yourself in?'

The word 'yourself' was stressed. She looked past him to the outer door to indicate the extent of the intrusion. 'Come at last!'

'Cat caught any mice?'

She screwed up her face. '*You* said that cat was house-trained!'

'Mouse-trained!' corrected Michael. 'You've been feeding her!' he accused. 'You should have kept her, as I said, without food all day and shut her up in the kitchen all night with the mice!'

'Not one mouse has she caught!'

'You can't be sure of that. She'd eat them up. So they're still with you?'

'Come and see for yourself.'

As she opened the kitchen door, several mice ran from under the sink from three large plates loaded with fish and the contents of at least one tin of cat food and other scraps. A rice pudding basin was overflowing with milk.

'She hasn't eaten much,' she remarked, looking at the food with concern.

'There's enough there for three cats for three weeks and ten mice for a year.'

Musty made straight for the plates which she immediately snatched out of his reach. He started sniffing under the sink, letting off a series of high pressure snorts and sniffs and taking into the depths of his being, the exciting smells of an unknown number of tiny but inaccessible creatures. ·

'I did shut her up. And let her out each morning. She didn't catch one.'

'She would eat some she caught despite all this food.'

'This morning, she rushed out of the kitchen, leapt into the sitting room, then into my bedroom and then, when I opened it, shot out of the front door and away and left me to clean up after her. Now she's disappeared. She hasn't come back as she usually does.'

'She'd be desperate! You overfed her and shut her up.'

'Well good riddance to her!' she said, pettishly.

Then Michael saw her expression change as the thought passed through her mind that the cat had gone for good.

'Good riddance to her,' she repeated but this time in a tone of voice that quite contradicted her words.

She hurried back into the porch to the front door and opened it. 'She's always come back before,' she said, anxiously this time. 'Why hasn't she come back?'

Deprived of the plates overloaded with food and the milk, Musty had been wandering all over the flat, sniffing hopefully. Suddenly he started barking fiercely and rushed through the porch and out of the front door past her. Michael was startled by the look of horror that appeared on her face. He had caught a glimpse of a fourth face, a face with which he was totally unfamiliar. Agony and apprehension were written all over it.

'Don't let that dog hurt her,' she cried out fiercely, clutching at his arm and pushing him after Musty out of the door. 'Stop him. He's driven her away. She was coming back! She'll never come back now! I've lost her!'

Michael ran out calling Musty, caught him up and put him in the Land Rover, barking indignantly. To his astonishment, Dorothy Kennedy had actually run out after him into the pouring rain, calling out in a voice that he had never heard before, 'Pussy! Pussy! Puss! Puss! Puss!'

As he caught Musty, she caught the cat and took it down from the top of the peat stack where it had taken refuge. She held it close in her arms, was loving and fondling it and there were tears in her eyes. He left the subject of mice.

'Have you been to Carnach yet with Mr and Mrs McPhail?'

Musty had been left, much to his indignation, in the Land Rover and Michael was seated at the dining room table with a cup of tea, a plateful of rock buns and one on a plate in front of him.

She did not answer him. She had almost certainly not left the flat – not crossed the threshold of her front door since her arrival, except to run after him to rescue the cat.

She was living, as ever, in a state of siege, relieved only by the vans, the postman, the McPhails and himself. She went to a drawer and got out her pension book.

'I've had it transferred to Foghar Post Office,' she said, holding it out to him.

'I see you have got the new cowl to the chimney?'

'It hasn't made a bit of difference. That chimney will always smoke. Anybody would think I was a kipper,' she laughed.

She was quite different and happy and kept watching the cat lapping up fresh milk from a china saucer in front of the electric fire, not from the overflowing enamelled rice pudding basin which she had restored to its place beneath the sink.

'Good! And you've made the book out correctly,' he said, checking. 'I'll bring it to you later on today.'

He left her and returned to Mary Ella. He was excited and drove much too fast, anxious to climb that height again that they had reached together. He sat down opposite her instead and worked. He worked very hard and well and didn't say a word to her but he was infinitely happy.

Musty, when not lying asleep in a corner, sat upright on the table between them looking out of the window, so that in working hours their three heads were to be seen by the passer-by: Musty's in the large centre sash window in front of Mary Ella's typewriter, Mary Ella's and Michael's through the two smaller ones on either side of the bay. Musty growled when anyone passed.

It was not all work. They always had three breaks: one at eleven, one for lunch and one in the afternoon. On these and other occasions Mary Ella when she wanted to attract his attention, used to signal by making the bell on her typewriter tinkle rhythmically by passing the carriage backwards and forwards three times. Michael would look up, dismiss work from his mind and become wholly conscious of her. At eleven o'clock they had a cup of instant coffee together. At one o'clock she left the house and went away to her aunt's for lunch and in the afternoon she made them both a pot of tea. They had both morning and afternoon breaks in the lounge which she had furnished very comfortably with warm colours, carpets, curtains and chairs which made the visitor relax instantly at the sight of them. Only for the first few days, until they had caught up with the work, did they keep to regular hours and made the breaks short.

Mary Ella did not return to Glasgow to live with her aunt and uncle now that her father had died and no longer went near his house. Their work had benefited enormously from her brief visit to London. She had developed a system of exchanging information with Margaret Smith and Elizabeth, which enabled them to do more and more work on the island. This meant that Michael had to visit London less often. Michael found, as had her uncle, that she was much more than a secretary and they very soon recovered lost ground. They had time to spare which they spent crofting. Mary Ella always accompanied him, introducing him to friends and relatives in need of a spare hand.

'I'm glad you didn't go and look after those brothers of yours,' he said to her in one of the short breaks, soon after the funeral, before they had caught up. 'I gather they were rather savage to you before you went to Glasgow.'

'It was never a happy home after my mother died. They were violent and knocked me about until I grew strong enough to clobber Murdo one day. Then he stopped. Alec and Ian did too. That was a year or so before I went to Glasgow. My father had become less and less rough physically as I ceased to be a child and he became more and more dependent on me. But he was never kind. Nor were they.'

'They made you do all the work?'

'Most of it. Indoors and out. Not so much made me as left it to me. Nothing would have got done otherwise. Aunt Morag helped me as much as she could. She has always been very good to me but she had a large family and a household of her own to keep going.'

'You should have been called Cinderella instead of Mary Ella.'

'Nobody thought of that!'

'Tell me about your mother. I saw the photograph of her in the sitting room of your father's house.'

'The room you were afraid I'd furnish this lounge like?' she asked giving him a steady look.

'I said I was sorry for that and I've done nothing but express unstinted admiration for your efforts here since.'

'And what else should you be doing?'

'Only sackcloth, ashes and a pilgrimage to the Holy Land will satisfy you, I suppose.'

'You were asking about my mother. She was good and loving.'

'If she hadn't had you, she would have had a very unhappy life.'

'She had her faith.'

'Which she passed on to you?'

'She would be the last to claim to have done that.'

'Why?'

'She believed that we must each of us find that for ourselves. She felt it her duty to set an example and bring us up to know the Bible and say our prayers. The rest was between us and God.'

'Malcolm said that the only thing Christ and Calvin have in common is the third letter of the alphabet. By the way what does being born-again really mean?'

'It means becoming spiritually awakened, responsible, not at sea, static or drifting like seaweed or just moving about like fishes looking for food.'

'Sharks!'

'Or animals, only we are not so innocent and beautiful as they are.'

She was innocent and beautiful, he thought. He wanted her just as she was. He didn't want her ever to change. He was sure that she was as she had always been. Always the natural, unregenerate Mary Ella. As if she had been reading his thoughts, she answered the question in his mind.

'Nothing in us changes but the spirit with which we live our lives. We meet the same things, the same people, the same events, the same circumstances. Being born-again means we don't get lost in life but find ourselves, our real selves – what God sees and can alone see. Not the mess we make of what he created by self-will denying him. The spirit of love with which we meet life inspires everything we do and meet. It masters every situation. We don't lose our individuality or our personality, only the unadulterated, unloving careless spirit which previously animated it.'

Michael looked into the lively, beautiful face opposite him, at the eyes full of intelligence, kindness and laughter. He contrasted it with the darkness in that of her eldest brother and with the signs of an inner struggle with suffering that told plainly on the face of the photograph in the velvet frame of her mother. She was not an example of the prevailing, stern, unloving spirit of Calvin that domi- nated religion on the island. Instead, she exemplified the kindness and care for others he saw in so many faces there and in so many lives, despite being born into that harsh, unyielding intolerance that sprang like a trap and gripped with teeth of steel – malicious, divisive, cruel and obscur- antist. How was it that Mary Ella had not the least trace of it in her? Was it her five years in Glasgow?

★

In July, he and Mary Ella abandoned the office completely for the moor, to loading and bringing in the peat by tractor and trailer and to stacking it. The construction of the stack itself was an art. Peat stacks had to withstand all kinds of weather and keep out snow and rain, so that at all times of the year there was peat sufficiently dry for fires and stoves to be kept burning all the year round. After the fourth load was brought back to the growing stack, one of the women of the house would return on the empty trailer with refreshments for all the helpers. She would stay while they loaded the trailer and then served them all while they waited its return. She would then go back with the next load to rejoin the stacking party. The only occasion Mary Ella was away from the office on her own without him was when she helped her three brothers get in their peat and worked at their stack, acting as their hostess and took out the refreshments. The two had just helped her aunt, Mrs MacLennan, get in her peat and the whole congregation with getting in the Minister's peat and building his stack at the manse. The more hands, the quicker the turn around. The peat was loaded carefully to make it secure and firm, so that none fell off as the tractor drew the trailer over the uneven surface of the moor and down the rough tracks to the roadway. The total number of loads varied from eight for a small stack to sixteen.

Angus MacDonald did not fail to remind him of his promise of help with the haymaking – always a time of anxiety because of the uncertain weather and the need to turn it often to dry it. It was more often dried by the wind than by the sun, spread out on long frames, unless there were signs of a long spell of good drying weather. The harvesting of oats and the threshing and the digging up of the potatoes came last in the season.

Michael had not been invited to the manse for tea since the evening he had found Mary Ella's three brothers waiting for his return to the old manse – the evening the Minister and Mrs McAvoy had suggested one of the flats at Foghar Farm for Dorothy Kennedy. He had been away some weeks and much longer than he had intended owing to the robbery, and the whole community had been fully engaged with work on their crofts since his return. He had now been back a considerable time without seeing them and was wondering whether it was for him to make a gesture by attending Kirk. The Minister preached in English once on the first Sunday of each month (the rest of the service being in Gaelic, as was the singing of the metric psalms). There was no organ and there were no hymns. Any music other than the singing of the psalms in a loud chant peculiar to the Western Isles was considered profane.

'Would you take me with you when you go to Church next Sunday?' Michael asked Mary Ella at the end of the month, the next Sunday being on August the First.

She looked up at him in startled surprise, blushed deeply and then look pleased. 'To the morning service?'

'Yes. I haven't seen your uncle for some time. I would like to show respect to him and to your grandmother by attending Kirk at least once a month.'

He noticed a shade of disappointment pass over her face at his explanation but she still looked pleased.

The church was not large but absolutely full. Up with the elders on a raised pew just below the pulpit occupied by the Minister, he recognised Mr McPhail. He was in the most prominent position immediately below the pulpit and suddenly rose and began to sing alone in a high-pitched nasal voice, the opening line of one of the metric psalms. Michael realised that he was the Precenter. Suddenly all about him, Michael found himself surrounded by loud wailing intonation, like a human imitation of the drone of the bagpipes. The whole effect was quite unique. Everyone of every age knew the psalms by heart and gave their loudest and best wail under the leadership of Mr McPhail. There had been a strong gale blowing while they were gathering outside the church. The strange, weird sound was caught up and swept across the sea and the moors and up into the vast skies. The prayers and the sermon were both very long. Mr McAvoy delivered a powerful denunciation of sin with hate in his voice which made everyone uneasy but as he ended, his voice grew quiet and gentle and he finished on a note of hope and love. The service lasted an hour and three quarters.

There were smiles and nods of acknowledgement on their arrival together, from families entering the church. Afterwards, when they were leaving, there were further nods and smiles, especially to Mary Ella and a few words in Gaelic that made her blush.

The following week, the Minister called by just after she had gone to lunch with her aunt, with a message from his mother inviting Michael to tea that evening.

He was not, as on the previous visits, ushered into the sitting room but into the parlour across the hall opposite, which he saw for the first time. He was not, as before, left alone; the Minister did not go off to the kitchen and join his mother but invited him to sit down and stayed with him in the room. Michael wondered why his reception was so formal. Musty had gone straight into the sitting room and taken his usual place on the rug before the fire, until he realised the new situation and ran across to join Michael in the parlour.

The first thing Michael noticed was an oil painting of the Captain's ship by Torquil Morrison steaming across the Minister's wall but much more dramatically. The sea was rough and the wind swept the smoke from her funnels. With rugged waves, a cloud-strewn sky, smoking funnels and sea birds circling in the wind, it was full of movement, not lifeless like the coloured print in the Captain's parlour.

Members of the crew were busily occupied along its entire length and the Captain very clearly identifiable by his upright stance on the bridge and his peak cap. His features were those of an active young man; clean-cut, not bloated and distorted as he had last seen the original, both before and after death. By his authoritative bearing, the artist had succeeded in giving him absolute command of his ship. Michael expressed approval but the Minister did not even notice his remark.

'Have you had any trouble from Mary Ella's brothers?' he asked directly.

'Not since that night.'

'You will have taken the wind from their sails.'

'In what way will I have done that?' asked Michael puzzled.

'Your taking Mary Ella to kirk. I expect they have been too fully occupied drinking up all their father's liquid assets and converting everything possible in the house into cash for drink to make a nuisance of themselves.'

'They are not an attractive trio. I enjoyed the service.'

Michael was still very puzzled.

The Minister showed a trace of impatience but at that moment, Mrs McAvoy called them in a cheery way to come for their tea. They left the parlour for the living room and all trace of formality disappeared. Their relationship resumed the friendly and familiar course of his previous visits. At the end of the meal, there was no question of their returning to the parlour. Shortly after, the Minister's reason for taking him there became clear from the words between mother and son in the kitchen.

'Did you speak to him, Ian?'

'I got nowhere, Mother. The man's not got the least idea of the talk he has been creating.'

'Nor has Mary Ella it seems.'

'The lass should know better. She knows what it means

to take a lass to kirk, but I have doubts that he does.'

'And he has had no trouble from her brothers?'

'He is not at all concerned about them.'

'Under her spell?'

'And she his.'

'Can he really be so guileless as to think they can spend day after day together without causing talk?'

'Well! Well! I'll be joining the two of them in wedlock before the year is out.'

★

It was Musty rather than Michael who led the way home. The next morning when she arrived, he found himself immensely shy of her. He felt shy for the first time in his life. Elizabeth had dazzled him: she had not made him shy. He knew that he was a coward. He had been all these months enjoying her presence, loving her and did not have the courage to come out boldly and tell her. He could not bear it if she refused him. It was too wonderful just being with her as they were, day after day. He could not bring himself to risk losing her, and destroying that happy life they were having together. He again quietly told her he was going to see Dorothy Kennedy and would be back soon.

He was stopped on his way up to the farm by Mr McPhail, waving him down on the track up to the farm.

'We can't persuade the old lady to leave the house. She's not been out once, though we have offered to take her to Carnach every time we have gone there since she came. It is not healthy. If she's left too much to herself she'll become crazed.'

'She used to watch television a lot and often has her wireless on.'

'She has it on all day,' corrected Mr McPhail, clearly well acquainted with his tenant's habits. 'She never answers a knock on her door and never admits us. Leaves messages in the porch. But we always hear it. She has it on very loud sometimes. We can hear it in the flat above when we are there. We air it every day.'

'I'll suggest she gets a television.'

'There are a few in the district. Morrison's at Carnach will sell or rent her one and put up an aerial for her. There are other tenants coming to the flat above who might share the expense with her.'

'Have you told her about them?'

Michael knew only too well how this would unsettle her.

'I haven't had an opportunity to but when Mrs McPhail saw her yesterday she already knew. She always puts the correct rent in the porch on a chair for us to collect without disturbing her. But that time she needed change and was out in the porch asking if we had any. She would have seen them when they came to see the flat.'

Michael was not at all happy when the door opened at a single knock, promptly and wide, to reveal not the face that sank a thousand ships but the one with which she had passed with third class honours in psychology which he had not seen since her retirement. He was even more surprised to find the cat in her arms – an obviously thoroughly contented cat that didn't stop purring. *But,* Dorothy Kennedy was not purring or at all contented. She spoke very discontentedly and with determination and finality. She was leaving Foghar Farm.

'I won't stay here with people thumping and bumping over my head. I want a place of my own.'

'I was in touch with your agents recently. They have advertised your house again. Why not withdraw it from the market and go back? It's a good house, in perfect condition and easy to run. You will save further expense of buying and selling and have television again.'

'You are always on about that dark, gloomy place! I don't want that woman next door always knocking on my door again and poking her nose in, wanting to know what I am doing and how much money I've got. She only posted my letters so that she could read who they were addressed to. I want a place of my own with my own television. I'm not going to pay for an aerial to be put up on someone else's property. You sell that place and I'll buy a home of my own here.'

'It's not at all easy to get a place of your own here. Most of the houses have felt roofs and need re-roofing and completely modernising. Renovating by a contractor from the mainland is very expensive. There are a few crofters skilled enough to make a living out of such work but they are in great demand. You might have to wait a long time. They usually work in pairs. Most of the crofters do their renovating themselves or get a grant. Mr McPhail did all the work here and only got help with the electricity and plumbing from one or two of them locally who have gathered experience of both over the years.'

'Mr McPhail,' she said contemptuously. 'I've never seen such work. Just look at that kitchen! Stupid, long narrow place with the sink away at the back in the dark and the mice coming in by the score through the holes and tunnels made for the pipes.'

'The mice are still there, are they?'

'They'll be back. Plenty more where they come from.' She was stroking the cat lovingly.

'Shall I find out what is for sale on the island, then?'

Mary Ella undertook to do that for him and started telephoning directly he got back to her. 'She's in luck! Arduachdran Castle and estate is for sale. That's most of the island,' she laughed, looking at him from the phone. 'It has just come on the market. If she buys that she'll be our feudal superior.'

Both shook their heads, laughing together.

'I don't see her as a chatelaine! Nor as my liege lord! Too much of that already and she's not the hunting, fishing and shooting type.'

'There are two houses for sale that have just been feued and separated from their crofts by a law, only very recently introduced. Otherwise, there are two crofts for sale with houses.'

They contemplated Dorothy Kennedy as a crofter with even greater hilarity.

'One of the feued houses is at Foghar and is coming on the market next week. I can't think which it is. It is odd that we haven't had word of that. I should have thought my aunt would have been the first to hear about it. The other has been on the market for nearly eight years and is thirteen miles from us at Closach on Tamhasgail Rock. That's no place to live at all. I'll get the particulars of the one at Foghar.'

'Better get the particulars of both. It is too far away and she won't consider it but if we didn't tell her anything about it and she came to hear of it from the McPhails or the Postman or one of the vans, she wouldn't rest till it was hers.'

'It isn't the distance that is against it,' said Mary Ella. 'It has a sinister reputation. The whole place has. Closach means carcass or carrion, and "tamhasgail" means ghostly or spectral. It is very old. Up to about the middle of last century, the people of Closach made a living by wrecking. The house stands right at the top of the rock, right on the edge of the cliff, immediately overlooking the sea with nothing but a sheer drop to the seashore for miles along the coast on either side of it. One of the bedrooms that looks straight out to sea is what is known as the "Wrecker's Window", where they used put the light to lure ships on to the rocks. The road up to the house is very steep and the houses, close upon each other on either side, hem it in. No light from any of them can be seen at sea, only the light from that house and that window. Foreign ships mistook it for a lighthouse until one was built well north of it about a century ago.

'No one ever survived a wreck on the Tamhasgail Rocks and all the wreckage and bodies got sucked into the dozens of caves or on to a few very small beaches when the tide is out. There is no easy access to caves or beaches except by boat but it is believed that there is an inland way or ways known only to the inhabitants of Closach. There was a wreck there in the last war when the Arduachdran lighthouse was not in service. No one on board survived it. There is no one on the island that doesn't believe it was the light from the window that caused it. Everyone is convinced too, that the access to the shore or caves is still known and is kept secret because there may be another war.'

'Trust her to get fixed up in a house like that!' said Michael. 'We must contrive things so that she buys the house here in Foghar. You must find out which it is and all about it, if there is anyone local who will undertake to renovate it and if she can get a grant. If there is no one local who will do the job, check up on contractors here and on the mainland. I'll get in touch with the agent selling her house and try to get some idea what she is likely to get for it and when.'

'If she gets a grant, the council will require a new roof, doors, floors and windows. It will certainly need rewiring and the bathroom and kitchen modernising. If contractors do the work, the cost will be enormous.'

Mary Ella spent the rest of the day in the Land Rover and on the telephone. The house was an old croft house, long since vacant and the reason why no one knew it was coming up for sale was that it was considered unsaleable and very badly in need of renovation. The only good thing about it was that it was next to the Post Office and General Store. No one locally would undertake the work and only one of the two contractors on the island and one on the mainland were interested. Both gave very rough estimates. That from the mainland was astronomical and that on the island was five thousand pounds in excess of the maximum grant. Mary Ella also learnt that, not being born on the island or having lived on it long enough, Dorothy Kennedy did not qualify for any grant.

Michael telephoned the agents. The manager told him that he had that morning received an offer five hundred pounds less than Dorothy Kennedy had paid for her house, that this was the only offer made for it so far and that he had that morning written advising her to accept it.

'I think she should either stay where she is at Foghar Farm or go back to her own house,' Michael said to Mary Ella that evening before they finished for the day. 'I shall try again to persuade her to go back to her own house. There really is no one you can think of who would do the work here?'

'Only my three brothers!'

'Do they do that sort of work?'

'If they can get it. They renovated Morag Morrison's house while I was away in Glasgow and did a very good job. They are good at their work when sober but no one likes to employ them because Alec never sticks to his word and to the terms he has agreed. Once all the materials have been bought and the owners are committed, he bullies them and bargains for more money an hour or says he wants a contract for a particular job, re-roofing or harling. He can't be trusted not to try to extort more money and break his original agreement.'

'What has Morag Morrison got that all the others ha-ven't.'

'Holy Terror! No one would dare try to do anything like that with Morag Morrison! Or turn up anything but cold sober! Men become cold sober at the sight of her! All three happened to be desperate for money to pay their fines!'

'I shall go and see her again and try and persuade her to go back.'

He went up to Foghar farm at once.

'How you do keep on about that house! All that dark, gloomy panelling and that traffic back and front twenty-four hours a day. I'm never going back there and I'm not staying here in this flat with those McPhails always nosing their way in. I want my own television and I'm not going to spend money on someone else's property. They should put up an aerial here. I'll buy that house at Closach!'

'It's thirteen miles away and been empty for years and will almost certainly need a great deal doing to it. Much much more than the house here in Foghar.'

'Then I want that house at Foghar. It's right by the Post Office and the Store. It's ideal for me. I can get my pension, do my own shopping and have television in my own house with no one calling in. I'll buy it whatever state it's in. Take me to see it. I'll tell the agent to accept that offer directly.'

She put on a smart hat, pinned a silk scarf round her neck, put on thin, brown, court shoes and a town overcoat while he waited. The rain was being dashed against the wide porch window, driven by a mounting gale. He drove her straight through it to the Post Office and left her waiting in the Land Rover where she was, in her strange, quite unsuitable town dress – an object of great interest and curiosity while he went into it to enquire from Mr Mac-Donald, who had the key. Mr MacDonald produced it himself.

Michael went and opened the door and signalled to her. She got out and hurried over to him through the rain. She went through each room seeing everything, observing nothing and failing completely to appreciate the work that would be required to transform it into a habitable dwelling place. Next, she insisted on being taken at once to see Mary Ella's three brothers, although Michael had warned her against them and given her all the reasons Mary Ella had given him for not employing them.

A dreary atmosphere surrounded and pervaded the Captain's house. It was heavy with symptoms of withdrawal and not only of the Captain. It was quite evident that the Captain's money was all spent, all his liquid assets realised and that the three brothers had been dry for some days and did not like it one bit. They were greeted with surly silence by Alec with Ian standing by his shoulder, and Murdo peering down at them from the landing. Something almost like geniality, the nearest he ever got to cordiality, thawed the hardness of Alec's face when the object of their visit was, with some considerable difficulty, made clear to him by Michael. The sudden realisation that the drought was about to break with the promise of whisky again for a long period, had the effect of getting them all, including Murdo, into the parlour where the picture of the Captain's last command had been replaced in its original position but awry. Had it really been steaming across the ocean, it would have dived to the bottom and been lost with all hands. Upon her learning that their father had commanded the vessel, any doubts Michael had put in Dorothy Kennedy's mind as to the wisdom of employing them were dismissed. She was quite determined to engage them. She showed no further interest in the house itself other than to see the owners at once, short circuit the lawyers and agree a price. They agreed to sell it to her at a price five times higher than the starting price advised by the Carnach lawyer. She returned to Foghar Farm, having bought a property which would not have fetched fifty pounds a very short time before, if it could have been sold at all.

'You're not to tell those McPhails,' she said as they passed their bungalow, unaware that everyone in Foghar would be in full possession of every detail of the transaction within minutes, rather than hours, informed by all those on the telephone. Some had already been rung up from the Post Office while they were on their way back to her flat and some well before.

'The next step is to get the plans prepared and the application to the Council for the grant.'

The next day, Michael called up again to tell her that he had arranged for a surveyor to go over the house and to make the necessary plans.

'Oh, that house!' she said, contemptuously. 'I'm not going to live there. It's too near those McPhails. I've bought that place at Closach. Rock House I think it's called.'

'You can't do that!' said Michael aghast. 'You've offered and agreed to buy the other house.'

'I have signed nothing through a lawyer. I have for Rock House. Mr McPhail drove me over to Carnach. It is all settled. He drove me to see those three brothers too. They have agreed to work on Rock House. Your surveyor can survey Rock House instead! Did you know it is a listed building but I can't get a grant?'

She had bought the house at Closach without even viewing it. The brothers had agreed to work there, providing she paid the cost of travel there and back each day. She admitted she had not informed the owners of the house next to the Post Office of her decision and asked him to do so. This was in fact unnecessary as they already knew. She also asked him to get her half a bottle of White Horse whisky as soon as he could.

Chapter Ten

Waddy

When, on the night of the break-in and attempted robbery, Elizabeth had disappeared into the darkness of her garden with Musty, leaving her father and Michael discussing Burma and the Arakan, Fairfield Broughton had not called Elizabeth out of the shadows into which she and Musty had disappeared on the night of the robbery so much as out of the past. She was back more than twenty years and not in the shadows but in the broad daylight and bright sunshine of a spring morning, back in her childhood with Waddy and Crystal, her yellow Labrador.

Fairfield Broughton, nearly as young as Elizabeth was now, was often abroad for long periods. He was continuing to build an empire, while the Empire itself was passing into history. His great fortune was springing up and spreading itself out, taking root all over the world and finding means of growth in the meanest and richest soil, nursed by his genius for production. At the end of the war, it was as if all those years of destruction had been winding up a spring in him. It was as if a detonator went off and set off an explosion of production, instead of destruction. Oil wells gushed, forest plantations spread, vast crops were sown and harvested of every kind, huge dams built, jungles cleared. Mines were sunk, skyscrapers rose and industrial and building estates spread out, both at home and overseas. Anything positive, anything productive acted like a marching song upon him. He had started a millionaire and therefore money was always a means not an end with him, a measure of achievement only. He sought neither power nor wealth, only production, especially in the depressed areas, in a world where almost everywhere was depressed. He was, as a result, always away and more often than not far, far away.

His marriage was not a failure. He adored his young wife but she had an incurable disease. It was quite apparent to them both that it only made her unhappy when she felt it acting as a brake on his vital and expansive career, which she did her best to follow closely until she died. If he stayed with her at Broughton for more than a few days, she grew quite irritable and worried. They both knew why. And so he would hasten off in despair to where he was most anxiously expected and needed. He was the dynamic heart of a great productive economic empire which drew all its energy and power from him.

Monica Broughton was a beautiful woman but not in the usual sense in which the word is used. Her body, paralysed by disseminated sclerosis, lay on a ripple bed. She could not sit up and her speech was badly affected yet she was alive with beauty. To stand by her bedside was to receive it like sunshine into the soul, no matter how coarse, rough and insensitive the character. No one left her without feeling strengthened and refined. She was more an influence than a person. It was impossible to describe any physical characteristic at all, except the impression taken away of an indescribable smile which told that in that useless body dwelt calm content. Her visitor – nurse, servant, friend, husband, daughter – came away morally elevated, purified. She was a living shrine. As energy, confidence and decisive determination emanated from Fairfield Broughton, so did something unspeakably lovely from Monica Broughton.

Elizabeth was eight when her mother died. Until that time, she was completely free as children rarely are. Her mother had the same effect on her as she had on everyone but the special gift that she gave Elizabeth was freedom in the unspeakably lovely and spiritual sense of that word but also as a child. She herself had to have a nurse but Elizabeth did not, and Monica Broughton managed, as far as she was able, that her own nurse should be as inconspicuous as possible in the house. Elizabeth was free because of the influence her mother had on her. She was free of the need of all those protective restraints, burdens and restrictions which by faults, shortcomings and heedlessness most children impose upon themselves. In the heart of the beautiful old house lay the vital, protective love of this scarcely living mother, to whose presence she had almost unlimited access. She had taught her daughter to read and write before her disability disabled her but first and fore-most to love goodness. She seldom left her mother for long and they read to each other and talked together of this beautiful world of theirs which belonged wholly to them and in which she was free to roam.

One part of her world she particularly loved, was the garden into the shadows of which she had disappeared with Musty that evening. Besides the presence of her mother in her life, she had two other dearly loved companions at that time. One of them was her dog Crystal, and the other was the gardener, Waddy. There were several gardens and other gardeners but the garden of the shadows was her own and Waddy was her own too.

Like her mother, Waddy had always been in her life and like her mother, he had also died when she was eight. But that is really true of neither as for Elizabeth, they never died or even faded away but continued to live – vividly and presently in dream and daydream, and in all the peaceful moments of her life. Like her mother, peace was within her and she carried that peace everywhere she went.

Waddy was like a living tree to her, with beautiful eyes and sheltering arms, and there was always the rustling of leaves about him and even the dead leaves were beautiful. His weather-beaten face, his great height when straightened, and his gentleness with her, the plants and flowers, even the earth he turned with spade and fork, the magic of the wheelbarrow, the motor mower and the broomstick, were the parts and he himself the centre, of this little world.

Elizabeth was perhaps even more beautiful as a child. She had that almost unearthly beauty that dwells in childhood and especially that rarefied beauty that dwells in children quite unsullied or corrupted by their circumstances and surroundings.

She and Waddy were closer than friends or even close relatives. He never stopped what he was doing, except to show her something interesting – a pretty flower, butterfly, bird or bee and he always addressed her as 'Miss Elizabeth'. They were aware of each other as was perhaps only possible at that period of time in England. He was for her something unspeakably precious in her life, an integral part of it, a friend in whom she had absolute confidence and for whom she had nothing but the utmost respect. To him she was 'Miss Elizabeth' and nothing of what she was was lost upon him. She was his little mistress – mistress of his heart – not because she was his master and mistress's daughter but in her own right, because of her intrinsic qualities and their special relationship. They were part of each other's lives; she for the first, he for the last years of their lives.

There was nothing in their world that they did not discuss. Elizabeth would come and see him at various times of the day and always before her ride on her pony in the morning. On her return, she would go to the kitchen for her glass of milk, and then she would take a cup of well sugared tea and a piece of cake, carrying it carefully with both hands, followed by Crystal, to Waddy in her garden.

When her mother was known to be dying and only six months before his own death, they had a long discussion about it.

'What happens when we die, Waddy?'

'I can't rightly say, Miss Elizabeth. Some talk of Heaven and of Hell, some of haunted spirits wandering the earth, some of other lives in other ages, other bodies, and some of entering other beasts and living things all together.'

The topic occupied some time and all these possibilities were discussed fully. Elizabeth brought the discussion to an end.

'Let's make a promise to each other, Waddy.'

'What shall we promise, Miss Elizabeth?'

'Let's promise each other that whoever dies first will come back and tell the other what it's like.'

*

The past Fairfield Broughton had recalled when Michael had told him of the meeting of Malcolm at the zoo with the man he had fought with in the Arakan was very different from the childhood recollection of Elizabeth. The Arakan was one of the most disheartening and desolating theatres of war there is ever likely to be. He had been all through that campaign: the mud, the monsoons, the leeches, malaria, the dense jungle, the water barriers and other difficulties of the terrain, added to which the wrong training, the wrong equipment and the low morale of the fighting force, tortured and twisted by the agonies of frustration.

By surprise and their mastery of jungle warfare, their swift, relentless advance through Malaya and the fall of Singapore, the Japanese had achieved overwhelming moral and military superiority. What had been considered an

158

impenetrable jungle and defence, they had filled with
menace and the deadly fear that the hunter brings to the
hunted. All its difficulties were at that time turned to their
advantage. They were braced by their success and their
fanatical belief that death in the service of a divine Emperor
brought them instant immortality, led to heroic action.
Their deliberate and merciless cruelty to those who fell into
their hands brought home to him the truth of the reports of
their invasion of China and savage cruelties inflicted there.
They ceased to be regarded as human beings but with the
fear and loathing aroused by reptiles or deadly insects like
the tarantula or the scorpion. They tortured before killing
any prisoners or wounded who fell into their hands,
slaughtered the wounded they captured in hospitals in their
beds. The cries of two of his men captured returning from
a patrol before they were killed still rang in his ears. It had
become an unwritten law that no one must ever be left in
Japanese hands, but must be rescued from them at all costs.
To leave a comrade in their hands was regarded as worse
than abandoning him to be eaten alive by ants or swallowed
by crocodiles, indescribably horrible and sinister. He had
come to regard them as repulsive and subhuman, of
another order and with revulsion altogether different from
his feelings for the Germans whom he had faced in the
Blitzcrieg and at Dunkirk. Though mortal enemies in battle
the Germans had remained fellow human beings, caught up
in a deadly struggle. They respected the Geneva Conven-
tion and international law. Even after he had learnt of
Hitler's terrible treatment of the Jews that feeling remained.
He had associated the Holocaust not with the race but with
Hitler and the Nazi party and the worst forms of human
prejudice.

The Japanese rejection of all normal and acceptable behaviour to other races, their attitude to death and their
deliberate and fiendish cruelty to those who fell into their

hands, man, woman and child, especially their brutality and cruelty to civilians in their invasion of China before the war and in their prison camps during it, overshadowed for many years the affection he had felt for the many individuals he had met before the war and had dealt with in business since.

Fairfield Broughton, as a young territorial sergeant, had won a DCM in the debacle leading up to Dunkirk. As a gesture of independence and self-reliance, which his father had been quick to approve and appreciate, he had not asked him to use his influence as the Colonel-in-Chief of his own county regiment to get him a commission, but had crossed the county border and joined its most famous regiment, which had in the great war won its glorious reputation for winning VCs before breakfast, as an other rank. Now as an officer in the same regiment he had come to the Arakan at a time when British morale had reached its lowest point ever in physical conditions which could not be worse.

In fact, under these conditions and in a hopeless military situation, the regiment had put up as fine an effort as ever, but not in its own eyes or those of High Command or of a propaganda press desperate for success. With air and naval superiority almost eliminated and after a sequence of terrible defeats which had knocked the breath out of the defeated army what was in reality a splendid achievement and a necessary, essential and unavoidable part of the climb back to moral ascendancy was written off from its start as a continuation of them.

There were minor successes but not even for those who won them was the bitterness of defeat removed. Fairfield Broughton, as a temporary captain in command of a company, had won an immediate MC for a brilliant sudden and successful counter-attack which had encouraged the whole battalion. However, it was one of the very few decorations won from a High Command which did not –

perhaps could not – recognise the much greater qualities required to stay the pace when all is hopeless and negative, and when defeat seems certain. To Fairfield, no less than to all the others, the very word Arakan was synonymous with a jungle covered in quicksands of despair, and endurance of the worst kinds of misery, both physical and spiritual, with cheerlessness, a sinking heart, sinking spirits and sinking health.

Later, with a bar to his MC and a DSO and as acting Lt. Col. in command of an infantry battalion himself not far from the Arakan, but in very different circumstances, he found himself with all that behind him. Akyab had fallen without a battle and the war had swung round and turned south. But for him, it was a continuation of the same campaign and the same struggle. Only weeks after the fall of Akyab, he was in very similar country, having been landed behind the Japanese and was advancing to engage them as part of the three-pronged drive in the great battle, for the recovery of Burma.

He was about to enter this particular field of memory that he was subsequently to visit so frequently. He had sent one of his most aggressive company commanders ahead of the battalion to take up the most favourable position he could, in order to enable the entire battalion to deploy for an attack on an important enemy supply depot. He had given him strict orders that under no circumstances was he to start the battle on his own, before the whole battalion had joined him and was in position to attack. His orders had been obeyed, although it had meant abandoning two excellent men – trained snipers – who had twice disobeyed orders and gone ahead of the leading platoon, just as it had made contact and drew fire from the enemy. Charlie Besant had, with the greatest difficulty, restrained himself and his company from an immediate advance to extricate them but, realising the importance of obedience to his orders, he had dug in and instead spent a watchful night sending out small reconnaissance patrols to get as much information as possible. He awaited as ordered, the arrival of the whole battalion the next day.

Very early on the morning of that day, Fairfield Broughton had ridden ahead of the battalion on the horse belonging to the officer in charge of the mules, risking enemy patrols and ambushes. He had his batman up behind him but, when they were nearly up with the leading company, he left the batman with the horse to wait for the battalion to catch up. Fairfield Broughton had carried on on foot, unescorted. In action, batmen served as bodyguards, enabling their officers to concentrate on maps, tactical reconnaissance and planning, while they kept a sharp look out for enemy patrols and snipers.

On his arrival, Fairfield Broughton told Charlie Besant that he would himself quickly reconnoitre and mark out company forward positions for the attack the next day. Surprise was important and on his own he would do this with less risk than with two or more men on the job.

Fairfield Broughton was a very young commanding officer, the youngest to reach that rank in the Fourteenth Army and he was not much, if at all, older than his company commander. However, they were a match for each other in spirit. Their voices became raised in dispute.

'You must have protection, Sir,' exclaimed Charlie Besant indignantly. 'That ground was swept by fire yesterday when I withdrew and I lost two good men – Keene and Harwood. There will be one hell of a bloody mess if you get killed.'

'I shan't get killed. Bobby Marshall or you yourself could step into my shoes and do just as well even if I did.'

Bobby Marshall was second-in-command and, at that moment, bringing up the rest of the battalion.

'There's not the slightest sense in risking another life,

drawing more attention and giving away our intentions by taking someone with me. I can move around much more furtively alone. If I don't make it, guide the companies in yourself into the best positions you judge right at the time. Put yourself forward, with Willis on your right and the other companies in reserve. Where we are now is best for Battalion Headquarters.'

'It's not the CO's job; it should be mine.'

'I know how you feel, Charlie. I'm not playing the hero or being bloody minded. The placing of the companies at this stage is really important. The two reserve companies have got to train and fight at the same time. Only you and Willis have any experience of commanding companies in action and you both have the most experienced NCOs in your companies; that's why I am placing you forward and the other two in reserve. Vane and Temperly have, neither of them, ever been in action before. I don't even like placing them in supporting positions without having examined the ground. The map, as usual, is utterly useless and can only direct them to the area. It doesn't give a hint even of cover or the least bit of tactical information.'

'Okay, Sir. You know what you are about. Don't take any risks. As you say, we are desperately short of experience in the battalion and over half of us are replacements.'

The CO slipped off into the jungle but not, as he thought, alone.

*

Every battalion has a cook sergeant and every company has a cook, usually a lance corporal and almost always acting unpaid. The company cook had produced mugs of tea, drawn from the biscuit tin in which he brewed it, including one for himself, and had been seated out of sight but by no means out of hearing during the conversation between the

CO and his company commander. On active service, and when in close contact with the enemy and action is imminent, every man is issued with hard rations and the only cooking the cook has to do is to brew tea. After that he has nothing to do. This was one such an occasion. He had brewed the tea, issued it and now he had nothing to do. He seized his rifle and slipped off into the jungle after his Colonel. Silently and skilfully following in his steps, observing all about him, he acted as his bodyguard and escort, doing the job of the batman who was waiting back with the horse for the battalion to come up.

The CO went very carefully, pausing every now and then to mark his map. All went well. The lance corporal could see from the way he pulled the flap over and clipped up the map that the job was done. He shot a keen observant eye all about him but caught sight of a Japanese sniper, tied in a tree, taking careful aim.

Fairfield Broughton was startled by the deafening sound of two shots fired simultaneously, one almost beside him. The next instant there was an ugly spurt of blood from his thigh, which he realised must be staunched at once. The next moment he was aware of a face he would never forget.

It was the face of a very young boy but expressed the calm determination of a much more mature man. Youthfulness had doubtless got him the appointment of cook by a suspicious company commander – suspicious that he was still much too young when he had joined up. Strength and independence of character and determination had got him, unsuspected and unquestioned, through the recruiting centre, well before the call up.

The lance corporal had taken off his belt and cut two lengths of bamboo.

'He's fired his last shot, Sir,' he said, pointing to the body hanging high up in the tree above. 'It's a lousy tourniquet but will do the job till we can get a better one.

I've shot the little bastard who got you. That's it. Hold on to that and release and tighten while I carry you. Not far to go and the shots will have alerted the company.'

His voice was quiet and confident and he had the tourniquet deftly in position. He abandoned his rifle, fifty rounds of ammunition and the map case, fell on one knee, took the CO under his arm pits and knees and with astonishing strength, lifted him from the ground like a bridegroom carrying his bride over the threshold.,

Fairfield Broughton concentrated on the tourniquet and remained fully conscious but rapidly becoming weak and dizzy – incapable of helping himself. He became utterly submissive to the other's strength of mind and body. He could not speak but did not take his eyes off the boy's face and read every bit of the strain and determination written on it. When they were within yards of the company but still quite hidden by the jungle, he lost consciousness and let go his hold on the tourniquet. The lance corporal let his weight slide to the ground and shouted. He heard a rush of men towards him, turned back and slipped away in the direction from which they had come.

When Fairfield Broughton was once more conscious of his surroundings, he was in the care of a forward surgical unit where the bullet was being removed. Suffering from excessive loss of blood, he was flown in a tiny, tree-hopping jeep plane in which he lay on a stretcher, his head close to that of the pilot to an advanced casualty clearing station.

Charlie Besant was killed in the ensuing action. The battalion was commanded by the second-in-command, Major Marshall. The CO had been found bleeding to death with a belt round his thigh acting as a tourniquet ten yards from where he had set out and no one was ever aware of the activities of the lance corporal. Despite all of Fairfield Broughton's subsequent enquiries, the company cook remained unidentified. He had disappeared and Fairfield

Broughton, later assisted by Elizabeth Broughton, had been looking for him ever since.

He had in fact, managed to recover his rifle, the fifty rounds of ammunition and the map case, which Charlie Besant found by his own when Major Marshall came up and took over. This enabled that gentleman to deploy the whole battalion, without delay, in excellent positions and ready for action, as the CO had planned. They attacked at first light in the morning. The cook could not recover his belt which got him into trouble but as they were about to go into action and during that action he was able to replace it, the whole episode was forgotten.

Chapter Eleven

The King of Sausages

Even though Michael lay awake in the night, longing for her and to be with her, when he actually was, he never revealed the revolution that had taken place in his feelings for her. As Mary Ella likewise had never revealed hers for him, everything remained as it had always been between them. His manner towards her had not altered in the least. He was loving and adoring all the time, and most of all when he was with her. She had no idea he had fallen in love with her or changed at all towards her. He had no idea that she had always been in love with him. He never revealed what he was feeling to anyone, except his kindness and good humour. No one had ever known what Malcolm's disappearance, so suddenly and unexpectedly, out of his life had meant to him. Now he gave not a hint of the powerful and disturbing feelings which possessed him and no sign whatsoever that when he was away from her, he was tortured by uncertainty, by the thought of a tomorrow without her, the fear that they might not always be together. The thought of one hour, one minute lost, let alone a day without her coming to the old manse quite appalled him. None of this was obvious.

'I feel awful letting those people down,' he said to her when he saw her the day after Dorothy Kennedy had reneged.

'The nature of Mrs Kennedy is well known about here

now. No one will blame you.'

'What a pity there were only just those two houses on the market!'

'You are forgetting Arduachdran Castle!'

'I suppose we must be thankful that thought never entered her head.'

'It may yet.'

'No. She will have to go to live on Tamhasgail Rock when the house is ready for her now.'

'She will regret it bitterly. Is she really committed this time?'

'Signed the dotted line.'

'There are few born in Closach that would care to live in that evil house. No one else on the island would go near it, let alone buy and live in it. I should not have a moment's peace if it was mine.'

'How much is the asking price for the Arduachdran estate?'

'They say the King of Sausages is asking three quarters of a million for a quick sale.'

'The King of Sausages?'

'Mr Pratt of Pratt's Sausages.'

'Is the income from the estate a big one?'

'The rents of most of the farms and crofts and all the feus on the island, plus the shooting, the salmon fishing, the deer and the running of thousands and thousands of sheep.'

'It is just like an estate in England.'

'Not quite. Crofters have rights: they can't be removed and have very low, fixed rents and the Crofting Commission protect those rights. There are a few independent crofts and a few small farms. The estate has no interests in Carnach.

'Who did he buy it from?'

'He didn't. His father bought it from a MacDonald. It

originally belonged to a chief of the clan of your own name who ruled the island until the sixteenth century. He offended the king and forfeited.'

'Will he have much difficulty in selling?'

'There will be others like the Pratts who want to get away from a business life and the rush of the city. The Castle is very beautiful, set at the far shore end of the sea loch. The only other dwelling near it is The Thorn in the mountains, above and beyond the Castle, in a small fertile valley in the heart of the estate. It is not very much bigger than a croft – just a very small hill farm with a superior dwelling house but has considerable mountain grazing. At the time when Arduachdran passed out of his possession, the King made the grant of The Thorn to the dispossessed chief in order to keep a promise made to his ancestor, that all the land granted for some great service done to the crown in former times, should never pass out of the possession of the family. The Thorn has never been part of the estate since. The present Mr Pratt has been trying to get possession for years, without any success. There is a local saying that when the island is once again in the possession of one family, that family will prosper. I think that is why he is going. It really has irked him. The descendants of the former chiefs retained considerable influence through it and actually continued to rule the district. Its possessors have never altogether lost their former dignity. The MacDonalds drew little more than the material benefits, resented and hated the grant. That is how it came to be known as The Thorn.'

'Surely the MacDonalds would gain full authority in time, through the power of the purse?'

'Yes, of course, but not all the influence and loyalty. MacDonald too, was careful not to damage his economic interests by trying to evict the previous chieftain's tenants and replace them with MacDonalds. He had no great wish to do so anyway, as he married the former chieftain's daughter. The Thorn was granted to her uncle. No woman could be chieftain.

'I rather fear that Dorothy Kennedy will prove another thorn but this time in the side of the people of Closach.'

'More likely she'll get badly scratched herself.'

'Let's go and see the house while it's empty, before your brothers get their hands on it.'

They drove from the gently sloping moorland around Foghar in the north, into the wild mountainous south, where they reached a narrow stretch of the Arduachdran estate protruding, like a tongue, into private crofting country over which neither the Crofting Commission nor the estate had any jurisdiction. Michael stopped at a junction with an estate road which led up through the mountains to the Castle.

'Let's turn up there. I'd like to see the Castle.'

'We would be stopped long before we could reach it, unless we had a viewing order from the London estate agent. Mr Pratt is very much the forbidding Superior – a keep out or get thrown out type of landlord. There are NO TRESPASSERS and TRESPASSERS WILL BE PROSECUTED and NO CAMPING notices everywhere. In fact trespassers can't be prosecuted in Scotland and PRIVATE PROPERTY is the usual sign.

'The sooner he gets back to sausages the better, but surely he would want people to see over it, now he is selling it anyway?' said Michael. 'What about The Thorn then? Let's go and see that.'

'It's not this way. It is right over on the other side of the Castle. The only road to it is past Prabar, before we come to Closach. Prabar is a small port nearest to the Castle, originally it was called the Port of Arduachdran.'

'Let's go there then, after we have seen Rock House. No, we jolly well won't! We'll go and see the Castle. This is the twentieth century. We can then go on to The Thorn beyond it. Let's take the Castle by surprise. Storm it! We can't drive all that way round because of a pratt by name and nature.'

Mary Ella shook her head doubtfully and was very soon proved right.

They passed over a cattle grid and headed up into the mountainous country in the direction of the Castle. They had gone past two turning points and were climbing and turning a difficult bend, when they came to a third, cut into the mountain side. A man with a dog and a gun stepped out of a hut, rather like a large sentinel box, just by it. He leant the shotgun against the side of the hut and advanced to stop them. He was not an islander but an English employee of Mr Pratt's. His manner was hostile and full of the confidence that full authority to forbid gives. He clearly knew his job. 'What's your business?' he asked curtly.

'We want to see the Castle,' said Michael.

'Your order to view.'

'We haven't one.'

The man said nothing but gestured them brusquely off with one hand sweeping forward and pointing in the direction they had come. Then with both palms raised, he impatiently and repeatedly signalled them to back the car. As he was standing blocking the way, he prevented them driving forward and using the turning point just by him. Musty, who was on Mary Ella's lap, emitted a low growl and broke out into fierce barking and made as if to get at him through the windscreen. She had to hold and restrain him.'

'Let's hope the next owner isn't another Pratt,' said Michael.

He steadily backed round the awkward corner and down the considerable distance to the passing point behind them.'

At Closach, all the houses, unlike the others on the island, were aggressively neat and white. There were no felt roofs and not a slate was missing or out of place. The guttering and drainage was so firm and effective that not a drop of water appeared to have overflowed from the recent heavy rain. Every door, window and gate was fresh with paint and each tiny front garden was scrupulously weeded, with cockle shells all in a row. They gave the impression of owners hypersensitive to their neighbours. Identical white muslin courtesy curtains were up in every window up the street, giving Mary Ella and Michael the uneasy feeling of being watched by diseased, sightless, sinister eyes – observing everything and missing nothing. There was not a soul to be seen.

Rock House stood like a dirty, sluttish old woman among a crowd of highly respectable, disapproving matrons. It had an air of total neglect, of abandonment and of not having been inhabited for years. The tiles on the roof, far from glistening and shining from the rainfall like the rest of the houses, had the original slates cemented together, giving the affect of the ruffled feathers of a rather scruffy old sparrow.

Mary Ella got out and knocked at the door of a house right by it, while Michael turned the car in the narrow cul-de-sac, so that they could drive straight off when they had seen over it. There was only room for a very skilful driver to turn but not enough on the cobbled road for two cars to pass one another, without mounting the very narrow pavements on either side of it. Michael felt their every move could be seen and heard. At one point, a hand stretched out of a window could have touched him. All the houses up the narrow street, except the house at the door of which Mary Ella was knocking, were built directly opposite each other, so close that they seemed to stare rudely and offensively at each other. The exception was this house which, instead of a house, confronted a giant rock – jutting up, jagged, vertical and gaunt. On its smooth face, about twenty feet from the ground in very neat, white capital letters was written, GOD IS LOVE.

There was no immediate reply to Mary Ella's knock. Michael had turned the car, got out and was standing by her before it was opened. The face of the man who at last opened it reflected the whole forbidding atmosphere of the place. He expressed no pleasure at the sight of them but quite the contrary and certainly none at that of the message imprinted so clearly on the rock immediately opposite him. He bore so little resemblance to the rest of the islanders Michael had come across, that he gave him the impression that the people of Closach were of a different race. He ignored Michael entirely and abruptly told Mary Ella, in reply to her request for a key that there was none; the door was open.

Rock House consisted of an original house with additions and extensions made at different times, none of them times of prosperity. The roofs of these extensions were of various kinds: rusty corrugated iron, felt, asbestos and an expanse of perished synthetic rubber tiles. It looked as if the rain was coming through all the roofing, except the main, slated roof of the original building where the cement was proving effective, though very unattractive.

Immediately opposite him as he opened the front door Michael saw a door into a cupboard under the stairs the first flight of which went straight up beside it. 'You never know what you will find in these cupboards,' he said to Mary Ella, opening the door. Looking in they saw an old man with a cap on his head, sitting on a lavatory seat. He shut the door quickly, pointed upstairs and followed hastily after her. A minute later, they heard him pull the plug, go out and shut the front door.

'So that's why the door is left unlocked. The place is being used as a public convenience during the vacancy!' he laughed. 'Why on earth don't they use their own?'

'Some of these houses won't have bathrooms or inside WCs – only Elsans. They are whited sepulchres.'

The bedrooms upstairs were dark and sordid. Throughout there was a stale, unhealthy smell and everywhere was damp. The house was furnished or rather had furniture. There were no carpets – only one or two dirty old mats. In the bedrooms were even dirtier old mattresses, stuffed with horsehair or straw from a previous century, lying on brass knobbed iron bedsteads with rusted old springs and bed irons. A large double bedroom had a window at either end. One very small one set deep and high in the wall, faced out to sea. It consisted of one pane of glass in a frame that did not open. The window ledge was very wide, as were those of all the windows because of the thickness of the walls. From where they were standing, only the light from it could be seen. The other window was incongruously very much larger and looked across a very narrow space, directly into the courtesy curtained window of a bedroom belonging to the house of the man with the loury face and abrupt manner they had just met.

'This,' Michael said, 'will be Dorothy Kennedy's bedroom.'

He stood on the mattress of the double bed but the small window was still too high for him to see out.

'That must be where the wreckers placed the fatal lamp. They must have used a small ladder. Stand on this.'

Mary Ella handed him a cane-bottomed chair. 'I'll hold it steady.'

He placed it against the rail of the bedhead, pulled himself up onto the seat by a brass knob and balanced precariously while she held the chair awkwardly but steady.

'You're right,' he said. 'It's just like looking out of a lighthouse. The wall of this room must be a continuation of the cliff face. The sea must be immediately below. I can't look down, only straight out to the horizon.'

The bedrooms were all panelled like ship's cabins and had coved ceilings but the panels had been papered over with wallpaper, now dirty and torn. Electricity had been installed many years before by an amateur and there was no power. Power points half way up the walls in several rooms were connected to the electric light current. Almost all the switches were broken and exposed and some were hanging from the wall. The place had obviously been vandalised at some time as several were missing altogether. Strands of exposed wire sprouted futilely and dangerously out of the ceilings. The whole house required rewiring.

There was no garden front or rear but running along the cliff to one side of the house, was a bleak strip of grass with two poles stuck in it. The washing line was missing and Mary Ella identified the large rectangular concrete slab between them as a septic tank. It was far too close to the house, cracked, with its outlet overflow straight into the sea a hundred feet below them. At the same time, Michael became aware of the pungent smell of pipe tobacco rising through the bare floorboards of the landing at the top of the first flight of the stairs. They went down to investigate but before they reached the hall at the foot of the stairs, the plug of the lavatory in the cupboard under them was again pulled, the door opened and another old man in a neat and well brushed navy blue suit, a navy blue cap on his head, emerged. They watched him disappear through the front door and close it carefully behind him.

To the left of the front door, they saw a door to the first room they would have gone into had they not been diverted by the unexpected presence under the stairs. The room gave them a feeling of welcome, despite the abandoned furniture and faded wallpaper. It was a large sitting room with a low ceiling and all the windows looked out to sea. Everything had so far repelled them, but this seemed instantly to welcome. It gave them a feeling of inviolable sanctuary from the desolation and discomfort they had found everywhere else in that house. It had a comforting, comfortable and peaceful atmosphere.

Someone has been infinitely happy here, thought Michael.

Someone has filled this room with love, thought Mary Ella.

They looked into it, then at each other and said nothing.

The narrow hall led into an even narrower passageway, past a door and into a large room, which must at some time have been the dining room, then past another staircase straight to the open door of the kitchen. The staircase was so narrow and went up so steeply, almost like a ladder, that they wondered how any furniture could reach what must have been servants' quarters. They themselves had not the stomach to climb but went on into a kitchen of great size, right across which, brilliantly lit by a sudden beam of sun, they saw a bathroom with its door wide open. None of the taps in the very small, short bath worked, nor did they in the minute washbasin. The pull plug of the lavatory, unlike that in the hall, was out of order. All water appeared to be cut off in that quarter of the house, except that which came through the roof. The bath was full of rainwater, with an old newspaper floating and dissolving in it. In contrast to the rest of the house, the kitchen and bathroom were bright with light coming through a great hole in the roof. Very little light came from a very small window – even smaller than that in the main bedroom they had just seen. It was as high above the washbasin and quite out of reach.

Michael caught Mary Ella's eye. 'This whole place is a very bad joke. Let's go.'

They said nothing until they were well on their way from Closach back to Prabar.

'What on earth will it cost to get that awful place into

any sort of order?'

'Thousands and thousands, even if she can get someone local to do the rewiring, the plumbing and install a proper sewage system. Contractors, if they would even look at the job, would be ruinous. It would be much cheaper to pull the place down and build a new house.'

'She will never be persuaded to do that. Your brothers couldn't possibly rewire, plumb and cope with the sewage system, could they? Have they got the necessary skills?'

'They had once. They were quite good when they lived with my mother, before my father had that accident and retired and for a year or so after that. But they have done little or nothing since he came back but drink.'

'Which will not have improved their work. If only she had stayed put in any one of the half dozen excellent homes she has left this past, goodness knows how many, years! The law of averages was bound to turn against her if she kept on moving. I greatly fear that she is about to meet her Waterloo.'

'A few thousand pounds more whisky won't do Alec, Ian and Murdo much good either.'

'Is there somewhere in Prabar where we can get some tea?'

'There's a very old hotel just before we reach it, which caters mostly for fishing holidays. It is full in the season and quite empty the rest of the year. It is rented from the estate and very expensive, as is everything on the estate – especially the fishing.'

While they were having tea in the hotel, Michael asked the waitress about The Thorn. She was a student on vacation and had never heard of it but the manager soon after came into the lounge and over to them.

'I understand you are asking about The Thorn? The Elder may be away at the moment. He goes off for a week or two every now and then.'

'The Elder?' asked Michael.

'The chap who lives there. There are, of course, other elders but he is called The Elder, with a capital T and a capital E like the place he lives in. I've only been Manager here for a few years and don't know him by any other name. He is greatly respected by everyone, even by Mr Pratt himself. He wouldn't mind you visiting The Thorn and looking round at all, if you want to but if you want to see him, I suggest you make certain he is not away. He never goes for long – at most a week or two. He belongs to the place and to the people, though he hasn't been here all that length of time but his family has. Nobody knows where he goes or what he does when he is away but it will be something good, something worthwhile.'

'Let's go there, as we have come this far?' said Michael, looking enquiringly at Mary Ella.

'Where are you from?' asked the manager.

'Foghar.'

'Foghar! Mr McAvoy will know The Elder. He comes to the Prabar and Closach communions without fail. There is a track which leads up to The Thorn between here and Closach. You would have just passed it,' he said. 'Never been up it myself.' He paused as if this surprised him and he must go sometime.

They took the turning, which was not far out of Prabar and almost within sight of the hotel. It led off the sea road and up into the mountains, following a stream which ran down from them. They found themselves entering more and more beautiful country until, after nearly two miles climbing steadily higher, they suddenly broke into a small plain, surrounded by mountains. It was divided by the stream, joined by another, swifter rush of water from another burn beyond it. In the centre of the plain stood The Thorn, a small, simply designed seventeenth century house with a ruined tower.

'I wonder who looks after these animals while he is away?' asked Michael.

'The sheep and the cattle just graze at this time of the year and water themselves at the burn. I expect some friend or neighbour keeps an eye on the place and feeds those hens and collects the eggs. They are free-range and wouldn't starve anyway at this time of the year.' Mary Ella pointed to about a dozen of them running free about the house.

'Quite a way to come. He must have good neighbours.'

'Sounds a good one himself, by report.'

'The name elder is a misnomer then. I always think of elders as serious, solemn, unsmiling men in fustian, dark grey or forbidding black – extremely conscious of a very angry God who is always on their side and very anxious to punish the wicked, especially me. Gave up the stool of repentance with extreme reluctance and not without a fight.'

'So do I,' laughed Mary Ella.

'What exactly is an elder?'

'There are two kinds – ruling and teaching. The word comes from the Greek, meaning an old man and therefore deserving reverence for the wisdom he has accumulated. Catholics use the same word. Priest is a shortened form of Presbyter. The Minister is himself an elder and an elder in Scotland is as important an office in the Presbyterian Church as a priest in the Roman Catholic Church.'

Laughing together brought them close, so close that Michael turned from the wheel and looked down at her. Their eyes met and he wavered and drove dangerously near the wrong side of the road – the seaward side with a drop to the shore of several hundred feet. With a swerve, he recovered the right side of the road. He had regained the refuge of his psychological shell but with an enormous wave of regret and sense of loss and failure, as if he had disappointed himself by shrinking back and giving up some exhilarating challenge, such as a high dive or an assault course, at the last moment.

Mary Ella, as her eyes left his, placed a hand caressingly on Musty who was lying on her lap. He got up, placed his forepaws uncomfortably on her collar bone and proceeded to cover her face and neck steadily with gentle licks with his small red tongue. She too was completely engaged in her own feelings and did not see that Michael was loving her – everything about her, every expression, every tone of her voice, her every movement. He had panicked again and feared his fate too much.

As they entered Foghar, the thought of Elizabeth Broughton, who had never been so far from his thoughts or for so long, momentarily reoccupied his mind, until Mary Ella quickly banished her. He had never made any comparison between the two and didn't then. He thought of each as if they lived in different worlds, and in a totally different way. He had always thought of them separately. He had only seen them together at Broughton, when his mind was full of Elizabeth.

There was a car outside the gate when they reached the old manse and sitting in it, waiting for them to return, was Elizabeth Broughton.

Chapter Twelve

Elizabeth's Thread

Elizabeth's quite unexpected presence on the island struck Michael as it had the first time he had seen her on opening the door of his flat in London. She dazzled him – took his breath away she was so incomparably beautiful. However often he saw her or thought of her, he was uplifted. An exciting mixture of emotions coursed through him – surprise, pleasure and then, oddly, dismay. What could she be doing there? He at once dismissed any thought that she had come to see him. Though aware that there was something about him that attracted and interested her which he did not understand, he knew that she was not interested in him as a partner for life. There never had been and never would be anything between them but that close, easy going but very real friendship and he knew, at that moment without a shadow of a doubt, that she was not that one woman Malcolm had said would enter his life. Mary Ella, sitting there in the car beside him, was. Elizabeth's sudden appearance did not alter in the least his feelings for Mary Ella.

Elizabeth was now as essential a part of his life, as Malcolm had been. In fact, when he was with her, she always brought his past life with Malcolm vividly alive, as if he were there and had never gone out of it. Michael knew that without her coming into his life, he might never have awakened to and been so certain of his love for Mary Ella.

Elizabeth and Malcolm lived continuously in a world he only shared when with them. Away from them, he resumed his own, less idealistic and more prosaic daily existence but wonderfully refreshed and in every way the better. Living with Elizabeth, he would find himself becoming more and more dependent upon her as he had been on Malcolm, not standing on his own feet. He did not want that. She did not want that. Malcolm had not wanted that either. They both wanted him to find for himself, and in his own time, that wonderful world in which they lived and breathed and had their being. Only then, would he breathe freely the depths, heights, freshness and freedom of existence. Why then was she there waiting outside his house on this remote Hebridean island?

'You should have gone in, not waited outside,' he said quietly. 'We are never out usually. I do hope you haven't been waiting long.'

'But the door isn't open!' laughed Elizabeth. 'I haven't been here long at all. My car is away getting petrol.'

'Oh, I'm so sorry. I completely forgot!' Mary Ella apologised to Elizabeth, producing a key. 'I had a Yale lock put on the front door after the windows were broken. We use the back door. We don't usually lock doors on the island.'

She turned to Michael. 'I forgot to tell you.'

Michael saw at once how her brothers' barbarous behaviour embarrassed her. He was glad he hadn't told her of Murdo's attempt to get in through the office window and its frustration by Musty.

'We have been house-hunting for an old friend of yours since we last saw you,' he said to Elizabeth. 'Dorothy Kennedy! We took the day off to go and see her latest volte-face. She has really landed herself in a mess this time. It's at Closach. We tried to see Arduachdran Castle on the way but were ordered at gunpoint off the estate by one of Mr Pratt's keepers.'

Mary Ella let them into the house with her key.

'That won't happen again. To you or anyone else,' said Elizabeth firmly. 'The red carpet for you next time, and soon. We can only have just missed each other. I have just come from there.'

'You know the Pratt!'

'I didn't. I came with an order to view from the agents in London and was asked to stay. Father has bought the place for me just as it stands. Tomorrow Mr Pratt and all his staff move out, taking only their personal possessions with them. Nothing will be switched off and I shall just carry on living there instead of him. The home fires will be kept burning. All the original furniture way back is still there. Mr Pratt is leaving Arduachdran as he inherited it from his father or grandfather. Of course they have added luxuries and extensively modernised it. Talking of furniture, I like this.' She looked around appreciatively. 'Can I see the rest?'

'It's great, isn't it?' said Michael enthusiastically. 'Mary Ella has done a superb job. Can you stay to dinner? A very bachelor effort!'

'No thanks. I've rather overwhelmed Mr Pratt with the swiftness and suddenness of our decisions. I have only tonight to get out of him as much information about the property as I can. I'm expected back to dinner very soon.'

'Why bundle him out so quickly?'

'Very discourteous of me. He just doesn't go with the place, which is marvellous.'

'Too much associated with sausages!'

'I don't mind his sausages at all, quite the contrary. We had some at lunch.'

'How did you come?'

'I arrived by air and was met by that car which is just returning from getting petrol and will take me back there. It was Mr Pratt's and goes with the place! Not the chauffeur. He goes with him. I decided at once before even seeing it.

The lawyers have settled it all between them. I have immediate possession.'

She smiled affectionately at Mary Ella.

'Lead on. By the way you two, I have orders from father to tell you that you are both to stay with him at Broughton. Make it your home whenever either or both of you go south. We won't have far to go now when we need to see each other over those tax schedules, will we,' she laughed, happily.

Michael stayed in the office while they went off together. He was puzzled how she could separate herself from Broughton. It reminded him of Malcolm and his suddenly detaching himself from his past, though Elizabeth certainly wouldn't be doing that.

The time was growing very near when he must go to London and see Margaret Smith. He had been putting it off. He must try to rearrange his work, so that visits there should become more and more infrequent, by transferring as much as possible to the island. Elizabeth's move would greatly facilitate this. The tax assessment of Fairfield Broughton's worldwide interests formed a large part of his work. Nevertheless, a great deal would always remain to be done in London and visits would always be necessary. However, he would make them slightly longer but less frequent. He made an immediate decision to go that Friday, leaving both Mary Ella and Elizabeth on the island. He would accept the invitation to Broughton that weekend.

'If you are getting in touch with your father, would you tell him I shall be with him on Friday,' he announced to Elizabeth when she and Mary Ella had returned from their tour of inspection.

The great beautiful car, with Mr Pratt's chauffeur at the wheel, had returned and was waiting for her outside.

'He will be delighted. Me too. I don't like leaving him on his own – this weekend particularly. He will be coming up here often but can't before we have organised a landing strip at Arduachdran. He has always been keen on forestry and will want to reforest here not, needless to say, blanketing the whole estate with ranks of spruce. I suppose you couldn't manage a visit to the Castle before you go on Friday, so that you could tell him something about it?

'Not before Friday. I must get an awful lot done to get away then.'

'Well, Mr Pratt's divorce and departure from the estate should be absolute by the time you get back. Perhaps it is better for you to see it for the first time after it has been completely depratted. You must come as soon as you can, and bring Mary Ella.'

*

Michael flew to London on the Friday. He was at Broughton the same evening, Musty back at his post of watchdog, even more puzzled how either of them could bear to separate themselves from Broughton, even for one weekend.

Events in the short time since they had met, had drawn the two men into a close and intimate friendship, deepened by their being alone there without Elizabeth for the first time. Her arrangements for their comfort were perfect and she was present in their thoughts and the almost continuous subject of their conversation. They found they had more and more in common, not least that they both shared the same attitude towards her when with her and when not in her presence. Both were men who liked to stand on their own feet.

'You must miss her terribly. Have you never thought of marrying again?'

'Marry again! I could never do that.'

The question seemed to strike him like a blow and Michael instantly regretted having asked it. He knew nothing of Monica Broughton.

'Monica was quite helpless for the last four years of her short life. Everything had to be done for her, who till then had never left anything undone that she could do for others. She was more conscious of others and more thoughtful of them than anyone I have ever met but in those last four years she became utterly selfless. She radiated goodness and love and she gave herself as never before. People always think people who die to themselves are boring. Monica was exhilarating, intensely exciting. You went from her presence refreshed and recharged, though shattered at the thought of leaving her. It inspired Elizabeth with the belief that there is divine purpose behind everything and that it is wholly good, however evil, cruel and base life may seem, and that there is a thread that leads unerringly through every life to eternal love. Most of us live from day to day. I do myself. We plan for the future but for Elizabeth, there is a thread running through every life. Thanks to her mother, she has found and followed hers easily. Not at all easy to find, let alone to follow, for the likes of you and me. The thread is startlingly clear to the pure in heart. Pharisees, as Christ said, are quite blind to it. Elizabeth is, like her mother, no Pharisee. She thinks meeting the right partner, as I did, is the most wonderful thing that can happen to her in time. You greatly interested her when you spoke of your uncle Malcolm, saying there only being one partner that is right for each of us in life.'

'But he stressed that, more often than not, sex, circumstances and impatience prevent their ever coming together in this life. The thread seems to me a solitary process. Marriage doesn't seem appropriate.'

'Elizabeth says man and woman are the instruments with which God creates life and they are divided in time, not eternity. The right woman and the right man, uniting in time remove all that stands between them in the course of true marriage. Following the thread together makes them one and whole. You are part of Elizabeth's thread, by the way. My mentioning you to her was a case in point. Elizabeth sensed at once that you were part of her thread. Your entering both our lives had nothing to do with the subtleties of my fiscal problems. Elizabeth wanted to meet you as much as I did and to bring your non-existent wife to Broughton. It wasn't chance that introduced you into our lives. It was her thread.'

'I can't see how I come into it.'

'I can only guess. Elizabeth doesn't guess. She knows.'

'By intuition?'

'My guess is that it has something to do with the war and your remembering Arakan that night, but it is more than that.'

He then confided to Michael the experience he had had when wounded in Burma.

'Your saving my life that night brought that startlingly to mind. Not that it is ever out of it for long. I've spared no effort to discover who and where that young man is and Elizabeth is every bit as eager as I to find him. She loves him ever since I told her about him as a little girl. It is her object in life as much as mine to find him. When she was little, she always said that she was going to marry him. She believes that marriage is the spiritual high road. He has been her hero and much more. In creating and trying to appreciate all the qualities she has in her own mind endowed him with, she has acquired them herself. She has measured his goodness in her mind and in her heart and has grown beautiful herself by doing so. It is quite extraordinary what that young man has done – that his action, deliberately undertaken before she was born, should have had such effect on her; that that young boy, tall and strong as he was, should not only give me my life but transform the quality of hers and give me so many other gifts in her.'

'What was he like?'

'Physically, he was tall and powerfully built but of lithe and muscular, rather than heavy, build. He was, I should say, a little taller than you and I are. My first sight of you brought him strangely to mind but particularly on the night of the robbery. It was as if I woke up and saw him. Possibly because of the psychological similarity of the two situations. He was very young – seemed no more than eighteen. His cheeks weren't pink and white but yellow because of the ephedrine we all had to take as a preventative against malaria. He was sun-tanned but he had the skin, despite all that, of a very young boy. He had certainly never put a razor to his face. He must have been glaringly under age when joining up yet his facial expression was unusually mature, full of character, strength and determination. He might have been drafted to India for training. It is highly unlikely that he was brought up and educated there and joined up when war broke out. He would almost certainly in that case have been an officer. I have never seen a face since, more open and full of integrity. He would scorn to take any credit for doing what he would consider an obvious duty. Usually in such a character, there is a deficiency of humour. Not so with that chap. With a seriously wounded man on his hands and a hornets' nest roused and angry within yards of him and despite my diminished faculties, I became aware that part of the extraordinary strength that inspired him was his being highly amused at the thought of picking up his commanding officer like a baby. Can you wonder that we won't give up? Ever. We shall find him.'

'But he may have been killed in Burma or died since.'

'I have thought that many times, especially when a new lead has led to blank disappointment but never Elizabeth. She knows he is alive. She won't even allow it to be intuition. She is certain.'

'She has joined you in the hunt?'

'Elizabeth has not only sought him, as I have, by physical means. She has sought him morally and spiritually, scaled the heights on which she thinks he is to be found. She has even studied and started careers he is likely to have followed, been outstanding in, and so easier to find and identify. She is convinced that the best way to find him is to become as like him as possible and then they will meet on the same heights and will recognise each other at once.'

'Why are there so few Monicas, Elizabeths and Malcolms in this world? So many of us?'

'How can we know there are so few? Certainly they seem thin on the ground nowadays but there must be many, quiet, peaceful, gentle, humble, loving men, women, and children too, in all walks of life, who suffer and are selfless who do nothing to be seen of men, everything to be seen of God. They save the world. Christ *is* the Saviour of the world, not *was*. But sadly, the vast majority of us are too preoccupied with the struggle to survive, sensual satisfaction, and indulging in developing personalities, to die to self. Or we hand over all responsibility to some guru, institution or sect. All the great religions sooner or later mislead, discourage or prevent their followers from thinking for themselves or following their Founder's teaching: become the blind leading the blind. We should take up our torches individually and follow the thread.'

'What good can one individual do following the thread?'

'Individuals whose selfless, self-sacrificing love lights and warms wherever it is, or goes, are the thread. Unlike fire, their light and warmth never goes out or dies but is accumulative and ever will glow brightly. Just meeting people like Malcolm, Monica and Elizabeth, we find something that we cannot possibly do without. Following the thread is knowing with increasing sensitivity and assurance what is the right action to take and what is the wrong. It is the spirit in which decisions are made. You and I are part of Elizabeth's thread. That means we shall, each of us, find something that we have either wanted or lacked which, when we find it, we will discover to be something we could not possibly have done without.'

Before the service the next morning, Michael sat isolated and conspicuous, alone in the old family pew, while Fairfield Broughton performed his duties as Church Warden and sidesman, handing out prayer and hymn books, welcoming the members of the congregation as they arrived and, later in the service, taking the collection and presenting the offertory. Michael missed Elizabeth's presence there. He thought of the conversation the previous evening and how odd life was becoming. What was that something that he would find that he could not possible have done without? Nothing had been quite the same since he had met Fairfield Broughton and Elizabeth. He had wanted nothing for a very long time. He had not entertained such thoughts since Malcolm had left him. He did not doubt now that there would be something. That encounter with Mr McAvoy had been no less disturbing. An awakening had been taking place since he had met them, an increasing awareness of other worlds, other people, other dimensions still beyond and yet more and more involving himself. Elizabeth had led him out of being cabined, cribbed and confined into freedom, not out of one into another form of confinement, not out of one set of opinions into another but out of clutching opinion altogether, into free, unrestricted thought where there was no judging, condemning or blaming but only the delight of discovery.

'When do you think you will go to Arduachdran Castle?' he asked on their way back to London. 'The way was barred by another man with a shotgun when Mary Ella and I tried to see it.'

'Not for a while. I want Elizabeth to absorb everything there first and make it hers. I expect we shall go back together from Broughton when next she comes south. We are on another scent, following a trail we have recently picked up which means a long visit to the archives of the Ministry of Defence. I know I should long since have handed all this research over to professionals and saved a great deal of time but they wouldn't have cared enough and been so anxious not to miss or overlook the least thing. Will you be here next weekend or are you off back to Scotland? How are things going with the leg?'

'I'm not sure. I shan't know how long I shall have to be south till I get back to the office but I shall certainly be with you next, and almost certainly the following weekend, too.'

He did spend the next two weekends at Broughton and might have spent a third but was so anxious to get back to Mary Ella that he worked very hard and late all that week. He had telephoned her early to say that he would not be returning till the Thursday of the following week but then made a sudden decision at the end of the week not to go to Broughton but return at once. It was too late to get in touch with Mary Ella. She would have left the old manse. He would announce his presence by calling and taking her to church on the Sunday morning.

He did not have his plane. He had managed to fly it back after his injury but had had great difficulty and pain getting in and out of it and so had decided to leave it on the island and travel by ferry and train. He could only take Musty by private plane. The physiotherapist, who had massaged the leg daily in London, advised him to walk as much as possible but had warned him that it would be unlikely that he would ever walk again without a stick.

He travelled overnight to Scotland and caught the last ferry to the Island on Saturday evening. The long sea crossing was very rough and he did not eat on the ship but had a late supper at the Harbour Hotel in Carnach. It was a two hour drive to Foghar by taxi. The road was extremely circuitous – skirting lochs, deep sea inlets, and mountains and, when crossing moorland, very bumpy and uneven, owing to subsidence in the deep layers of peat under the surface. He arrived at the old manse just after midnight, having stopped the taxi a mile short of Foghar to give Musty a walk and to exercise his leg. A huge bank of cloud hid a bright moon as he reached the gate of the house. It was so dark that he almost fell over the two suitcases he had asked the driver to leave by it. A gale was blowing hard against the front door which flew open as he turned the key in the yale lock and thrust Musty and the larger bag in first. As he turned to fetch the small case containing only his night clothes, a cloud passed and a flood of brilliant moonlight lit the front of the house and the narrow front garden like a scene on a stage. He was in great pain and very tired but paused to look up at the moon with pleasure and, turning back, he looked directly at the window where he and Mary Ella would be sitting opposite each other on Monday morning. Dangling out of the window and held a helpless captive was Murdo Murray.

He could see at once what had happened: the sash cords had broken, the heavy window had fallen and trapped him, trying to get in again and wreck Mary Ella's beautiful furniture. Only the lower half of his body was visible in the moonlight and his feet were off the ground so that he could use neither his legs to push nor his arms to pull himself up. He hung motionless and silent and had either given up shouting for help or had not dared to attract attention to what he was up to, or had found it useless as his voice would have been drowned by the gale. How long he had been there, Michael could not conceive and cared less. At that moment, a violent gust caught the front door and swung it open so violently that it struck the wall, rebounded and slammed shut. He searched his pockets in vain for the yale key which he had forgotten he had left in the lock. Frustrated and unable to get in or get rid of Murdo Murray, something in him snapped. A wave of uncontrollable anger swept over him at the thought of his trying again to hurt Mary Ella. He completely lost his temper for the first time in his life. His customary self-possession completely deserted him. He found himself raising Fairfield Broughton's malacca walking stick and striking the seat of Murdo Murray's jeans again and again.

He only stopped when the moon once more disappeared behind the clouds and they were in absolute darkness. Musty's muffled barking reminded him that he was inside the house and that the only reason why he could hear him above the roar of the gale was because he was so near and in his usual place on the table. He would be very close to Murdo Murray's head. The thought that he might bite the trapped man shocked Michael into his normal state of self-control. He was horrified at what he had been doing. He quickly found the key, turned the lock, switched on the hall light and burst into the office without stopping to switch on the light.

Musty was on the table, now neither barking nor biting but to Michael's surprise, he was ecstatically wagging his tail and licking Murdo Murray's face. The latter, his hair wildly all over it, was trying to keep him off with his hands. Michael climbed painfully onto the table, put a foot in the small of Murdo Murray's back, pulled up the heavy frame of the window, put his shoulder under it, stuck the malacca cane in the sash to hold it up, grasped Murdo Murray under the armpits pulled him in and slid him across the table. He then recovered his stick and lowered the window. A sharp stab of pain from his thigh shot through him as he sprang from the table to shut the door to prevent his escape.

As he switched on the light, the small figure came at him like a shot and landed a fist in his eye.

She would not listen to him although he held her and would not let her go.

'Darling!'

'I'm not your darling. Let me out of this place! Let go of me at once!'

'I love you!'

'Let me go this minute! Do you want another black eye?'

He hugged her to him.

'Only if you will listen. I thought you were Murdo. I thought it was your brother breaking in again. He tried to once before. I didn't tell you. I didn't want you to leave me. How was I to know it was you?'

She was stuttering and struggling with rage and fell back into the island English which she had modified in Glasgow.

'There's not the man with the least intelligence in the world that would know it but you. Let me out of here this minute or it is shouting above the roar of the gale I'll be. Let me out of here before I call every man in the village to come and throw you into the sea and be the drowning of you.' She struggled to get away from him.

'If you promise you'll be here on Monday, I'll unlock the door for you and let you go.'

'There's not a promise you'll get from me if you keep me here till dawn.'

'We'll see about that,' said Michael, beginning to get annoyed again himself. 'Here you will stay until you see reason. I'll not let you out of this room till you have given me your promise.'

He quickly pushed her away, turned, slipped through the door, shut her in again. 'I'll never let you out till you give me that promise. I love you Mary Ella,' he shouted through it.

Not another shout came from her, not a single bang on

the door. Michael heard nothing but the roar of the gale. At last he called out miserably.

'I love you, Mary Ella. I've been an outsize fool, my darling. I loved you from the moment our eyes met and did not know it. I know you may never love me but please stay here and work here and give me the chance to be less of a fool.'

The silence became more and more unbearable. He had never felt so alone. Strange thoughts passed through his defeated mind. He felt he had fallen into a strangely real world of struggle and misery, in which he had been vanquished and over which he had no control. He had lost everything that, with two eyes in his head, he should have recognised that he most wanted and had always wanted. He had been as blind as ignorance itself. He had found and lost what he could not do without. Bitterly at that moment, he felt that he had lost her without hope of recovery. Musty had been licking her face and loving her while he had been beating and hating her. He could not bear the thought of working in that office without her. She will never work here again, he thought, desperately. She will return to her uncle in Glasgow.

Not a sound came through the door. No reply, just the din of the gale rising and sweeping over and about the house. He must let her out at once. The great, heavy sash window frame was quite beyond her strength and she was hurt. He cursed himself for being so stupid as to lock her in and leave her alone. He opened the door. He had forgotten the two smaller side windows which had never been opened. Both had thought them stuck fast long since with paint. The one on her side of the table was staring wide open. The gale blew violently into his face. She had gone out into the darkness and he was alone.

Chapter Thirteen

The Eagle's Nest

Elizabeth Broughton was on her first adventure. She had always waited for the events of life to roll towards her like the waves of the Atlantic towards the shores of the island, upon which she was now living. They would break over her and she would feel the spray on her cheeks and the wind in her hair. She would inhale the force of the surf and transform the elements into her very being – into vitality and spiritual vigour. Nothing yet had ever disturbed her, everything had instead strengthened her serenity, but now she knew that, slowly and quietly and inexorably, it was she who was making the next move, it was she who was taking the initiative in the greatest event of her life. It was she who had come to the island.

It had not come like a great wave towards her.

She walked the estate without hurry and began to absorb everything about it. She was not even like an artist painting a picture, before the delicate stuff of his imagination is dispersed, like a mist in the wind. She remained calmly and serenely receptive. She was actively following her thread – that new trail which Fairfield had spoken of to Michael their first evening alone together. She had always met life with a thrilling undercurrent of excitement in her heart, which had not ceased to flow through her since she had emerged from childhood. She met it by relaxing – not by tension – as if it were an ecstasy. Her life had been wholly one of real prayer, which filled her with that vast energy and peace that flowed, unhindered, into and through her from the inexhaustible source of love. Life was not always smooth sailing. There were dark days for her, when the source of the love and gratitude that flowed from her dried up and she felt abandoned, reminded that nothing was her own except this suffering. She had been warned by her mother to expect such periods and to welcome them, as they always passed, and if she waited patiently, with humble resignation and unswerving faith, she would, however long they lasted, be infinitely the better for them. St Theresa had suffered one such spell that lasted fifteen years.

The castle was hauntingly old in a setting perfectly suited to the moods it evoked. Four corner towers firmly grasped the rock on which it was built and of which it had become part. Long years, with all the varied and strange means at their disposal, had subtly modified the defiant, once gauntly menacing building by every kind of storm and weather into gentle, rugged dignity. Its windows seemed to have grown wise and full of steadfast tranquillity. It too, waited patiently.

There were men those first few days after her arrival, who hung about the stables – local men, Elizabeth learnt subsequently, waiting for casual work. When none came their way, they disappeared and she was left alone. The car she had bought, together with everything else in the Castle, stood unused outside the great front door where she had left it on her return, the evening she had waited for Michael in front of the old manse. The previous owner had packed all his personal belongings into another large car and other estate vehicles and taken himself, and all that belonged to him, back into the world he had brought with him. Vanishing, he had left scarcely a trace of it and this the wind and the rain were steadily blowing and washing away.

Elizabeth listened: she listened to the wind and the rain,

inside and outside the house. After a week of quiet walking and listening she was spiritually acclimatised. Then she started a new day, by walking slowly along the flagged corridor leading from the front to the back of the house. She passed the open door into the great kitchen and paused to adjust the long rain coat she was wearing and to put on the sou'wester she was carrying, before going out through another door at the end of the passage into a stone paved courtyard surrounded by high stone walls. With the green wellingtons she was wearing, she was completely protected from the rain, except the tresses of chestnut hair which escaped and unfolded beneath the sou'wester. She went across the courtyard, through another door in the wall and entered a high walled garden.

It was a vegetable garden with a large greenhouse in the middle of it. Well kept gravel paths ran parallel with the walls, intersecting the flower beds; the centre one running straight through the greenhouse and out the other side, the whole making a neat geometrical pattern. Elizabeth made her way past the greenhouse to yet another door in the farthest wall at the end of the garden.

She passed through it, on to a track which wound round the mountainside in country, so wild and rocky that the thought of the tremendous labour it must have cost to create that garden struck her, and at once put her in mind of the need to maintain it. Her most pressing task must be to find a gardener. Across a stone bridge, she met another track that divided and followed the rapid river upstream and down. She followed this track upstream up into the mountain. Downstream she guessed it would lead to Prabar, the Port of Arduachdran and to Closach. Small, stunted trees flanked either side of the river, which had grown in the shelter of the channel the torrent had scooped out over thousands of years, as it had torn its way to the sea. About a mile along the river side, she came to another track leading invitingly away from the river up a narrow valley into the mountains. She accepted its invitation and it led her, higher and higher, to a level from which she could look back and down upon the river and track she had left, and beyond.

Half a mile further on and higher still, her attention was caught by a golden eagle in flight high in the sky, circling a distant valley between two peaks. Looking back again she saw, in the far distance below, the gleam of the river running through moorland scarred by peat banks and stretches of black bog where peat had been cut almost to water level. She looked beyond the wide, green grass-covered semicircle of crofts, divided into narrow strips by ugly, barbed wire fencing, running up to the houses surrounding Prabar. The old port, from that height and distance, looked very neat, with the masts of small fishing vessels and boats sticking up above the low roofs of the houses immediately fronting the harbour. Other houses were dotted along the coast, stretching away either side of it. She stood for a minute, watching the never ending, ever changing play between sea and shore and then finally the vast ocean swept her off into infinity.

A few minutes later, the track led round a bend in the hillside and on, past a solitary croft house with a wide and irregularly shaped croft – not a long strip like the crofts about Prabar. It was part of the estate and held on a tenancy leasehold, land won in the past from the rock strewn slopes, and enclosed by stone walls, built by the stones which had had to be cleared by generation after generation of hard toil in the struggle to exist. The track passed the door which opened straight on to it. As she reached it, Elizabeth for the first time met one of her tenants. He was standing in the doorway.

The struggle between clouds and sun had resulted in a complete victory for the former. The wind had dropped and a dull, uniform grey overcast the whole countryside. The rain was now falling in a heavy downpour. It was falling with steady, inexorable persistence.

'Can I come in and shelter for a minute?' she asked.

Elizabeth was tall but she scarcely reached his shoulder. Her beauty was of that kind in which moral, spiritual and physical perfection meet in one person, making command and persuasion superfluous but, more often than not, evoked eager compliance with her slightest wish in the most unpliant stranger. She was all the more irresistible in that she was herself quite unaware of the effect her presence had upon others and quite incapable of using the impression she made consciously in her own interest. It was this influence that had happily banished Pratt of Pratt's sausages from the island without protest.

Donald MacDonald was descended from one of his clan that MacDonald of Arduachdran had brought to the district. He had lived alone in the house since his mother had died a few years before. He was nearing sixty and, despite occasional bouts of heavy drinking, was at the height of his strength. The hands which held open his front door and then opened that into an inner room were enormous. Elizabeth was almost as impressed by his courtesy, as he was by her beauty. He did not take off his cap. He seldom removed it from the moment he put it on in the morning till late at night but wore it continuously inside and out. He had a settled expression on his face of habitual kindness and good humour, entirely free of Calvinistic gloom or moral disapproval. He was clean-shaven with wide open, clear blue eyes. His welcome was without words and was expressed by the skilful way he dressed the peats in the grate, the flames springing up and a cheerful warmth filling the small room into which he ushered her. He took a black kettle, hanging from a hook above the fire, and made a pot of tea. They quietly waited looking into the fire while it gathered strength.

The chair he invited her to sit in was a very old armchair – one of two of a very dilapidated three-piece suite of which the couch was missing. In fact, he slept on it in the next room more often than he did in his bed, up the very narrow and steep staircase. She sank so deeply into it that she was a little concerned about extricating herself later and handling her cup and saucer meanwhile. He asked no questions and she said nothing while he was making the tea. It was not until he had lost a great part of himself in the other chair and they both had a cup that she volunteered an account of herself.

'I have just come to live at the Castle. Mr Pratt has gone and all his staff with him. I don't want a staff, only some help in the house and a gardener. Did Mr Pratt employ anyone from Prabar?'

'If anyone wanted to earn a day's wage, they were almost certain to get it if they went up there any morning but never regular or permanent employment. He had some men, bachelors, like himself, who organised and ran everything for him. Some worked inside and some out. He left them in charge whenever he went to the mainland or abroad. They employed people from Prabar as and when they needed them, from season to season, and from day to day. He kept up some state there.'

'Did he have house parties?'

'Shooting and fishing and deer stalking. Mostly men. Very rarely did a guest bring his wife.'

'My life here will be very quiet. My father will come and stay from time to time. There is only one thing I am anxious about and that is the garden. I don't want it to get overgrown or to run to seed. It is in splendid order now and in full production but far beyond my needs. I would like to find someone to care for it and take it over, as if it is his which, in effect, it will be. You are not far from it, much nearer than anyone at Prabar. Would you consider taking it on? Would you have the time to spare from your croft?'

No one was yet aware that Mr Pratt had gone and few, if any, had seen Elizabeth and knew that she was the new owner of the estate. Donald, without the smallest change of expression, greeted this proposal as if the sun had broken through and the clouds and the downpour outside had vanished. The Castle had always been oppressive, exclusive, hostile and far too near. He had never entertained for a moment a thought of working there and had avoided all contact with the estate, beyond paying his rent to the factor. For the first time in his life, he felt as if paradise was just by and he was being invited to enter it. He decided at once to accept and was filled with pleasure at the thought that he would be working for her. Nevertheless, he did not accept at once.

'May I come and see it?'

'Of course. It's big but I hope not too big. There is an excellent greenhouse. Too much work for one, perhaps. It's better working on your own, though. Do you have much to do here?'

'Cutting the peat and shearing are busy times and I help The Elder up at The Thorn when he needs me, but that is not often. More often he helps me. We cut our peat together and that halves the time for both of us.'

'Who is the Elder and what is the Thorn?

'*The* Thorn is the last possession of the old chiefs, before the MacDonalds. *The* Elder is their descendant and lives there. He is always referred to as The Elder. The elders in Prabar look to him before even the Minister. The people and elders of Closach do not. The elders of Closach look to Ebenezer MacGregor who lives by Rock House in Closach, a very different make of a man. There is only one kirk and one minister for the two townships. It will be interesting to see which of the two the new Minister will look to for guidance in the district.'

'In which township is the church?'

'The manse and the Church were built exactly halfway between them on the road that follows the seashore.'

'What is the new Minister like?'

'I haven't met him. It is not three weeks since he came to settle in the manse with his wife and young children.'

'Do you not see him on Sundays?'

'It is three months to the next communion when I shall see him.'

'You don't attend regularly?'

'I used to attend regularly but not since my mother died. Alone, I have found that I am more aware of myself and of others than of God in church. I am nearer Him by myself here.'

'How often do you have communions?'

'Twice a year. The last was held by the old Minister. You are taken off the roll if you do not attend Communion. I always attend communions in memory of her. I have wondered about Ministers too, since my mother died. They sometimes stand in the way. The Kirk does too. A man is better on his own and in silence. The old Minister came to see why I had stopped attending every Sabbath and I told him it meant nothing without her. She was my only reason for going. She brought love into the Church. It isn't there without her.'

'What did The Elder say?'

'Don't come again until you can do that too. Open your heart to God. He will fill it with love.'

'You are not married?'

He shook his head. 'I've never seen the garden, but if it is big and there is a greenhouse, it should be profitable and produce all you need at the Castle, and cost you nothing.'

She knew that he was coming. There was often tacit understanding between Elizabeth and anyone she was with, especially with natural and lonely people like Donald MacDonald. She made it unnecessary for him to say so.

'I hope it will be all you could wish for,' she said, understanding at once that he had never worked for anyone and must be his own master. 'How soon can you come and see for yourself?'

'I'll come tomorrow morning.'

'There will be Pratt's sausages for lunch and mashed potatoes. He left a deep-freeze full of them and very good they are too.'

Elizabeth, her mission fulfilled, walked back in the pouring rain and went through the outer door, back into the garden. It looked different now. She had no anxieties about its falling away from the perfect state in which its recent owner had left it. The next morning, this was confirmed by the satisfaction on Donald MacDonald's face as he surveyed his new province. It was indeed in perfect order; not a weed was three days old and it was as if it Mr Pratt's administration had been active to the last moment before his departure. In addition, it was over equipped with every kind of mechanical assistance to be had that had passed the test of time and proved reliable. The greenhouse was heated to any required temperature by a self-regulating electrical heating system, with its own generator and power supply, which made it quite independent of the power cuts which plagued the island. High walls and the sheltering mass of the castle itself gave almost complete protection from the wind.

At lunch, they sat together at the huge kitchen table near the Aga on which Pratt's sausages had been fried.

'That's two things I've found in the Pratts' favour. They kept all the original old furniture intact, threw none of it out and they made good sausages and ate them themselves. What was the local feeling about them?'

'Entirely of their own making. There was the great divide. They were the rich and we were the poor. They came as visitors and strangers and put up class barriers between us and them. They never really came to the island. Didn't come to the Kirk but went to London for their baptisms, marriages and were buried I don't know where – not on the island. Mr Pratt, that has just left, was born here. He lived all his life more months in the year on, than off, the island and yet never grew part of it. Now he's away without a backward glance and not one of us bade him goodbye. But it is good that he didn't take the sausages away with him,' he finished, holding out his plate for another helping. 'Tomorrow I'll thin the lettuces.'

Had Mr Pratt's administration inspected his work when he left that day, it would have met with unqualified approval. Elizabeth did not even think of inspecting it.

Donald MacDonald always drove the mile and three quarters from his holding to the postern gate on his tractor. It was very old and had given him long service since he had acquired it second-hand from the mainland, many years before. Like many of the crofters on the island, he was a self-taught mechanic. When not in use, he had kept it cleaned and oiled and well maintained in his barn. At the castle, he found a workshop in one of the former stables where he exercised his mechanical ability, to great effect. He was able to maintain and manage all the motor and electrical equipment and kept the greenhouse as well heated and productive as ever.

Like so many of the crofters on the island, he was self-sufficient, very practical and could turn a hand to almost anything. He and his father had built and decorated their own house and were masters of many manual and technical skills. Both when young, had gathered wide experience at sea: both had served in the navy – his father in the Great War and himself in the 1939-45 war. They had found no difficulty in changing from pony and cart to tractor and trailer, but had kept both. They used the pony and cart for the jobs they could do better and more easily. One corner of his straw thatched barn was a neat harness room, glittering and smelling of polished brass and leather. In another, he kept a tool box, foot pump and equipment to charge batteries. There was never the least suggestion of haste or urgency in his movements. Watching him at work had the same effect on Elizabeth as watching Waddy at work, all those years ago. He had no watch but his time was always right.

He was the only personal contact she had made so far. She had seen the men waiting near the stables from a window in the Castle but had not spoken to them. They stopped coming, immediately it was known that Mr Pratt had gone. Almost all got permanent jobs on the estate from the factor who Elizabeth had instructed to employ them and only local men, on the island.

Days passed. She continued to explore, sometimes for the whole day, leaving him in the garden, a midday meal prepared and waiting for him in the kitchen. The car stood outside the front door where she had left it.

The castle faced east, its back to Prabar at the head of, and directly overlooking, a sea loch several miles back from the sea, with a very narrow entrance, hidden from sight by the rocks. It was a natural harbour, very well sheltered by the two mountainous land arms enfolding it. She wandered along the wild, deserted shore in both directions. At one high point, she looked down on the concealed entrance and then back across the sea loch to the castle. She searched along the west coast beyond that from Prabar to Closach and the great sinister mass of Tamhasgail Rock which rose above it. With the rain, driven by the wind, beating on her face, she felt that deep feeling of security that comes to some when quite alone in wild and remote country, in the dark stillness of night and in the height of human disaster.

One day, she felt an impelling urge to go once more through the door out of the garden. She was dressed as on that first morning but as the wind had fallen to a gentler breeze and there were patches of troubled blue in the skies and no certain indication of rain, she held her sou'wester in her hand. The tractor stood near at hand, turned and ready to take Donald MacDonald back to his house when he had finished for the day. Quite undecided, she wandered along the track by the river bank to Prabar, which she had not yet visited. As she reached the turning up another track to Donald MacDonald's holding, she again caught sight of the great eagle, high and aloof, but closer – more fascinating, and exciting. She did not go on downstream to Prabar but she found herself drawn to follow as before and continued on and past Donald MacDonald's croft, climbing higher and higher into the mountains. After a while, she paused to look back. Prabar had disappeared. She reached an easy pass between two mountains, crossed a narrow footbridge over a rapid stream splashing over rocks, in the direction of Closach and Tamhasgair rock. Over the bridge, the track turned and led along the other side of the stream and was joined by another track, which wound its way up from the road along the coast between Prabar and Closach, the road taken by Michael and Mary Ella. She found herself in a steading broader and bigger than Donald MacDonald's, with a larger, more imposing house on the other side of the stream across another stone bridge.

The house stood amid small fields enclosed by drystone walls, which sloped steeply and unevenly down the mountain sides on either side to the burn. The track led to the house and stopped. No one answered her knock at the strong, solid door and no dogs barked. The only sign of life were the hens scattered all about the house and yard in front of it, scratching and pecking and, as she followed upstream past the house up into the mountains, she saw cattle grazing and in the distance sheep on the mountain-side. After the recent heavy rain, the burn was high and, where it narrowed, a torrent. The sound of falling and rushing water grew greater as she left the steading behind her and made her way up, climbing and jumping over and onto rocks and stones, crossing and recrossing the stream. The way became more and more difficult as she followed its course up into the mountains. The more difficult the challenge became, the more determined she became to meet it.

After some considerable time, she came to a jump that demanded all her powers and brought a breathless smile to her lips. She measured the distance across which she must jump and leapt. The water was swirling so powerfully round the stone upon which she landed that she was almost dizzy and hypnotised watching it. She paused and closed her eyes before reckoning her next move. Then she looked and saw that she had reached her limit and could go no further. Directly facing her was a six foot wall of smooth rock, part of which formed a waterfall and over the ledge beside that, the stream was flowing and falling. It was only possible to climb by narrow clefts, few and slippery.

Looking up to her left, she became aware, with startling suddenness, of a pair of boots firmly planted immediately above, scarcely eighteen inches from her head. Stretching her head right back, she found herself tracing from feet to head the figure of a very tall man, made infinitely taller by the angle from which she was looking up at him and the fact that he was looking up himself. Following the direction in which he was looking, she saw that he was intently observing the great eagle. It was dramatically close, descending from the sky into precipitous obscurity near the summit of the mountain, landing, coming to rest on a ledge. For an instant they saw it together, then it disappeared and was lost in dark shadows into which their eyes searched in vain.

He turned and looked down on the beautiful face below looking up to him. From beauty in the sky he gazed on beauty at his feet. She was breathless and flushed with the excitement of achieving the stepping stone on which she stood. Everything happened in an instant of time. Looking up she found herself in another world. They saw each other for the first time with unique objectivity, without association, unselfconsciously, before they had lost their sense of solitude, recovered that awareness of another human presence that transforms and distorts reality, before they once again became imprisoned in personality. They also saw each other for the last time but as neither ever forgot that moment, it was never lost. Each had seen a vision.

They could not speak with the din of water rushing and falling but, with an unmistakable gesture he beckoned her to come up to him and at the same time showed her the way. He pointed to a cleft in the rock where she could put a foot, a hold for one hand and, as she came, he grasped the other. She had no idea what to do after that. She found herself doing exactly as she was told with complete confidence. With one arm outstretched to him, he caught her up, slipped his hand under her other arm and, grasping her in the small of the back, swung her up beside him.

She saw his face. It was the face of a leader who commanded neither by force, fear, nor persuasion but by imperturbable reassurance and understanding. The eyes that looked into hers were full of understanding. She felt that enchantment that comes with being understood completely.

'You once picked my father up like that, Malcolm Gunn,' she said, as he gently drew her closer and closer.

She shut her eyes and found his lips on hers and experienced her first kiss.

'I will show you the Eagle's Nest,' he said at last.

Chapter Fourteen

Sudden Departures

Jesus Christ declared that the Sabbath was made for man and not man for the Sabbath. On the island, man was decidedly made for the Sabbath. The Fourth Commandment was kept with formidable and forbidding authority over man, woman and child and every dog, except Musty. No work whatever was permitted and no pleasure of mind or body sought or savoured. On the stroke of midnight all activity, save church attendance, Sunday school and Bible reading, was anathema. Malcolm had once told Michael that the real Sabbath was not a sacred day but a state of mind, an inner calm in which we should try to live not one but every day of the week. This particular Sabbath was neither a day of rest, nor of spiritual recreation for Michael.

He had broken it three times without compunction before it had really got started. He had taken Musty for a walk. He had opened the front door to put him and his cases into the house. But the third time left him, though outwardly calm and collected, inwardly in a state of mental and moral disintegration, having to spend the next twenty-three and a half hours to all appearances, spiritually on charge and composed – contemplating the terrible damage he had done by his inexcusable brutality. He felt powerless to take one step towards repairing it, no hope whatsoever of pleading a case that showed every sign of being irretrievably lost, and still less for the foreseeable future, of entering

210

what Malcolm had described as the Sabbath rest of the soul.

He did not call for her and went to church with certainty in his heart that he would get no more than the sight of her and that nothing to his good would come of that.

She was not even there.

Two hours alone in the pew were even more soul destroying. What little sleep he had had, had been very disturbed and he found, when he got back to the old manse, that he was quite unable to work as he usually did without compunction on the Sabbath. This made his situation even worse: should Mary Ella not come the next morning, and she had given him the emphatic impression that she would not and never would again, he would have to return to London almost immediately and stay much longer to reorganise the secretarial position with Margaret Smith.

She did not come the next morning.

He was on the point of going to find her and confront her indignation with distraught appeal and despair when he saw her aunt, Mrs MacLennan, hurrying to the gate. He ran to meet her. 'Mary Ella went off to Glasgow by the early ferry this morning. She had an urgent call from her aunt on Saturday. Her uncle is ill and needs her badly till he is better. She has told me to tell you her key to the front door is on her desk by the typewriter. She forgot to take it with her when she left on Friday and couldn't get in on Saturday night. She got into a terrible state trying to. She came home in a state of shock and was really unwell all yesterday. We didn't know you had come back till I saw you in the Kirk yesterday. I wasn't expecting you back till Thursday and to give you her message then.'

Mary Ella had not given the least hint of anything being wrong between them or of what had really happened. She must have pulled the front door to and shut herself out. It wasn't safe, as he well knew, to leave the manse unlocked because of her brothers. She must have been reaching for the duplicate key to the yale lock when the sash cord had broken and trapped her. Nothing of his increasing misery showed on his face. She had been thinking only of him, trying to get in to leave a message on his desk explaining her sudden departure to Glasgow and not expecting him to return till the following Thursday.

'Did she give you any idea how long she would be away in Glasgow?'

'She said she hoped only about a week and that she would let you know if she is kept longer.'

He thanked her, but was too unhappy to ask further questions.

'I must go away myself,' he said. 'Wait a moment.'

He found the key and gave it to her. Then he pulled himself together. He would go to London at once. But he must first visit Foghar Farm. He had not seen Dorothy Kennedy since her change of mind and his and Mary Ella's visit to Rock House.

The door opened immediately before he could knock. She almost pulled him in and shut it quickly. He got the impression that she had been keeping a constant lookout for him or to avoid someone else.

'I must get away from this terrible island. I must move at once to Closach and get that house in order, so that I can sell it and move back to England.'

'But it's in a terrible state. I've seen it. It's quite ghastly. It will take months to make it habitable. Months and months, if not years, before it will be fit to live in, even if the grant were through and the Murray brothers could start right away.'

'They have already started! Or say they have. They have been here demanding wages every Friday night and I have already paid them for lots of materials. They are quick enough for their money those three. I've had a huge bill for that taxi too, which takes them to Closach each morning and fetches them back each evening.'

'They can't have started! There is no electricity. It'll need rewiring before electricity is connected and someone from Carnach must do that. And that will be very expensive. You can't possibly move in. The house also needs new sewerage. At present it goes straight into the sea. The place is uninhabitable.'

'The house has already been rewired. They weren't on the work minutes before that Alec was up here demanding a power point to make his tea. They got the electrician from Carnach. He's done the whole job. I'll have to make do with the present sewage system. The sea has been good enough for years and is near enough there, isn't it? The Murray brothers say it is anyway.'

'Haven't you seen the house?'

'I'm going to move right away. I shall see it soon enough.'

'But I've got to go back to London right away and won't be back for at least three weeks. It will take at least the next three weeks to get a room or two fit to live in. You can't move till I get back. I'll hire a small van locally and get the brothers to help and we can choose a good day. You must go with the first load to see the carpets laid. Do think again. The house really is quite uninhabitable. The Murray brothers may be unwilling to help you move, of course.'

'I pay them, don't I? No need to wait till you're back. They can move me right away. I must get away from this place.'

'Mr and Mrs McPhail really care and will look after you. They are real Christians if ever there were.'

'Funny sort of Christians. All they want is their rent. I don't like any of these people. They can't speak English! They're foreigners.'

'You are very mistaken. They would do anything for you.'

'Sham, all a sham and it's no use pretending it isn't. You get me that van. I want to move, mess or no mess.'

He could see that she had reached a state of total incompatibility, even quicker than usual. 'All right. I'll see about hiring a van and try to see the Murray brothers too. I haven't much time... you are very unwise.'

This time he had a cup of tea but Musty did not get a rock bun. She had already packed things into cardboard boxes, obtained for her no doubt by the ever obliging McPhails, and was already living in a state of acute discomfort with almost everything out of use. He was very uneasy about leaving her at the mercy of Alec, Ian and Murdo but had no option. He had to go to London. He telephoned Elizabeth on his return to the old manse to tell her that he was back but had to return at once and would not be able to come over to Arduachdran for at least three weeks.

'I do hope you won't be away so long.' There was an unusual note of excitement and disappointment in her voice.

'I wish I wasn't going at all but I've lost Mary Ella. Her uncle has been taken ill and she has gone for an indefinite period to Glasgow and Dorothy Kennedy has just reached boiling point again which has already lost me a day.'

'Father is arranging for landings at Carnach until something can be fixed up here. All should be ready in about three weeks. I'll arrange for everything to be comfortable for you both at Broughton. Keep in touch. You might be able to fly up here with him.'

'If you're speaking to him today tell him, if he is free, to lunch with me on Wednesday. Usual time. Usual place. I'll go there anyway.'

'I'll do that but do get everything finished, Michael, and come back as soon as you possibly can. There is something very special I want to see you about that affects us both but it must wait till we meet. I haven't told Father yet about it either.'

This time he felt her excitement rippling over the phone and caught it himself. 'I can almost promise then. We must all three keep in touch. I shall make every effort to. How is Arduachdran?'

'Quite wonderful. I shall tell you all about it when I see you.'

As he approached the Captain's house that evening, he felt more and more uneasy about Dorothy Kennedy's having anything to do with the three brothers. It was obvious that they would cling on to her like leeches and would spend every penny they could lay their hands on on drink, and their work would be all the worse as a result. To his relief, he was not invited in but kept at the door. Fortunately, it was Alec who opened it as he did not have to wait, as he would have done if one of the others had come. It would be a waste of time to talk to either of them. Everything would have had to be referred to him. Alec was heavy with drink as usual and in an ugly mood.

'We're not furniture removers. It costs money to move. Tell her I'll do the job for fifty pounds. No! Seventy-five. Much less than it would cost her professionally.'

'You must arrange all that with her. I am away to London first thing tomorrow morning and won't be seeing her again before I go.'

'That ruin isn't ready for her yet,' Alec shouted after him. 'It's going to cost her plenty to get that hole right.'

'She will expect you tomorrow at nine,' Michael said over his shoulder. 'I estimate it will take three trips to move her to Closach.'

He did not wait for any assurance that they would do the job. It was certain they would, for the money but quite as certain that the move would be neither a happy nor a comfortable one. Early next morning he left the island.

Chapter Fifteen

The New Minister

The morning after her meeting with Malcolm, Elizabeth stood looking out of the window of the bedroom she slept in, at the top of one of the four massive towers of the castle. She had spent most of her time since coming to the island looking at the world outside. At Arduachdran, unlike Broughton set in the heart of a forest, she could see vast seas, skies and the world surrounding her from a commanding position but Elizabeth had an even greater command of the much vaster psychological world within her.

She had been greatly blessed. She had been born in circumstances which had enabled her to find herself, her real self, when very young. She had observed herself and the world objectively, appraisingly without criticism but with greater and greater understanding. She had become aware of herself, the world and other people from this commanding position. She had got to know herself, not lost herself. The world had never snatched her, swept her off her feet or taken her from herself. She had never put on any of the disguises, masks, or cloaks or put up any of the smokescreens, the temporal unreality, that blinds and hides others from themselves and which they come to believe to be reality itself.

The price she had paid had been loneliness. She had lost her mother as a child and she had only seen her father for short visits and during school vacations. Only in recent years had he spent more time with her at Broughton. Thrown on her own resources, she had learnt her true position in life, in the world and in the universe. From her mother, she had learnt real suffering and real love, and that life does not depend upon external circumstances but upon the spirit in which they are met. Above all, she had learnt that without love, life is dead, that love is closer to us than the breath we breathe and is ever present, ready to sweep in and transform every situation, state of mind or body, grief, illness, pain, poverty, even paralysis. She learnt that real life is a wonderful, exhilarating pilgrimage to the source of all love. She had been lonely. Now she was lonely no more. She and Malcolm would now be making that pilgrimage together.

They were to meet again tomorrow at Kirk. She had had every intention of becoming one of the community in which she had come to live before they had met. He was already a leading member. She decided to start very early to walk to Prabar so that she could visit a cousin of Donald MacDonald's on the way. Donald MacDonald had told her about her when they were lunching together. He cut her peat and ran a few sheep for her on her croft.

'Martha is but a poor thing,' he said. 'Simple and good. She has for nearly forty years cared for a niece, born blind and badly deformed to her sister who emigrated to Canada with all the rest of the family soon after the birth. The child was so physically disabled that it was impossible to take her with them, so Martha had stayed and has brought her up on the croft. She is now a grown woman, as helpless as ever, but very intelligent. They are lonely, have few visitors, and Martha dearly loves a visit.'

The croft was on the way to the church and quite near it. It happened that the new Minister, whose time had been fully occupied since his recent arrival settling his wife and young family into the manse, also decided to make his first pastoral visit. He decided to visit Martha and her niece on foot. He arrived very shortly after Elizabeth and they met by Mary's bed. Martha left Mary and Elizabeth to greet him and Elizabeth immediately took her hand and murmured that she would see her again very soon before Martha, delighted to have both visitors, ushered him into the room. After the visit, Elizabeth and the new Minister walked to the church together and parted at the front entrance, the Minister to make his way to the vestry door.

They were about the same age. He was perhaps a year or two the younger. They got on well together. He accepted her invitation to visit the castle the next day and have lunch with her, and meet Donald MacDonald who was one of his congregation. He excused his wife because of her family commitments. He was a quiet, rather timid man, not as yet confident in the performance of his ministry and very much in awe of the congregation and of the elders in particular. Like all the ministers on the island, he was very well educated and learned in his profession – a doctor of divinity with a good knowledge of Hebrew and New Testament Greek.

Elizabeth found herself alone in the midst of the throng which always gathered outside and just within the church doors, before moving into the body of the church and filling the pews. It was a very large congregation with no financial problems whatsoever. Many threw a kindly look in her direction but more wore what can only be described as 'the Sunday face'. Although not cheerful, the look was not gloomy, nor resigned, nor even pious and, being only worn on Sundays, can only be described as 'the Sunday face'. Many wore 'the Sunday face' at funerals but there was another 'funeral face' which was quite distinctive but only to an expert physiognomist. Few present had the will to distinguish the one from the other. It would be rare to see a 'funeral face' on a Sunday but there might be many 'Sunday faces' at a funeral.

They all made their way through the main door and down aisles to the left and right. There was no centre aisle. Elizabeth became aware of Malcolm inviting and directing her to a seat. They were to meet after the service. He then disappeared into the back of the church only to reappear with all the other elders on a raised pew, facing the congregation and looking down on them. It was immediately below a lofty and commanding pulpit, occupied at the same time by the Minister who announced the first psalm. The precentor rose and so did his voice and the service began. It was all in Gaelic and very long.

She waited for Malcolm at the entrance to the church and they walked back together towards Arduachdran Castle but took the turning which led directly to The Thorn.

'Did you really come to the island to find me? How did you know of my existence? I recognised you the moment I looked down and saw you but only from my dreams. I could only hope and pray that our paths would cross and we would meet, not set out to find you myself. You had to come.'

'It has never been haphazard. I started looking for you as a child and have followed a thread ever since – never given up or let go of the thread. Intuition has helped and luck too, though I call it destiny. Michael was part of it and led to the last breakthrough. We never gave up. That's the secret.'

'We?'

'My Father and I. You saved his life in the Arakan.'

'Good Lord! Are you the CO's daughter? But how on earth does Michael fit in.'

'My father thought highly of him. He has most unusual qualities. Physically he is very like you. Intelligent. A strong character. Very independent and hard-working. He has height, breadth and depth, too. He is a brilliant accountant and a tax expert. My father and I discussed him and decided to try to get to know him. I wanted to because I had a presentiment; I knew it was right the moment I saw him. I was also interested in his work for my father and its effect but mostly it was intuition and my thread leading me to find you. It was he who told me that you would be waiting, that there was only one woman in the world for you?'

'Has he found the right partner yet?'

'Yes but quite overlooked her so far. He hasn't found himself yet and so doesn't know what to look for. She'll find him and teach him.'

'Like you have found me and will teach me?'

She laughed. 'He isn't just waiting. He is looking. Anyway, it was his telling me what you had said that put me on your track. That and his mentioning your meeting someone at the zoo and overhearing that you had fought in the Arakan. My father and I redoubled our efforts. He has never given up or stopped looking for you and I have been with him since before I can remember.'

'How wonderful!'

'You were right to leave Michael when you did. How did that come to pass? Did you inherit The Thorn?

'That wàs just what did happen. Surprising because my grandfather was the youngest of five brothers who all had sons of their own. He was the first of them to die too. It had been in my mind to go for some time but I wasn't sure where or how or whether I should. I had always been drawn to the island when I first heard my grandfather came from it. I knew nothing of The Thorn, though. I gather the grant is in the royal archives in Edinburgh. I had always thought highly of crofters. There is real independence. I first learnt all about The Thorn from a letter I received and opened in the train on my way to work one morning. It was delivered to the flat first post which I always opened on the train. Rarely more than one or two letters. I learnt I was the heir, beating Michael himself by half an hour at most, his father and I being twins.'

'That'll be why you are so alike.'

'I made up my mind there and then before leaving the train. In fact I got off at the next station, not at my usual station. I wrote two letters, actually letter cards, at the nearest post office and then went straight to the lawyers in Edinburgh. The family wasn't rich, but it wasn't poor either. They had made much more than a living at The Thorn all those centuries evidently. Finding myself with both a healthy occupation, a home, and I already had a good income, I started a new life here. I sold my partnership and made looking after Michael part of the agreement.'

'I am puzzled at your being an elder.'

'I took up the whole life, not just the bits I fancied. Some are born elders, some seek to be elders and some have eldership thrust upon them. It is the highest office in the land if you are summoned to it by the Holy Spirit and perform it in the spirit of love.'

'Do you always give *the* answer, not *an* answer?'

They had at this point just crossed the wooden bridge. Prabar was out of sight and they were quite alone. There was quite a long pause.

'Yes, you do,' she said, getting her breath back. 'You will like my father,' she said, after another silence.

They had linked hands as they crossed the bridge together. It was just wide enough for two to walk abreast.

'You are forgetting he was my commanding officer in the war. I liked and admired him greatly. He was a splendid leader.'

'You will meet very soon. He's been searching every possible avenue and every public record since the war. I haven't yet told him I have actually found you and that we have met each other, but we had tracked you down at last, identified you and learnt you were living on the island.'

'So you bought the whole place so that I was in the net and couldn't escape! When shall I see Michael? Does he know I'm here?'

'Michael has been living in the north of the island at Foghar for the best part of this year and neither of you have had the least idea you were both on it. He has been drawn back to the home of his ancestors too. Talking of homes of ancestors, you will like Broughton. Michael will be staying there with my father this weekend and they will almost certainly be coming here together.'

'Why did you buy Arduachdran?'

'For the same reason you sold your partnership and came to The Thorn. We must discuss all that. I haven't quite decided what to do with it. I was thinking of something to help children; handicapped or convalescent or single parents with children in desperate need of a holiday or a change or to get away. A change that doesn't just come to an end but transforms their lives that they can and want to repeat. It must cost them nothing. Just comes out of the blue. There is something wonderful about a mother and child, or children, battling with life and love on her own. I want to use the estate, whatever I do with the castle, as much as possible to help the great unemployment problem on the island, one of the worst in Scotland; staff it with islanders and also with some of the single parents.'

'We will give Michael The Thorn when he marries.'

'No! We are going to live at The Thorn. He and Mary Ella will be perfectly happy at the old manse which she has just furnished beautifully for him.'

'I thought you said he hadn't found any one?'

'No! But I am quite certain she has!'

'Like you did me?'

'We are going to live happily ever after!'

'I might have become a hardened bachelor and you find me very difficult to get on with.'

'I might find you hard work, but I like hard work.'

'So do I. Marriages only fail because one or both don't work hard enough at them, or at all.'

'Or take each other for granted.'

'In short, don't really love each other at all but go on loving themselves exclusively.'

★

The Minister did not come to the castle for lunch on the following day. Instead Elizabeth received a letter from him. At about nine o'clock on the Monday morning, Elizabeth saw from her third storey window, upon which the rain was beating vigorously, a mini car driving up from Prabar. It had arrived by the time she reached and opened the front door. A man she did not know, who made no attempt to introduce or explain himself and did not smile, got out and handed her a letter. He then abruptly turned and got straight back into the car. She watched him drive off in the pouring rain before opening it.

> *Madam,*
> *You have been accused, before a special emergency meeting held at the kirk last night, of breaking the Sabbath yesterday and it was agreed that as a new and welcome member of the Kirk, you should answer this charge without delay. Myself and the elders of both Closach and Prabar therefore propose to call upon you this very evening at eight o'clock.*
>
> *Alasdair MacPhie*
> *Minister of the Parish of Arduachdran*

Elizabeth's first reaction to this formidable letter was to discover that she had not one but two consciences, one towards God and one towards man because whatever it was that had offended the one, had not offended the other. Her conscience towards God was as clear as it normally was, because she had now for a very long time tried to live continuously in the presence of God and that meant living with love in her heart. Her conscience towards man was different. She did not live her life continuously aware of her fellow man but only of that love. Her second reaction therefore was to ask herself what she could possibly have done to offend Alasdair MacPhie. It was her first experience of being formally accused of anything. Her third reaction was to accept the fact that she had offended.

She should not, of course, have walked up to The Thorn with The Elder on the Sabbath. She should not have kissed him gently on the cheek, just past the wooden bridge, when he was not expecting it, nor perhaps should she have allowed him to take her in his arms moments later but none of this could be the offence of which she was accused before the Presbytery. No one but Donald MacDonald, whose croft they had passed, could have seen them together and he would have had neither the will, nor the opportunity to report them. She knew that he kept to his house on the Sabbath, except twice a year when he attended communion at the kirk, and he could not, had he seen them, have reported them to the kirk without opening himself to the charge of having broken the Sabbath too. Nor could he have done so this Monday morning early, having arrived at the Castle to work in the garden half an hour before. Anyway, the letter stated that the meeting had taken place and the charge considered last evening after the evening service. The track to The Thorn led only to the homes of Malcolm, Donald himself and then over the bridge and round the mountainside to the castle. There was no one else living in either direction but the three of them and no one else could have played peeping Tom without also breaking the Sabbath.

At lunch, she placed her problem before Donald Mac-Donald but despite his lifelong experience of the district and the people, they failed to discover the nature of her offence.

'It would be much easier if I knew what it was before they came, but unless The Elder can enlighten us when he comes this afternoon, it looks as if I shall have to wait till they are here. We are going to examine the archives in the muniment room and see if we can unearth any more about the original grant of Arduachdran from the King and the subsequent grant of The Thorn. By the way, I have thought of one way we can help Martha and Mary and that is by sending a good supply of fruit and vegetables from the garden regularly.'

'You've seen them already, have you?'

'Yes. I went yesterday on the way to church.'

'You went yesterday?'

'Yes. Why not?'

Then it dawned on Elizabeth why not.

'That is why the Minister isn't sharing this meal with us today,' said Donald MacDonald.

'But the Minister was there visiting them with me! We met by Mary's bedside. He arrived after I did and then we left together and walked the short distance to the church.'

'He will have been sanctimoniously skinned, gutted and gently fried by Ebenezer MacGregor, one of the elders of Closach and their chief spokesman. He, the Minister of all people, to go about any business that has not to do with the worship of God upon the Sabbath. Ebenezer will have boiled him in holy unction and they will all have prayed together with him till late in the night that this blot on his soul, that this blight upon his young ministry, may pass away.' Donald MacDonald lowered his eyes from the heavenward direction and gave Elizabeth a great grin.

'Tell me more about this Ebenezer MacGregor? Remember I'm next on the menu.'

'He lives on Tamhasgail Rock, the highest point in Closach right next to Rock House. Closach is notorious for wreckers. They used to put a lamp high up in one window to lure the ships to their destruction on the rocks which stretch for miles in all directions. For the sins of their ancestors they have formed a very severe sect, although remaining part of our communion, dedicated to cleansing their souls to the third and fourth generation of this particularly horrible form of original sin.'

'What sort of man is he, apart from religion?'

'He is never apart from religion. He spends his life on the look-out for sin. The least scent of it and he is off like a hound and when he catches it, he jumps on it like a cat on a mouse.'

'One minute a hound and the next a cat! What a man! Must be a warlock. Donald, I suspect you of playing the parts of Bildad, Tophar and Eliphas the Temanite, all rolled into one and overdoing it a big bit. You're trying to panic me, get me in a state of mortal fear. There can't be such a man as that still in the twentieth century.'

She could see that Donald MacDonald was enjoying himself but he continued disturbingly convincing. 'He is the devil himself in holy orders is Ebenezer MacGregor. He sniffs out sin as a terrier does a rat and is himself a master of every shade of it, from that which is as black as the night to a spot on the sun. He is like the rub of a cheese-grater for company and like sandpaper when at his smoothest. Scratch, scratch, scratch. He leaves you raw and sore. I pity that poor young minister.'

'Never mind the poor young minister. Spare all your sympathy for the poor young chatelaine of this castle.'

'Is that what you are calling yourself? It is not a chatelaine but a poor, humble penitent you must be this very evening in this castle.'

'Get off to your garden. You are no help or comfort at all.'

Malcolm arrived later in the afternoon and they had tea together.

'What shall I do? What shall I say to them?' she asked.

'You mean what will you say to me. I have had my formal summons to the meeting. Most of the Prabar elders were not there last night. Ebenezer MacGregor had it all his own way. Norman MacLeod brought my summons to it in his mini this morning. He had to walk from the wooden bridge. You forget you are speaking to The Elder, I must say I was deeply shocked, Elizabeth.' He shook his head sadly.

'You are no better than Donald MacDonald.'

'The Navy gave Donald MacDonald a sense of proportion and developed a natural sense of humour. His mother had brought him up to have a horror of sin. The sea has knocked sense into a lot of them. They are coming because they are all curious to see you and the castle. And you more than the castle. The Pratt's never admitted anyone and no one wanted to come. The whole thing is a blessing heavily disguised. There is good in all this. They wouldn't be coming to the castle if they did not regard you and want you as one of themselves, of us. It means they have accepted you. They would never have sent a letter to, let alone come to see the Pratts.'

Elizabeth looked at him with delight.

'Ebenezer MacGregor's intentions are wholly evil of course. He is a nasty piece of work. Wants to wrong-foot you from the start – get you to make the wrong response. He has spent a lifetime rousing hate and anger in others. He is the most dedicated hypocrite alive. If he doesn't get evil for evil, he writhes and is a tortured man. You will know what to do. Heap coals of fire on his head.'

'I've always thought that rather uncharitable of St Paul.'

'So have I but get heaping. The man's a Uriah!'

It was with gentle dignity that evening that she welcomed the Minister and the elders and ushered them into the long and lofty dining room of the castle. She indicated to the Minister that he should take the chair at the head of the table and the rest should place themselves at either side. She herself went to the foot of it. When they were all seated, she remained standing and the Minister rose to his feet and they stood facing each other down the length of the long table. The elders flanked him to within five places of Elizabeth.

'Madam,' the Minister addressed her. 'You are charged before the Presbytery here present with breaking the Sabbath, in that you paid a social visit upon the Sabbath day last to the house of Martha and Mary MacDonald. How do you plead?'

'Guilty.'

This reply and their reception was clearly unexpected and there was absolute silence. It was at last broken by a man with a dark face that looked as if he had never smiled. He had black, glittering eyes which looked to his right and below waist level and not at her at all.

'Words!' His lips curled in a sneer. He drew in his chin as if drawing back from something contaminating. 'Fine words. It is penitence in the heart that is required of you. It was not to worship God that you went on your way to the kirk yesterday but to win for yourself a false reputation for goodness and love of your neighbour. It was the wickedness of vanity and worldly pride. It was to be seen of men.'

Elizabeth said nothing but stood still. The silence that followed was broken by a white-headed old man with blue, dreamy eyes and a very sweet and gentle expression. He had with all the rest been looking straight at her from his seat. He now looked away from her and addressed them all mildly.

'Only the Lord can search the hearts and behold the imaginations of men. We cannot know the thoughts or the mind of this maiden. The Son of God said that it is lawful to do good on the Sabbath and He fulfilled the law by love.'

Ebenezer MacGregor who sat immediately opposite him at once cast his eyes to his right and spoke to the edge of the table where the old man sat. 'Six days shalt thou labour and do all that thou hast to do but the seventh day is the Sabbath of the Lord thy God. God is no respecter of persons. Is there one law for the people of Prabar and another for the people of Closach?'

It was clear that the old man with blue eyes and white hair was one of the elders of Prabar. He found support from another – a small taciturn man of middle age, with a faint trace of amusement on his face.

'The disciples went through the corn fields on the Sabbath day and plucked the ears of corn, and the man with the withered arm was healed on the Sabbath.'

'We are not upon the shores of Galilee, nor are we in the temple of Jerusalem, nor is it two thousand years ago when such things might be. It is of Prabar and Closach we are and in the parish of Arduachdran in the twentieth century. We should know better. The Law is written on tables of stone and cannot be erased. The woman has offended, is to be condemned and must do penance. She has herself admitted her guilt and guilty she is. I call upon the Minister to command that she leave the room while we determine what that penance should be.'

Elizabeth directed a look of enquiry toward the Minister who bowed his head in agreement.

They kept her waiting for a very long time. Elizabeth spent it enjoying the stillness and quiet in the great hall of the castle. No sound came from the room she had left. Malcolm appeared at last and beckoned her to re-enter. She quietly resumed her place standing at the end of the table

230

opposite the minister. All the elders rose at her entrance and Ebenezer MacGregor was surprised to find himself rising with the rest. The Minister spoke.

'It is the decision of the Presbytery that you be admonished. Arise and go to thy father and say unto him, "Father, I have sinned against heaven and before thee and am no more worthy to be called thy..."' he hesitated, '"daughter". They that wait upon the Lord shall renew their strength; they shall mount up with wings as eagles.'

★

The next morning, Elizabeth did at last get into the car which had remained where she had left it on her arrival after leaving Michael and Mary Ella at the old manse. She drove to Prabar and began to visit every house and introduce herself. She did not need to. Everyone knew what had happened the night before and why, and everyone knew that she had been to Kirk on Sunday. Without one exception, she was received warmly. Doors opened wide and greeting was spontaneous and genuine. For the first time in her life, she experienced what it is like to be accepted into a community as one of them. At the end of the week, she felt as at home with the people as she had come to be with the mountains, the sea and the moors at Arduachdran. Malcolm had been right.

Elizabeth sensed that an entirely different spirit existed in the two main parts of the parish of Arduachdran. It was not just a religious difference, such as was all too common on the island. She wondered if it had always been so. The scene that had taken place in her dining room was quite unique.

She was particularly drawn to one woman who looked very preoccupied as she opened the door but instantly showed such pleasure at seeing her, that Elizabeth felt her heart beat quickly and excitedly. She knew immediately that she had found a friend.

'Come in, Miss Broughton. You are very welcome. I'll fetch my father. He will be so pleased to see you. Just wait by the fire till I fetch him.'

She came back with an old gentleman with white hair and blue eyes whom Elizabeth recognised at once.

'Could you tell me the names of the other elders who were present last night?' she asked him.

'The seven from Prabar go by the name of Gunn without exception,' he laughed. 'And Catriona and myself are both Gunns. How else should we all be called,' he laughed. 'Five of those from Closach are MacDonalds, one MacGregor and one Gunn. Not a difficult question.'

The new Minister was the only one upon whom she called who was a little embarrassed. He made no reference to the occasion and accepted her invitation to lunch the following week as if nothing had happened.

Chapter Sixteen

Closach Closes In

'I am flying to see Elizabeth and Arduachdran next week-end. Coming with me?'

Michael was spending his second weekend at Brough-ton. He had made no mention of the situation between himself and Mary Ella to Fairfield Broughton. He wasn't at all certain what it was himself. Had Mary Ella left him and gone to Glasgow because of his brutality or was her uncle's illness the reason for her sudden departure as her aunt had said? Or was it both? The desolate sinking feeling that he had lost her kept recurring and sucking him back, like a giant receding wave, into misery. He found some relief in Fairfield Broughton's company: he was so positive and enthusiastic with his vast worldwide interests and exciting plans for the future but Mary Ella had made a great im-pression on him too. He clearly regarded her as one of their intimate little circle and was impatiently looking forward to her return and seeing her again. He kept expressing his admiration and liking for her which delighted Michael but also painfully reminded him of that dreadful night and how he had hurt her.

'I must fly back tomorrow,' he replied, suddenly making up his mind as he spoke. 'She may have come back from Glasgow or her aunt may have some idea by now when she is likely to return.'

'Can't you give her a ring?'

'Don't know where in Glasgow she is or her uncle's name. I must also check up on what is happening to Dorothy Kennedy. She was heading for disaster when I left. About to sink her own ship ten fathoms deep. Usual suicidal behaviour. She's as obstinate and pig-headed as ever. She really has made a fatal move this time and fallen into very dubious hands indeed.'

'What about your leg and the plane?'

'I've just had a week's rigorous physiotherapy. Should be able to get in and out of it with less difficulty and fly it more comfortably. I shall fly it back to the island but leave it there for a while. Can I fly back here with you? Or are you staying on?'

'Come and stay at Arduachdran and get to know the place. Elizabeth particularly wants you to and bring Mary Ella if she's back. Elizabeth has something very important to tell us that concerns us both. She is keeping it till she sees us. Of course, I'll fly you back. I am only going for the weekend. I expect to be there again the following weekend for an indefinite stay. Stay with us at Arduachdran and I'll fly you back here on the Monday and back there again the following weekend.

He could tell at once from the look and feel of the place that she had not returned. The old manse was empty and dead. He did not go over to Mrs MacLennan to ask after her again. He did not want to draw attention to the situation. The office was desolate and unbearable. He left it the next morning for Foghar Farm and met Mr McPhail on the way up who told him that the move had taken place as arranged.

'It's bad all I hear of her and of that house,' he said. 'There is little or nothing that those three Murrays have done. They idle about and spend the time they should be working drinking the money they have not earned. The people of Closach have little to say that's good of them.

234

They don't like having men from Foghar working there at all.'

'Should I have got Closach men?'

'You could not have done so. You couldn't have got one.'

'Then why resent others doing it?'

'That's their way. There is no reasoning with the wrong-headedness of the people of Closach. They will eat her up between them. It is not a good thing for her being among them, especially her immediate neighbours, the MacGregors. I fear they will help themselves to large slices of her till they have carved her up. Any help she gets from them she will pay for dearly. In the bad old days, unfortunately not so very long ago, they had the whole district at their mercy and had absolutely none. Ebenezer MacGregor lives in the house next to Rock House on one side of the road and his sisters a little further down the road on the opposite side. The four of them grew rich on the poverty all around them, especially in the hard times. Ebenezer was the youngest by far, the Benjamin of the family. Terrible man but a saint beside his three older sisters, two of whom are still alive, the oldest nearly one hundred.

'For generations, the family ran the only store and general shop. Everyone was poor and starving and they grew richer and richer exploiting them, getting them to cut their peat, build drystone walls and dig potatoes. They even had the womenfolk carrying heavy baskets of groceries to sell for them in outlying districts, in return for a few groceries themselves. They employed no one except on casual labour and paid in kind and never in cash. All anyone earned working for them went to pay for their barest needs in the MacGregors' store. They had a great many in their debt and drove more than one family to emigrate. Martha, who lives near the kirk at Prabar, was the only one of one family to stay to look after a younger sister's badly handicapped child,

Mary. The wife of another family died in childbirth producing a tenth child. The father was struck with the palsie by the shock. Kirsteen, the eldest, took over and has brought up all her brothers and sisters. The MacGregors gave the eldest boy, only fourteen, hard labouring work to do for a pittance, a shilling for a very long working day and only casual, though he was working most days. If they didn't deduct it from the family debt to the store, the lad would take what he earned home in kind to his sister. He never saw any cash.'

'I'd better go over and see her. Perhaps her moving into Rock House and being on the spot will have the effect of getting the Murray brothers to work.'

Mr McPhail said nothing. The answer was clearly written on his face.

After a very long wait, the door opened even more narrowly than usual and an entirely different face from any he had known did not greet but just looked at him without any welcome whatsoever. It was the face of a sick woman. It was grey and she wore a grey silk scarf, held as usual round her head and under her chin. There was not a sign of the three brothers.

'Whatever is the matter?' he cried. 'Where are they?'

She did not answer and he realised with a shock that she was about to shut the door in his face. She was not taking him for granted as usual, she wasn't taking him at all. She was quite changed towards him and her attitude was hostile. They were completely estranged. But suddenly, just as the door was nearly shut, she changed her mind and opened it in the same way she had so often done in the past and turned and led him down to the kitchen. They had to squeeze past her electric cooker, washing machine and refrigerator and the rest of her kitchen furniture which had been dumped in the long passage. She threw open the kitchen door and they stepped over a fallen piece of wood studded with rusty nails down one side into broad daylight. It was open to the sky. There was no ceiling and no roof, just a huge gaping hole. Rubble, bits of plaster, rafters, slates and strips of roof felt covered the floor, the Rayburn, the table, chairs and furniture, left by previous owners. Everywhere was covered with dust. It was as if a bomb had fallen. Heavy rain and violent gusts of wind had stripped accumulated layers of paper from the walls, some of which stood out and waved dismally over the whole desolation like filthy, undignified ghosts or muddied washing blown off the line. The way to the bathroom and WC which, as in most of the houses on the island, was on the ground floor, was completely blocked. The thought immediately struck Michael that she must have had to use the WC under the stairs. As if in answer she pointed back down the passage.

'On my first morning here I came downstairs to find that the place was being used as a public lavatory.'

'You aren't looking very well,' he answered gently. 'Don't you think I should get a doctor. I think you should let me take you to the old manse until all this terrible mess is cleared up and this house is ready for you.'

She ignored his invitation. Her response was an angry outburst.

'I have sacked that Murdo. He's not a man. What do I want with three lazy louts when two can do as little as three. All that money each week for wages for this! I shall send the other two about their drinking when and if they come today or tomorrow. They will all three be here on Friday bullying for wages they haven't earned for work they haven't done. They aren't builders. They are wreckers! Thieves! Cheats! That's what Mr MacGregor calls them. Wreckers!'

'I'll try to get you someone else. You really should think of moving back to Foghar.'

'What you think is neither here nor there. I have handed

all my affairs over to Mr MacGregor, a church elder and a very nice man who lives next door and to MacGregor and MacGregor, solicitors at Carnach. He thinks it utterly disgraceful the way I have been treated and that I was very ill-advised to buy this house.'

She conveyed very forcefully in her manner who it was had ill-advised and treated her disgracefully.

'He and his wife called the day after they pulled this roof down and said they were very concerned.'

'What are you doing about meals? How are you cooking? The house is uninhabitable. You really must move back to Foghar Farm.'

'To you and those dreadful McPhails? That's your advice, is it?' she said scornfully.

'The McPhails are good, kind people and will take great care of you.'

'Mr and Mrs MacGregor are the only people who have been good and kind since I came to this dreadful island. There isn't anything they won't do for me. Mr MacGregor is a very religious man and a total abstainer but he saw at once what I needed and got me two half bottles of whisky and some cigarettes.'

'That was sensible of him.'

'That Murdo Murray saw one of the bottles and asked me how I'd got it and had the nerve to tell me not to have anything to do with him! Called the people of Closach a lot of murderous wreckers and said if ever they got their hands on me, they wouldn't let go until they'd skinned me to the bone. A nice one he is to talk. He said Mr MacGregor used to drink hard himself when his mother and sisters weren't looking. Drank in the bothan whenever he could and told the other drunks there that, if ever he got his hands on Rock House, he would set it up as a tavern and call it 'The Wreckers Arms' to attract tourists. Likely story. He said that he would fleece them as he and his sisters and their family have fleeced the community for generations. That's the sort of elder he is, he said. I sacked him on the spot. He was very drunk. Then his two brothers came in and the three of them finished the bottle and went off. I expect they have been drinking ever since and that's why they are not here today.'

She led the way back to the hall. She was speaking to herself all the time now, as if she couldn't stop. 'I've had this yale lock put on the door to stop people using the place as a public lavatory, and to shut your Murray brothers out, too.'

As she said this, to Michael's surprise she clicked the yale lock up so that anyone could walk in. Then she started up the stairs to show him other horrors in the bedrooms, he presumed. He was about to follow her when they heard voices outside.

'That's them now,' she said, her voice quite changed.

He never saw what she was going to show him upstairs. Suddenly a man, followed by a woman, came straight in without knocking, the man opening the door for the woman carrying a tray with a pot of tea and some scones and butter. Michael recognised the man next door. Both were very put out at the sight of him and were clearly quite unused to playing the part of Good Samaritans. The woman was completely flummoxed; she found herself quite incapable of dealing with the altered situation and had no alternative but to carry on as if Michael wasn't there. The man just stood with an ugly stubborn look on his face and left the situation to her.

'Dorothy! Dorothy!' the woman called out absurdly, as if Dorothy Kennedy was invisible, and not immediately on the stairs in front of her with Michael between them, so close to her that the tray was directly under his nose and he could smell the freshly baked scones. All three then completely ignored him, although Dorothy Kennedy had to push past him down the narrow staircase to join them. They were all four crowded uncomfortably together in the narrow hall, until she squeezed by them all, opened the door into the large sitting room past the lavatory under the stairs and ushered the other two in. Michael caught a glimpse of a fire burning and of a room invitingly warm and comfortable before they went in, the door shut and he was left alone. He was struck by the darkness in their faces as they passed him. They were like lamps that had gone out or had never been lit. 'You can measure the love in the heart by the light in the face,' Malcolm had once said to him.

As he opened the front door, Musty came out of the kitchen door into the blocked passageway, paused, cocked a leg at the electric cooker, and went out. Michael shut the door behind him, regretting that the bolts were not outside. It was Thursday. He decided to go straight to Arduachdran and return to London with Fairfield Broughton on Monday.

He found no one about the castle until wandering along the passageway past the open kitchen door and across the courtyard into the garden he met Donald MacDonald. The thought of seeing Elizabeth and the sight of Donald MacDonald was like walking out of the shadows into the bright sunlight.

'She'll be back soon. She is visiting in Prabar. All is ready for you and Mr Broughton but neither of you are expected till later. Perhaps you might like to look around meanwhile. That door leads out up the mountainside to my croft and The Thorn. You cross a bridge over a stream and follow the track up the stream on the other side.'

It was a wonderful walk. He passed Donald MacDonald's croft. There was no one in again at The Thorn so he made his way back to the castle.

Donald MacDonald told him that Elizabeth had not

returned but would certainly be back soon and suggested that he went over the castle. He walked through the open door into the great kitchen first, which he had passed on his way out and, after looking round, he crossed over to another open door revealing a narrow, winding staircase which disappeared up one of the towers. As he reached the bottom, he heard footsteps coming down and waited. A man's legs appeared and then the man. He gave a violent start as he saw Michael quietly standing there. Then his face became alive with pleasure. Michael's as usual revealed none of the intense emotion this sudden and totally unexpected meeting roused in him and that in an instant he had been stormed and recaptured.

'Have you found her, Michael? Not been too preoccupied? You haven't overlooked her, passed her by?'

'No,' he answered truthfully. 'I certainly haven't overlooked her or passed her by. What about you and what on earth are you doing here?'

'I am going to marry Elizabeth.'

'Elizabeth!'

'We shall all be together here this evening. Her father telephoned that he was coming today, earlier than planned. I think he was coming tomorrow.'

'That's right.'

'She is worth waiting for, isn't she Michael?'

At dinner that evening Michael told them of his visit to Rock House that morning.

'You don't mean to say you carried on after I left, Michael! You poor mutt! She was always so incredibly rude and ungrateful. How is the poor old thing?'

'Still incredibly rude and ungrateful! She carried on with me! You always said she was good for the soul. I've never been sure I had one but carried on just in case.'

'It isn't charity,' said Fairfield Broughton. 'Certainly not duty. Must be *noblesse oblige!*'

'To carry on where I left off shows a truly noble spirit – stoic and heroic. Marcus Aurelius Michael!'

'I wonder why she picked on you two?' asked Fairfield Broughton.

'That has always puzzled me, too,' said Malcolm. 'She suddenly introduced herself about six months after Michael left the Wonderland Home and became whatever it was she became in our lives. No words can describe it. She had never met me at all. I had never even seen her before.'

'Quite extraordinary! Very odd indeed! We must have her here, Elizabeth, and ask her straight out,' said Fairfield Broughton.

'How such a woman ever got an appointment to an orphanage full of children needing love, the one essential qualification for the job, and hung on to it all those years, dishing out textbook psychology instead, defeats me,' said Malcolm.

'I don't think she even liked children. It was just a profession and a job to her,' said Michael. 'I wonder if she ever had any children of her own?'

Michael and Malcolm looked at each other, struck with the same thought simultaneously.

'Where has he been all our lives?' asked Michael.

'Was there ever such a person?' asked Malcolm. 'She has never mentioned a Mr Kennedy. Has she to you?'

'If she had ever had any at all, I should suspect him of being a figment of her imagination.'

'How very odd that neither of us ever before gave the existence of such a character a thought. Not one little thought. This is the first time he has even become a suggestion. No Mr Kennedy has ever entered our minds, appeared in person, conversation, recollection, reference or published memoirs. Quite extraordinary! How much nearer to nonentity can you get! Not even to have been a thought. Not even a casual thought. Not even implicit. Not even a resurrection from the dead! No body!' said Malcolm.

'He may still be alive!' Michael suggested.

'No! Almost certainly died of a surfeit of rock buns,' laughed Malcolm.

'Or ran away!' said Michael.

'If not dead. Still running!' said Malcolm.

Elizabeth had not said a word so far but sat at the head of the table aloof, looking incredibly beautiful. 'Quite blind, both of you. Don't you realise who Dorothy Kennedy is? Who Mr Kennedy is?' She had a mischievous look in her eye which both detected at once.

'Go on, Elizabeth,' said Malcolm grimly. 'Tell us. Don't keep us in suspense.'

'All the evidence points quite conclusively in one direction and one direction only, quite, quite conclusively. The chaplain's name was Kennedy. Michael, when your grandfather died of a broken prospectus, your grandmother married him. She ceased living in sin with a potential prelate and regularised their union. Ask yourselves this question. Why should a professional psychologist of lifelong experience, fasten on to you two the way she did if she wasn't obeying the instincts of a mother?' She turned to Malcolm, 'and of a grandmother.' She turned to Michael. 'Why otherwise choose you two, who for twenty years have between you, made a hash of one move after another for her, you two whom she could, as a trained psychologist, see at glance couldn't move a chicken from one hen house to another?'

'His name was Reginald Carpenter,' said Malcolm.

'Before he changed it to Kennedy,' said Elizabeth.

'I hope, Elizabeth, this is your perverted sense of humour and not that infallible intuition of yours,' said Fairfield Broughton. 'Otherwise, I fear I may have to declare cause and just impediment why you and Malcolm should not be joined in Holy Matrimony. Your banns are to be read in church on Sunday at Broughton. I must decline to give you away. Some alliances should not be encouraged, some should be actively discouraged, some should not be permitted under any circumstances whatever. The mingling of the strains of Broughton with those of Dorothy Kennedy come under the latter category.'

'Imagine lots of little grandchildren the living image of Dorothy Kennedy running all over the castle,' said Michael.

'And all the visits from Granny with baskets full of rock buns,' said Malcolm.

'I am serious!' said Elizabeth. 'This is not a laughing matter. Ask yourselves! Why should a woman, wholly apathetic to children, take that job unless she had had some tragic and painful experience such as having to choose between her school chaplain and her twins? It is not a question of intuition. Just common sense. Putting two and two together. Though my intuition does point in the same direction and is, as you have heard my father say, Michael, infallible. And I should add that I do not like either the tone or the manner in which you are receiving this tragic revelation of your parentage and grandparentage. It is so flagrantly unchristian. I am a changed woman since last night, thanks to Malcolm. I have been checking up on the commandments recently and there is one pretty relevant to yours and Michael's case, Malcolm. Not the Fourth about keeping the Sabbath, the one bang next to it: Honour thy father and mother, I repeat *mother*, Malcolm. And that, Michael, includes grandmothers as being mothers once removed. I rather fear that I shall have to report this transgression to the Presbytery. Perhaps you as The Elder will see Ebenezer MacGregor for me, Malcolm. We'll have the trial and the severe admonition here after dinner in the dining room tomorrow.'

'What happened to the chaplain?' asked Michael with

interest.

'He shot himself, of course,' said Malcolm. 'No man with any self-respect could survive making a mistake of that magnitude. The only remedy he had was to take himself off to some secluded spot and hang himself by the neck until he was dead.'

'I must dash over to the old manse to sort out a few things before coming with you on Monday,' Michael said to Fairfield Broughton on the Saturday morning. 'I shall call in on Granny on the way back.'

'I'll come with you.' said Malcolm. 'I'd like to see the place and my mummy too.'

They met Mr McPhail bringing some sheep off the machair back to his farm. He frantically signalled them to stop. 'The old Lady died suddenly last night,' he called out coming over to them, leaving his sheep scattering and starting to browse along the roadside to crop the fresh grass there. 'Mr and Mrs MacGregor found her dead in her bed this morning. They were taking breakfast to her.'

He was fully briefed to the last detail with Closach gossip by bush telegraph and a relative living there. Ebenezer MacGregor and his wife were full of righteous indignation and were claiming to have played the Good Samaritan and friend in need of a much abused woman.

'You and my wife and I are the accused. Between us we drove her to desperation.'

'Desperation!' exclaimed Michael. 'It is not suicide, is it? Can't be. She is just not the type. We drive her to desperation!'

'Ebenezer MacGregor went personally to Carnach on Friday morning with her instructions to a lawyer to draw up a will and brought it back to her to sign. He fetched two Closach neighbours to witness it. It is significant that he was not a witness himself. He drove back to Carnach a second time the same day and deposited the will with the lawyer, the senior partner in MacGregor and MacGregor. Her body has been taken away for an autopsy to establish cause of death. Prabar is puzzled as to why such a self-centred and grasping character as Ebenezer MacGregor should go to such trouble for a very strange and eccentric old lady upon whom scarcely ten days before he had never set eyes.'

Dorothy Kennedy's body was taken away for an autopsy to establish cause of death but was returned shortly after Michael had left for London, without an autopsy having taken place as she was belatedly declared by the doctors to have died in the night of heart failure. Ebenezer MacGregor took over and assumed full responsibility for all her affairs, including her funeral. She had given him power of attorney. She was buried by the people of Closach the very next day after the body was returned to Rock House. Ebenezer MacGregor took the principal part in the ceremony, assisted by the new Minister. Neither Malcolm nor Michael and no one from Prabar, attended. No notice was given of when it was to take place. Every man in Closach turned out to carry the bier of the woman who had lived among them for so short a time but whom not one of them had seen except Ebenezer MacGregor and the old gentleman, who in a grey hat instead of a cap, was quite unrecognisable without his pipe, the fumes of which had attracted her attention downstairs after her first night at Rock House.

On Wednesday of the following week, there was an announcement of the sale of all the furniture and effects of the late owner of Rock House which, for the same reason as the funeral, was attended only by the people of Closach. On the Thursday, the house was quite empty and bare. The only sign that she had ever been there were the new electrical fittings in the large sitting room, the desolate wreckage in the kitchen and the new yale lock on the front door. Everything she had possessed was distributed throughout Closach.

Chapter Seventeen

The Green Snake

On the Monday of the following week Michael was back and alone in the old manse. His visit to Arduachdran, reunion with Malcolm and the death of Dorothy Kennedy had not for one moment relieved his intense longing for Mary Ella; but he could not bring himself to go over and ask Mrs MacLennan when she was expected or for news of her. He could not have borne to hear she was not coming but had returned to Glasgow permanently. Now shamelessly superstitious, he was fearful lest the least hint or suggestion of doubt of her returning might influence reality. There must be no psychic, psychological or physical obstacles put in the way of her coming back to the old manse. His heart leapt at the thought of having her there. He could not settle down to work and was glad when he was interrupted by a knock on the front door. It was the Minister to invite him to come round that evening for tea with himself and his mother.

'Why did you never tell us you were of the island and the nephew of Malcolm Gunn?' asked Mrs McAvoy over tea.

'I knew that my great grandfather came from the island, but not that my uncle had returned to it.'

'It is in the blood to return. There's many that come back to die that were born here and there's many that, like yourself, were born overseas and yet felt the claiming hand fall upon them drawing them back in spite of themselves.'

'He is greatly respected, your uncle Malcolm Gunn,' said the Minister. 'Wise beyond his years, long before he had the years to be wise. Do you know the lady he is to marry?'

'Very well indeed.'

'Don't you think it shame for the uncle to be married before the nephew?' Mrs McAvoy was looking at him severely but he could see there was laughter in her eyes.'

'Heartily so. It is very lonely at the old manse.'

'Well you won't be lonely there much longer. Sandy is quite recovered and Mary Ella should return any day and be back at work before very long.'

Like headlights suddenly switched on, the future suddenly flooded with light but not a trace of his delight did he reveal. Instead he turned the subject in a different direction. 'Did you yourself never think of marrying?' he asked Mr MacAvoy.

Mrs MacAvoy answered for him. 'There never came a maiden the way of the manse. But that is not to say that she would not have been welcome and found herself wanted.'

Though now far from hopeless he was not yet free from acute anxiety and apprehension. Her uncle was better but there had no certainty she would return to the island, still less to work at the old manse. The days passed slowly and he found it more and more difficult to work and took to stopping early in the afternoon and getting away from the emptiness out of the old manse without her.

In the early months on his walks Michael had kept to the cliff tops. The physiotherapist had told him he could not exercise his leg enough in every way so now he not only went further but made his way down and along the shoreline at the foot of the cliffs. This meant climbing up and over rocks separating the pebble beaches, inlets and wide sandy bays along the shore and sometimes up to the cliff top and down again, especially when the sea was in. His walks grew longer and longer and always took the same direction past the place where they had first met.

The green snake still lay where he had found it and she had told him to put it down and he always passed it both going and returning. He never touched it but left it where it was.

The second week was coming to an end. He had lost all hope of her returning soon as the Minister and his mother had led him to expect. On the Saturday afternoon he went out earlier than usual and walked much further and on his return had reached the bay from which both the Minister and Mary Ella had climbed to the top of the cliff, the Minister right by the snake and Mary Ella a short distance behind. The small bay was enclosed by precipitous rocks, worn smooth at the bottom of the cliffs by the sea, from which Musty could jump down into the bay, but the little dog could not jump onto the ledge Michael had to climb onto to get out: it was too steep for him and Michael had always lifted him onto it. This afternoon Musty had gone off on his own when Michael reached the bay. Lost in thought he jumped down, walked along the shore and then climbed onto the ledge, forgetting him. There was the noise of the sea breaking upon the rocks and the brushing of the wind past his ears and both drowned all sound of his approach, but not of the song. Looking up he saw Mary Ella sitting where he had been standing when they first met. She was singing softly to herself.

Their positions were reversed. He saw her as she had first seen him, unaware of his presence and thinking herself alone and unobserved. The song she was singing gently reached his ears, and the sea and the wind acted as a wild orchestral accompaniment. It was so beautiful that he was entranced. Although not a word of it was comprehensible to him its meaning was so clear that his heart was filled with it. It was of love and sadness and yet it had an exciting note of hope and gladness creeping into it now and then, but the overall effect was to fill him with an excruciating tenderness. She was exquisite sitting there singing to the sea with a far away gaze.

The spell was broken by Musty's indignant barking. Michael turned away quickly to get down to him to stop him betraying their presence. His leg made it more difficult to climb down than to climb up. Musty wagging his tail and staring up at him, his head on one side, waited patiently until Michael scooped him up and set him on the ledge and together they returned to where she had been singing. She was gone and so was the green snake. He looked anxiously in both directions. He was just in time to see her disappearing in the direction of Foghar. She was not however alone. Musty with a little yelp darted after her and they both disappeared out of sight behind a rise on the machair, Musty at her heels.

Michael, with instant vitality, the most powerful of human instincts, regardless of his leg, raced after her but Mary Ella had got a good start on him, despite a hurried pause to give Musty a little pat of welcome. This, however, he considered to be wholly inadequate and was her undoing, for, as she hastened on her way, he emitted a bark which was unmistakably one of indignation which, as she continued on without paying him further attention, turned to the howl of the wounded spirit. He stopped and began to bark and howl. Mary Ella could not go on. She stopped, retraced her steps and, stooping down, picked him up. When Michael reached her she had put him down after kissing him and he was now on his back, relaxed and blissful, under her caressing fingers.

The only barrier now between her and Michael was the line of her cheek and the way she held her neck turned away from him revealing a pride which gave her no protection whatever.

'Oh Mary Ella, darling little Mary Ella, how I have missed you. Oh so much!'

She said nothing, but continued beside him and they made their way together to Foghar in silence.

'Mary Ella, having you here beside me is such tremendous happiness. Stay with me always, always be with me and never, never go away from me again.'

'Had it been me that you loved 'tis not so long you had been in declaring that love. It is Elizabeth Broughton that you love, that came to the island to find you. Had it been me you had not said it to me now for the first time.'

'It is not the first time that I have said it, Mary Ella. I told you that I loved you the night that...'

'It is nothing but a brute that you were to me that night, like my father and brothers had been to me.'

'I told you I loved you through the door that I had locked for fear of losing you, but you had gone out of the window and did not hear me. It isn't the first time, indeed it isn't. I've been in hell since you left, thinking of all those wonderful weeks when you were with me and the blind idiot that I was.'

Mary Ella said nothing.

'I shall fetch you for church tomorrow.'

Mary Ella said nothing.

When they reached Mrs MacLennan's she went in and the door was shut. Musty came away without any fuss.

The next morning Michael went, as before, to take her to church. She came away quietly by his side as on the machair the day before and they sat together in the Church, as before. Musty quietly waited, his head between his paws, at the old manse with his eyes fixed on the front door.

Mary Ella said nothing. When the service was finished, they walked back again together in silence till they reached the door. She went in again and it was shut upon him.

Michael was conscious of a curious sense of peace and happiness when she was silently with him but that same silence cut into him with a sharp, excruciating pain immediately the door shut and he was left alone without her. All through the night it seized upon him whenever he became conscious in the darkness, awake from uneasy sleep. It was long time until, worn out and restless, with the comforting thought that she was near and on the island, peace came and he fell into deep sleep.

In the morning he went down to Musty and to breakfast at eight o'clock. He dreaded the coming of nine o'clock when he would finally know whether or not she was coming. He went to the front door and opened it, clicked down the yale lock catch and left it open. He could suffer no barrier between them. In the same imbecile frame of mind he opened the office door too. He left both ajar.

He could eat nothing for breakfast and made himself a cup of tea. He looked round for Musty to give him his customary drink of milk. There was no sign of him. He sat down in silence holding the hot bowl of the cup in the palms of his hands. Then, rather dully, he called him 'Musty.'

He did not come. Instead he heard the distinctive tinkle of the bell of the typewriter three times as the carriage was pushed backwards and forwards. As he rushed in he saw Musty sitting on the table looking out of the window. Mary Ella in her place at the desk and, beside the typewriter, the green snake. The next moment she was no longer at her place at the desk.

'For the third and not the last time, Mary Ella, darling Mary Ella, I love you.'

'I heard you the first time,' she said.

Musty barked at someone coming down the road.